The Last Day
Before Forever

by

James Bailey Blackshear

The Last Day Before Forever

Cover Art by *The Wild Rose Press, Inc.*

The Wild Rose Press, Inc.
PO Box 708
Adams Basin, NY 14410-0708
Visit us at www.thewildrosepress.com

Publishing History
First Edition, 2023
Trade Paperback ISBN 978-1-5092-5209-1
Digital ISBN 978-1-5092-5210-7

Published in the United States of America

Somewhat reluctantly, all the children but Misla began to back away. Still holding zas hand, she led zam up the steps. Feelwin held the door.

"I have to go now," she said.

Bragen could see inside. There was someone else there, but otherwise the building seemed empty. Zie looked back. The children were walking across the field toward another building. Like a soft breeze, a hollow feeling passed through zam. Misla squeezed zas hand.

"It is ok," she said.

As she spoke, the ring around her neck faded, then turned a brighter orange. She looked up at zam. Bragen bent down. Those hazel-colored eyes seemed to suck something out of zam. Her mouth turned up. Bragen knew this was something pleasant, like a language, but could not relate it to anything zie knew.

"Where will you go now?" Zie asked.

"Back to school. I will be with my friends there."

"What do you do there?"

"Learn."

Bragen knew the word, but only within an animal context. How a rooker learned to fly. A baby sly-tail's first venture out of its ground hole. How forest and desert animals adapted to their individual environments. That was what Misla was talking about, but probably something more. What?

Still bent over, zie asked, "So, what could you teach me that you have learned?"

Misla reached over and placed her arms around zas neck and whispered, "Not to be afraid."

Praise

Awards from previous publications:

Will Rogers Gold Medallion Award

Westerner's International Co-Founders First Place Award

Dedication

For Barbara

Chapter 1

The report came in during the tenth hour of the third moon. A scorptor spotted bones tangled up in a growth of blueweed on Mythgarden Point. Bragen swung away from the Dimensional and looked up at Vatch.

"Bones," zie said, trying to shield zas thoughts. *I should know this.* "What kind of bones?"

"Well, you tell me," Vatch replied. "The scorptor followed protocol and let your genius, what's zas name, Cloyden? Let zam know. Zie was over there pretty quick, and took some samples. Zie's your archy. You didn't know?"

"We take samples of some sort every day," Bragen replied, avoiding a direct answer. "I was finishing up your permits when the digaspatch came in. How did you…"

"Zelio. Zie met Cloyden on the beach. Saw zam pull them out of the vines. The ones with the thorns. What is it again?"

"Blueweed," Bragen answered.

"Yea. That. Zelio is my site supervisor."

"I know," Bragen said.

"So, then your supervisor left. I got the report, same as you, the only difference being I opened mine. Non-definitive. *On bones.* I thought you would be there by now."

The message was only a few minutes old. Vatch's

office was just down the hall. Bragen opened it. A nondefinitive bone reading alluded to unknown DNA, which was ridiculous. Among archys, non-definitive was code for mitochondrial. Such readings were impossible, as only lower species, such as mammals contained mitochondrial DNA. Found in both males and females of several sub-species, only females could pass this genome to the next generation. *Females.* Archodials usually ignored nondefinitive readouts and ran them through the lab before reporting anything. Vatch messed that up. Which meant a pile of red tape awaited zam.

Bragen studied the screen. The Dimensional was in its third cycle, blipping back images of the aerodrome. Zie watched as a parade of dozers and grinders rolled out of the transport's belly. Several were already lined up on the tarmac, ready for delivery to Mythgarden Point.

"That's not possible," Bragen said. Zie had led this project for five years, now just days away from completion. Zie watched blue and silver rays wash interstellar particles off the heavy equipment.

"I know," the construction czar agreed. Vatch ran New World Designs, the company contracted to complete ten lifeways on Apollis. Mythgarden Point was the first. "A long delay could ruin my projections. Not good."

"Cloyden doesn't make mistakes," Bragen said, as much to zamself as Vatch.

The supervisor raised zas hands and stepped back. "Don't blame me. You have to fix this and quick. You know the implications."

Yet if your teammate, Bragen thought, *had not been so quick to stick zas nose in it, I could have managed this.* Zie visualized the topography around Mythgarden Point.

Most of that region was made up of canyons, arroyos, and dunes. Desert terrain. But not the target zone.

"Irrelevant," Vatch said, reading zas thoughts.

"What?"

Bragen shrugged. No one had to tell zam what this meant. Cloyden was just doing zas job. Still, the issue had to be dealt with. *Who else knew?* Zie studied the construction czar's awkward stance, a sure indication of impatience. To this point, Bragen's day had been filled with successful operations, final assessments, visualizations, and approvals. All done post-haste as a part of zas final duties on this sun-blasted planet. *Bones in blueweed?* A disaster.

Bragen stood and stretched, avoiding Vatch's probe. An hour earlier zie'd anticipated the snap-back that awaited the conclusion of this project. Zas next post, Romo, already took up a lot of zas thoughts. Now? Zie had to pull a grommit out of zas hat. Not the first time zie had done that. Zie looked back at Vatch. "Let's go."

"I can't believe it," Vatch thought. "The equipment is arriving at this very moment! Six crews will be here next week. This doesn't require a remboot. Someone needs to be cleanwaved."

Bragen closed zas mind and organized zas thoughts. "Let's see for ourselves."

On the way out, zie grabbed zas visor brim and the tharsonome that hung on the back of the door. Together they walked down the tubular metal hallway toward the hoverdeck. They passed the same digitals of construction sites zie'd seen five years earlier. All Vatch's projects, from Menomis to Lark.

Stellar Law governed what happened before colonization. The Council promulgated a series of edicts meant to ensure that grinders and other machines did not destroy evidence of previous life forms. The same law applied to every planet. Funding allowed archodials like Bragen, archy for short, to perform full-blown colonization assessments that generally took five years. After completed, the real work began. Phase One analysis included green-lighting construction of the aerodrome, the dormitories, and onsite labs. Phase Two included the lifeways. Bragen was finishing up those reports.

Shortly after receiving this assignment, many of Bragen's peers intimated that zie would never return. Being sent to this largely uninhabitable planet was zas real punishment for the earlier fiasco. Afterwards, Bragen was given two options: do the five years on Apollis or go in for a remboot. Zie'd preferred not to start over. Now the job was done. Or almost done. Zas cohorts were wrong. Yet a non-definitive could screw that up. Maybe Vatch was pranking zam.

A billion silver stars punctured the yellow-green sky. The third moon would soon disappear and the red morning would begin, bringing the heat.

A two-seat Silverstream hovercraft floated on the tarmac, orange steam rising off its lifters. The signal waved them forward. On approach, a small metal step sliced through the craft's jellyton-like skin. Bragen and Vatch slipped into the vehicle. The hatch closed behind them. The lead archy pulled on the visor and placed the tharsonome in the compartment next to zas seat. Two seconds later they passed through the last vestiges of the atmosphere and entered deep space.

Despite the heat, Apollis was an interesting planet with plenty of unexplainable anomalies. Bragen led the spade work, peeling back the top-soil and cutting trenches across the lifeway. Despite the scuttlebutt concerning zas supposed banishment, zie'd enjoyed those early years. But the bloom was off that rose. Zie was ready to move on.

As thought-prompts prepared them for arrival, Bragen recalled zas first meeting there. Five years earlier Acendor, a member of the Council, placed a piece of amalgamated metal and a few fossils on the display table. Both were found by anthrogenecistmavwa2209, a part of the Solient Expedition. The fossils reminded Bragen of those zie had found on Lark, and brought up files concerning an earlier discovery on that same planet. The Silverstream's Dimensional brought up an image of Mythgarden Point. They started their descent.

Cloyden greeted them on the tarmac. A few moments later they were in the tunnel that led to the lab. Zelio was also there. On the way, through a series of body movements, Bragen cautioned zas lead to be careful. While the Warp was not as strong on Apollis, the Local worked just fine. Using slight movements of zas own, Cloyden acknowledged zie understood.

The new bones were on a folding table in the middle of the brightly lit room. Vatch gave them a cursory glance, then stepped back. Bragen's grad work was completed on Arion, which included Uhlman and early Synthon biochem. Zie was an experienced archy, having completed field surveys on three other planets. While no anthrogenecist, zie loved paleontology. Zie squatted down for a closer look. Not much there, but what zie did see gave zam pause. Part of a skull, mainly the cranium and what looked like an orbital socket. A femur. A few teeth. *Teeth.* A tingle went up zas back. They did not look right. Not quite dormant. Or dormant enough. Zie kept zas eyes small and zas thoughts flat.

Bragen was fortunate enough to have visited the Mawoan Exhibit before it was shut down decades ago. Castigated by most but visited by nearly everyone in the field (until it was removed), the theoretical skeletal conceptualizations displayed there were considered fantastical at first, and later deemed unthoughts. Similar to early Uhlman skeleture there were certainly outrageous differences, particularly when it came to teeth. As a student zie was most interested in the sessions that focused on pliable membranes, called sinews, that were attached to the jaw line. But zie remembered the teeth.

Now in Cloyden's makeshift lab, zie stared at the teeth. They were too big. One appeared to be an incisor. Which was impossible.

"Where was the scorptor?"

Cloyden pointed at the Dimensional. A red star glimmered on a narrow beach that lay at the bottom of a sheer cliff. Zie ran zas finger across a crease that seemed to cut into the rock. "Right here in the blueweed. There had been a solar storm during the first moon. Not long after, several large waves swept into this space and apparently flushed them out."

Bragen stared at the screen. "So... There is a cave there. We knew that, right?"

"Yes. The blueweed was trapped in the crevice that led out to the beach. Beyond the crevice is a small cave. It is in our early reports. We gave it a Phase One two years ago. The storm pushed enough water into it to wash out a pile of debris. Riverin is in there now."

Bragen put on a pair of skin gloves before removing

the tharsonome from its case. Each fossil, grayish-white, was the color of the second moon. All the fossils were slightly pitted. The edges of the skull-fragment were delaminated. Zie ran the tharsonome over the teeth. The device turned green. Zie looked at Cloyden, who nodded. It never turned green. Zie turned it off, then back on. Zie ran it over the femur. It turned green. The same with the skull fragment.

Without speaking, Bragen popped the reader open and retrieved a clamp-like device and inserted it into the handle. Then zie slipped the device over the orbital socket fragment. Barely perceptible metal pins penetrated the bone. The tharsonome turned green. That was the first time Bragen had ever seen that. Nonspecific DNA. Everyone knew what that meant. Not Uhlman. Certainly not Synthon.

"Damn!" Vatch cursed. If these readings were verified, New World Designs' projected goals were out the window. And much more than that. Non-specific DNA did not exist in the Prometheus. Officially, Mawoans were fiction. Lore concerning such a race existed, but for the most part remained outside the Warp. That was why the exhibit was shut down. Much of what Bragen knew of such creatures came from unthoughts, always shielded. Being caught participating in such activities could damage one's career. It was the same with any profession, yet was particularly so within the archodial field.

Vatch continued to complain, "This means I'll have to hold off on the crews."

They all looked at the Dimensional. An image of Mythgarden Point appeared.

"What goes where?" Bragen asked.

7

Vatch pointed to the screen. A blue star appeared on the top of the cliff. Several ran down the edge to the beach. "The apartments overhang the cliff and run down the escarpment to the shore. This is where the waterdrome goes. Was going to go. Council designated this spot for the capitol building. They'll want their own eyes on this."

Bragen knew that. Zie thought of Lark and the Genesis Investigation. *Their own eyes.* In other words, an oversight committee. "Right," zie thought. "Well, you take the hovercraft back to the base and do what you have to do."

"You're not going back?"

"Not yet. Cloyden can bring me later."

Vatch frowned. "They will want to talk to you."

"I know. Tell them I wanted to study this a little deeper before I report."

Vatch looked at the fossils and the tharsonome. "More than this?"

Bragen turned to Cloyden. "Your team is in the cave?"

"For a couple of hours now."

Half-joking, zie said. "Let's go find some Mawoans."

Already on zas way to the hovercraft, Vatch stopped and looked back. For a moment it looked like zie was going to say something, but then waved dismissively in their direction and said, "Zelio, you stay with them," then left.

****

Synthons evolved from Uhlmans. Rawnswawn argued that Uhlmans evolved from Mawoans, making that clear in zas digibit, *Escaping Extinction*. This work detailed the excavation that made zam infamous. It occurred during a much earlier dig on Lark. This anthrogenecist claimed the twelve-thousand-year-old bones zie found there established this outlandish link. Rawnswawn's findings rocked the Prometheus, yet subsequent investigations on Lark did not corroborate zas findings. Over time, academian's, anthrogenecists, and archodials began to deride the "Mawoan to Uhlman" argument for two reasons. One, no one could replicate zas findings. Two, Rawnswawn went beyond zas original argument and made another.

Zie claimed zie had found trace amounts of an admixture that included mitochondrial DNA. The anthrogenecist's new theory posited Uhlmans were linked not only to Mawoans, but to an unknown species, which meant Synthons were too. Which meant Rawnswawn was arguing Synthons were related to beings who bore their own offspring.

Like a great tidal wave, zas conclusions washed over the scientific community. Most immediately discounted this more extraordinary claim and looked for ways to blank-spot it. Even so, a select few secretly pondered zas theories. Over the years Rawnswawn developed a following that argued, while the Mawoans probably never existed, it seemed likely that Uhlmans were once procreators. Such ideas often circulated surreptitiously through the Warp, letting loose what the Seers called contagions detrimental to the Common Benefit. One by one, such ruminations were eradicated from the Flow. In the beginning, Inducers pointed out the errors that made such conclusions ludicrous and made sure everyone knew of the consequences for participating in unthoughts. At great risk, discussions concerning mitochondrial DNA persisted. Such whisperings eventually made it to both Watchers and Inducers, which took actions to blank-spot them.

Long ago, the Stellar Council replaced Rawnswawn's report with one of their own, deemed, *The Final Report on the Lark Discovery.* This document explained that the DNA in question was contaminated by improper handling practices, which led to an embarrassing mistake. While the anthrogenecist's original work remained important, zas conclusions were wrong. All thought-flows regarding non nonspecific DNA were banished from the Galaxial Warp. Over time, Rawnswawn became something of a joke. Eventually, the story changed. The readings were not a mistake, but a part of some fantastical hoax that became embedded in the collective memory.

The Galaxial Warp shaped the One-Thought, the Flow that permeated the Prometheus. Legitimizing any thoughts concerning mitochondrial DNA were banished. Current thinking on the subject was formalized in Sarkasian's treatise, *Mawoan Myths and other Fables.* This tome castigated Rawnswawn's theories, arguing that anyone who followed them were practicing black-market thoughts. Sarkasian, a hard-core centralist, took the anthrogenecist's research apart line by line. Most importantly, the theories concerning procreation were eliminated from serious thought and regulated to the world of flips and whispers. Few of Bragen's peers knew who Rawnswawn was. One had to be careful.

****

Cloyden's base station was set up on the beach. Shyden and Loydback were busy tacking down tarps that led to the crease. Riverin stood by the vehicle and waited until Bragen and Zelio dismounted. This was where the blueweed was found. Together they walked toward the two archys.

"Anything new?" Bragen asked.

"It doesn't look like they were just washed out of the cave," Riverin replied.

"What?"

Riverin pointed into the five-foot wide opening that ran up the edge of the cliff. "They fell out of the cave's ceiling." Zie pointed to the red tag at the mouth of the crevice. "This is where the bones were found, stuck in the blueweed. Follow me."

Cloyden walked toward the splintered face of the cliff. The five-foot wide opening narrowed as it neared the top. Several cart-loads of soil and rocks were piled near the entrance. One held orange bags of tagged artifacts.

Cloyden nodded toward the bags. "There are more bones in there and some other stuff we have not been able to identify. Larger pieces." Zie walked into the crevice. "If not for the solar storm…"

Bragen knew this. "So, it's a cave-in."

"Yes."

"More non-definitive readings?"

"Yes."

A minute later they passed through the crack in the cliff and stood at the mouth of the larger opening, and looked up. Cloyden said, "We've installed a shoring brace, but watch it."

More a void than a cave, its height was lost in the darkness until a lightglobe floated by, revealing a weirdly twisted column protruding out of the top of a partially smooth ceiling that did not look natural. The pole ran down at an angle, penetrating the slick floor.

"What is that?" Zelio asked, as much to zamself as anyone else.

Bragen took a closer look. It was shiny and wet, swirling rills of blue-black metal wound its way up, the lightglobe's shimmer reflecting off its surface. While the object was completely alien, zie remembered one of the artifacts presented to zam on zas first day on Apollis looked like this material. That piece of metal had been found about five miles east of Mythgarden Point.

Other protrusions jutted out of the roof of the cave. Only where the column penetrated the ceiling did the surface appear too smooth. None of it looked stable. Cloyden said, "That's a lot of weird stuff. It is one-hundred feet to the top."

Bragen nodded. Zie understood why the pattern sweep had missed it. *Too deep.* Very intriguing. This was what an archy lived for. Zie looked back toward the beach, then up. "We need to get on top."

"Right," Zelio agreed, looking around. "Not sure how stable this is."

Bragen ordered another geomorph stability shot of the outcrop. Zie needed a better idea on what was in there before they proceeded. Zelio, reading zas thoughts, nodded.

There was no mystery as to why Mythgarden Point was chosen for colonization. A massive outcrop that pushed into the sea created the formation that rose above the cave. Heat was not much an issue along the shore, but that was not the case a mile or so inward. The draw was to the west. To the ocean. Spectacular views of the Aguila Coast ran north and south, its white beaches dotted with granite boulders once a part of the cliff face that ran for miles in each direction.

Highland Red Grass ran east away from the point, descending toward the mainland. Not more than a short walk east, the grass began to wither. Two miles inland the fertile top-soils were replaced with sand and rocks. At that point the rusty colored land began to undulate, its rolling surface broken by jagged arroyos and shrub covered hogbacks. Apollis was the closest planet to the sun that had been designated for lifeways. Most of it would remain uninhabitable. All the designated colonies would be established along the sea.

Once on top, Bragen started to visualize a new base camp, one devoted to finding a connection to the cave. Something had to be there. Cloyden began to shoot the geomorph. A strong wind rippled through the grass.

As was the case anytime Bragen began a new project, zas mind forgot about the Warp and concentrated on the task at hand. Putting aside the delays such a discovery entailed, zie began to organize the new work schedule. The archy started a new thought, then shielded it. *Not worth it*, even within Apollis's weakened Warp.

Like all Synthons, zie was always aware that an Inducer's presence was a possibility, and tried to compensate for that. But if the fossils were nonspecific, which was of course, an impossibility, zie could not help but think about those crazy fables. And the wizened.

Standing in the midst of a brief flip, zie recalled those fantastic conversations about smell and food. Conversations that could get one a remboot. Long ago the Stellar Council ingrained in zam that the past was not the past unless you could hold it in your hand. Zie removed the flip.

Bragen stood midway atop the outcrop looking toward the Aguila Sea. The point was approximately two-hundred feet wide. Zie noticed that Vatch had jumped the gun. Several construction flags jutted out of the ground, indicating where zas grinders would start.

Inspecting the ground, zie kept in touch with the outputs Cloyden's geomorph accumulated. The sound of the sea and the soft undulation of the grasses flowed past zam. Zie turned and walked east, toward the sandy plains.

The Silverstream sat on a flat spot near a low dune. Shyden was running a rayrake back and forth across the area. While they established a safe zone away from the outcrop, Riverin and Loydback continued their work down below, sending Digitals and artifact details back to Vatch. Bragen was not ready to return to base. Zie wanted a little more time on the ground. Once back zie would have to face the Council. The rayrake began to beep.

Shyden looked up. Before he had a chance to say anything Bragen was next to zam. "What is it?

Like Cloyden's geomorph laser, a rayrake was a ground penetrator, but did not have much depth capacity. Shyden held it sideways so Bragen could see the image. A lined structure of some sort ran west under the soil toward the sea. Zie pointed the rayrake down and painted a phosphorus blue dot on the dirt. Then he held it in a horizontal position and walked into the grass and toward the edge. Every so often zie stopped and painted another blue splotch on the ground. Shyden was in knee-deep grass before zie stopped and waved the rake in a circle. After first looking at Bragen, zie painted another dot at the corner then walked to his right. Every five feet he painted another dot on the ground.

Cloyden's Silverstream rose over their heads, shooting the same area. Bragen watched as zas lead wove zas way back and forth across the sky. The third moon was gone. A tinge of red painted the horizon, a part of the rainbow of colors that rimmed the planet's curvature. Fifty-feet later Cloyden turned and started toward zam.

Bragen watched zas approach. *Maybe that explains it.* The original shoot was focused on the construction footprint, nearer the point. These new features were further east. It may not be the answer the Council was looking for but zie did not have a better one. It seemed clear the area Cloyden and Shyden now scanned was beyond the original contract. As to what was exposed as a result of the cave-in, that was obviously too deeply embedded to be detected on a regular survey. At this point zie was just glad zie had not given Vatch approval to start grading. What a nightmare that would have been.

Thirty minutes later Cloyden landed by the other hovercraft. The sky was mostly red. All wore their visors, which told them when it was too hot. Such devices wouldn't be needed once the dome was in place. All three stood just outside the rectangular series of blue dots that marked the ground. Now about one-hundred feet long and fifty feet wide.

The geomorph reading was the same as the previous shooting, except for the area east of the cliff edge. But Bragen did see something that directly aligned over the cave-in, a small gray circle. The only one on the scan. Within this circle there appeared to be other anomalies, but it would have been easy to mistake it for a buried boulder. Zas memcore noted that was how it was identified in the original shoot. Bragen was no longer so sure. Zas visor beeped. "So, it begins up here, whatever it is," zie said.

"Ok," Bragen sighed. It was getting hot. Zie wanted to expose the circle but didn't have time. There was much ahead of them, especially to the east of the build site. Additionally, the anomaly had to be investigated. "Let's get back. On the way, I'll assemble the report. Cloyden, you and Shyden ride together. I will drop down and pick up Riverin. I am sure we'll be back soon enough."

Everyone nodded, knowing their roles and what was about to happen. Something new and unexpected had changed their plans. They had no idea of the impact the discoveries would have on the project. They did know the Council would not be happy. Especially since it involved Bragen.

Chapter 2

Mawoan Myths and other Fables: Chapter Six.
Digibit 51. *It began with Rawnswawn's discovery. As
early as the last years of the Ruul, notions of its validity
came into question. Even so, there was time enough for
unthoughts. Ingestion? Propagation? It all began when
a trace of the Truth was twisted into Wrong Thinking. A
mistake that led to the fables. By the time any reboot was
halfway through its cycle such mammalian fantasies
were discredited. It was an anatomically impossible
argument. So let us examine the myths.*
****

Bragen was on the Dimensional as soon as zie
returned to the conference center. Vatch and zas foreman
were already there. Bragen focused on what zie would
include in zas report, determined to keep it brief and to
the point. With echoes of the Genesis Project dancing in
zas head, zie detailed the tharsonome readouts, the
bones, and material artifacts that had been retrieved.
Everyone could see them.

The Council maintained oversight over colonial
expansion. It was made up of several anthrogenecists,
archodials, and government officials from the
Prometheus, which reported directly to the Hive.
Specific cases required that three representatives hold
hearings on changes to ongoing contracts and disruptions
regarding colonization activities. Acendor and Acendoth

were from Menomis. Linweil was from Thon. In a properly flat wave pattern Bragen recapped what had happened and then reviewed the data that was already in their memcores.

This included information on the non-specific DNA. Zie noted that it was unfortunate that they had not found the rest of the skull. In addition to the other finds, mammalian bones of a range arth, a desert rink, and an erzatz had been found. The range arth had been extinct for a thousand years. After a long pause, Acendoth broke the silence.

"What age is the tharsonome?"

"One," Bragen replied. Zie knew this was coming. They were bound to question the device. "I checked readouts and they appear to be satisfactory but from past experience we know they cannot always be trusted. On this planet, heat is not our friend."

The tharsonome's readings had already been delivered to each, via the Galaxial Warp, so whatever zie knew, they knew. Apollis's sun was particularly hard on tools but Bragen had no reason to doubt the data. Yet that was the case on Lark. "Cloyden's provided the same results."

Linweil spoke up. "Tell us about the artifacts."

Bragen looked at the table. Zie could only guess. An enclosed turbine the size of zas hand sat inside a foot-long rectangular metal box. A series of swivel switches penetrated its exterior shell. A three-foot long tube, broken off on one end, lay alongside it. Within the tube was a twisted blue-black metal similar to what was embedded in the cave floor. Similar to what zie had been shown when zie first arrived on Apollis. Zas extractions had all occurred in the last few hours. Images flashed on the Dimensional.

Both tharsonomes indicated these objects contained a molecular structure alien to Apollis, but not necessarily the rest of the galaxy. Bragen noted the material seemed similar to what Mavwa found in an arroyo, five miles to the east. That archy made this discovery 1,300 years ago. Bragen recommended that Council compare Mavwa's analysis to these artifacts. Zie planned to revisit this old site as soon as possible.

"We'll call a Full Council," Acendor sighed. "We have no choice. Looks like everything is on hold."

Vatch stepped in front of the Dimensional. "So, who pays for this? Should I stop the crews from showing up? Can't we get another opinion?" Then a quick thought to Bragen, "Looks like a fiasco."

"We will look into it," Acendor answered. "But as you are aware, such delays are always stipulated in these types of contracts. We have already arranged for a team. They should be here before the next third moon. What you have to understand is that this could be bigger than a construction contract. I do not even know how to describe what this might mean."

"Let's not get ahead of ourselves," Linweil cautioned.

"Who is coming?" Bragen asked.

Acendor looked at Acendoth. "We are still discussing who the Council Coordinator will be but the main team has been assembled and is making preparations as we speak."

Bragen nodded. In other words, quickly. If this followed normal protocol zie would lead the excavation but the Council's rep would have oversight and more importantly, would be popping in and out on a regular basis. "Ok."

The artifacts and bones would be shipped via starlight capsule to Wahlgahlen, the processing center on Arion. Revised protocols regarding the lifeway needed to be initiated. They would talk again. By then Bragen would have met the Council Coordinator to discuss the go forward plan.

After the meeting, Bragen, Vatch, and a few members stared at each other a moment.

The construction czar broke the thought-jam. "So, this crew will bring more sophisticated equipment, right?"

Looking at Cloyden, Bragen replied, "There is no way both of our tharsonomes are wrong. Everything hinges on the Wahlgahlen analysis."

"Right," Vatch replied, stomping out of the lab.

Bragen continued staring at Cloyden, trying to focus zas thoughts. Any archy worth their salt would relish this opportunity, but everyone on zas team knew what another false reading would do to zas career. How was the Mythgarden Point excavation related to Mavwa's Gulch? And what about Rawnswawn? Was it Synthon or late Uhlman artifacts they had found? Zie could not wait to get back in the dirt.

****

The revised Phase One began just as Bragen expected. The dirt work remained under zas control but every third moon zie met with Linatin, the newly appointed Council Coordinator. They had worked together before. Professional, yet a bit self-absorbed, zie clearly seemed to enjoy looking over Bragen's shoulder.

Vatch, like a ghost looking for someone to haunt, remained close-by, watching the dig and keeping up with the daily reports. Zie was not the only ghost. The excavation dominated the Galaxial Warp.

Even so, sixty moons out, official confirmation of the tharsonome readouts remained unavailable. That was odd. Readouts from Wahlgahlen were usually available ten moons out. Cloyden and the others kept asking Bragen about the delay. Zie was troubled but continued to focus on the work. In fact, Bragen had an odd feeling that if they stopped exposing features the project would be trashed for some as of yet unknown reason.

****

Bragen remained on zas knees, looking at the painted blue line that ran toward the edge of the cliff. Zie pushed the sharply pointed spade into the soil, then squeezed the handle. This elongated the blade's tip. Just as it had all evening, the handle began to vibrate once the tip penetrated a foot into the soil. At that point it ran against a hidden, compacted surface. Zie moved forward a few more feet and got the same results, then stood and backed away. Riverin and Loydback then moved in and began the hard work of clearing around the identified feature. By the time they finished, two feet of top soil was piled on each side of the exposed remnants of what used to be the lower courses of a wall. A wall that had been created out of the surrounding earth.

This last exposure brought them to a corner. The second moon painted a slightly silver sheen over their work, which stretched almost one-hundred feet behind them. At some places the wall was three feet tall. At others it was only two. There were other features as well. Two additional stem walls angled off, indicating compartments they had yet to uncover. Blue lines scattered in various directions. Linatin arrived each evening as the third moon descended to discuss the day's findings. From those conversations and the images zas memcore detailed, the Council Coordinator returned to base and made zas report. This included the observation that zas own crews had been unable to find the same features without Bragen's help. The archy taught them what came to be called, "the Bragen method."

The arid soils they worked in were brittle and chalky. An archy unfamiliar with this spade technique was apt to penetrate the target, in the process destroying a part of the feature. Thus, early in the excavation Bragen would get on zas hands and knees and run zas tool over and through the dirt, outlining the wall that lay hidden beneath the surface. After some training, everyone got the hang of it. More features were exposed every moon.

Bragen still planned to visit Mavwa's Gulch but Linatin wanted the excavation completed first. There was also the business of the anomaly up by the point, yet that too would have to wait. They were under pressure to meet a Council deadline related to an upcoming Planetary Reveal. This was to occur once the main features were outlined. They were ten moons away.

Bragen was fine with this, but wanted to wrap up the preliminary exposure and get on top of the cave. Zie worried zie would not have enough time to investigate that area, as well as Mavwa's arroyo before the big show. Zie'd put in for an additional three moons but Linatin nixed that.

"They have to make a decision on funding," the coordinator explained. A decision was imminent. Bragen understood. It was always the case with such a project, yet this particular lifeway's setting was quite spectacular. Mythgarden Point might be delayed, but it would never be cancelled. There was already talk of incorporating the ruins into the build-site, with an Uhlman museum situated within the halls of the Apollis government building. But that was getting the cart before the steedfell. As time passed, the absence of a report took up a lot of zas free thoughts. Yet free-thoughts were few as zie strove to complete the excavation and waited for the tharsonome results.

****

The Phase One was not finished until the first revolution of the moon. All told, the features were one-hundred fifty-feet long and twenty-five feet wide. An imposing site. Whatever had gone on there, it was quite an operation.

Other than the perimeter, nothing was standard about what they uncovered. The most puzzling aspect of the features were the spiderwebbing of interior walls that ran between and under the exterior courses. The crew followed one of the stem walls ten feet beyond the exterior footprint before stopping. Their schedule prevented them from chasing after the ever-expanding nature of the dig. Thresholds from the perimeter and adjoining rooms were unusually large. All were at a loss as to why no additional alien material or bones were discovered above the cave, just the brick-like blocks.

So, what was it? Every morning Bragen and Linatin discussed the day's work, mapped it, and flowed the data to the Council. They agreed the features were unusually old. Independent blocks were no longer being used by the mid-Uhlman period, replaced with permablends and shadedomes. Roof structures and other features reminiscent of that period were absent and therefore the dating process proved more difficult to pin down. The sought-after readouts from the cave were key to understanding not only that planet's history, but the history of the Prometheus. Linatin continued to report that an announcement of some kind was fast approaching. In all likelihood, the coordinator offered, the news would be delivered during the Planetary Reveal, a sun away.

The excavation's official title was Bricksite1. Each brick or block was dimensionally exact. Each perimeter corner throughout the project aligned perfectly with the next. There were some ancient Uhlman sites laid out in similar fashion, with one hypothesis being such corners were meant to align with an unknown galaxy during a certain season. The sun was just peaking over the distant mountain range when Bragen brought up another subject zie was interested in pursuing.

"I think we have time," zie said, referring to peeling back the topsoil over the rounded anomaly that sat over the cave.

"You know it's too late," Linatin answered. "They'll be here when the first moon rises, ready for the show. And remember, there should be news about the readouts during the ceremony. The rest will have to wait. They want it to look neat."

"Neat? This is a working excavation," Bragen said. "You already know, don't you."

Linatin shaded zas thoughts. "It's all a mystery. As to the other, we just have to wait. I think you have your hands full until this is over." This seemed pretty final, so Bragen dropped it. It was true. There was so much to do. Reveals, or shows, as Linatin called them, were more trouble than they were worth, but they were put together to help with funding approvals. Bragen followed the coordinator over to the newly constructed podium. Together they admired the ruins.

"This is impressive, Bragen. I have to hand it to your crew. You've done amazing work here. I am sure the Council will be pleased. I know my crew is. Are you ready for Romo?"

Bragen looked to the sea. The sound of waves crashing against the rocks below filling the pause that gave zam time to think. Zie was already supposed to be on Romo. "It might be that Romo is a long time from now. There is still the report to write. Someone else might have to go to there."

Linatin nodded. "Certainly, that is possible. Let's go over the blips."

Both put on their visors. There was really nothing they could do that could not be performed at the base lab, but the significance of what was about to happen prompted them to walk around the site as they conversed, aligning their information and formulating the final presentation. At last, Linatin squinted at the rising sun and began to walk toward zas hovercraft. "I guess that's it. We better get out of here."

Bragen nodded, but zas gaze went to the point. "In a minute. I'd like to walk it one more time."

The Council Coordinator hesitated a moment, then nodded. "Ok. See you back at the base for the Brief."

Bragen waited until the hovercraft had disappeared into space before wandering toward the sound of the waves. Zas crew was also gone. Zie could feel the heat at zas back. Near the edge of the cliff zie studied the circular blue markings that ran through the prairie grass. This was the area of the small hump in the soil. A boulder? Buried under thousands of years of soil? Zas hand itched. Looking toward the sea, zie fought back the urge to bend down and insert the spade that rested in zas hip holster. *They would know.* Time for that later.

But zie did not move. The sound of the waves entranced zam. Zie looked east. The visor was still in the safe zone. Not far beyond the excavation another ocean, this one consisting of sand and rocks, loomed in the distance. Dunes, plateaus, and arroyos. There was one arroyo in particular that zie pictured in zas mind. Once again zie checked the visor. Bragen walked to the hovercraft. There was still time. What would it hurt?

****

Council report: Lark1010genesisproject... Summarization by Archodialmajore1074. *Details provided in two parts. Phase One clear. Phase Two halt. Archodialbragen1031 uncovers artifacts of unknown origin (see packet details). Majore works with Council, acquires approval for Phase 3 excavation. Original conclusions that produced an alien presence were deemed inaccurate (see packet details). Phase 3 stopped. Construction approved.*

****

A band of Highland Red Grass separated the coast from the Eroded Plains of Apollis. These grasses once swept east across the plains, running all the way to the mountains. Ancient river beds and striated canyons once carried seasonal snow-melt down from the distant peaks each year, eventually falling off the edge of the escarpments and into the sea. Evidence of long extinct vegetation remained, as did the bones of various mammals who once roamed these prairies. Yet this history did not include an Uhlman presence, let alone Synthons.

Bragen still puzzled over this, put the hovercraft into low and floated east toward the arroyo Mavwa had excavated. In ages past, Uhlmans did scatter across the galaxy, perpetuating their race from Lark to Thon. They were followed by the Synthons. Who came to Apollis? Whomever it was did so before The Record. Aside from the logistical questions, there were implications concerning the Galaxial Warp. Zie understood that this was why the Council was spending so much time on the readings.

****

As the hovercraft zoomed along, the far mountains seemed to grow taller. Bragen was in search of a particular isolated peak that jutted out of the prairie, a landmark of sorts that guided interested parties to the deep ravine. Once zie spotted it, zie placed a blind on zas thoughts and pointed the geomorph laser over Mavwa's Gulch. It took a moment for zam to find the embedded icon and let go with a pattern sweep. The icon (a location marker) signaled back, initiating an input. At the same time, zie visualized zas first Planetary Briefing on Apollis. Information flooded in. Original reports about Mavwa's findings and subsequent readouts regarding the material excavated and delivered to Dalimath. While there was nothing odd about the data, in fact nothing about it had changed in thousands of years, something was missing.

Outside of the hovercraft, another top-of-the-line Silverstream, the heat was unbearable. The sky had begun to resemble the sun. Bragen noted that zie had ten minutes of safe time remaining. Zie lifted the craft another ten feet and painted the broad ray down the arroyo in both directions. Once done, zie scanned across a section of the gulley. Mavwa did not have the same type of sophisticated scanner when zie did zas investigation. Instead, zie used archaic rayrakes and other, less responsive handhelds. Old-fashioned dirt and shovel work. Good for a few feet. Bragen centered the scan on the icon and then bored deep into the ground. Zie began to get hits. Six feet. Ten feet. Twenty feet. Metal. Something like digaforms. Zas visor gave off an alarm. It was time to leave.

Bragen flipped on zas extraction component and let it sync over the target. Once complete, zie switched it off and removed the flip. Zie knew it had pulled something out of the ground but did not have time to open it. So zie stored it, then turned the craft around and shot toward the Point. Zie decided to return on a different course, so flew to the coast, spotted Manebeck, then veered north, following Aguila's white beaches. An instant later zie was in deep space.

****

Council transcript: *Lark1010genesisproject*

Councilravenal: Status?

Majore1074: Stellar Council approved my transition seventy-four years ago.

Councilravenal: Where did you go to Academy?

Majore1074: Rawen Lift.

Councilravenal: On Thon. Why so far?

Majore1074: There were several surveys going on there, preparing for lifeways.

Councilravenal: How many excavations have you participated in?

Majore1074: One hundred and eight.

Councilravenal: Before you got involved in the Genesis Project, had you been involved in such...

captures?

Majore1074: Only one.

Councilravenal: Did this other one turn out to be valid?

Majore1074: Yes.

Councilravenal: And where was that?

Majore1074: Dwarth. An early substation. I believe the archy was Cyrus.

Councilravenal: So, what happened there?

Majore1074: Early readings indicated unique lifeforms could have existed there.

Councilravenal: As in…

Majore1074: Yes. Once the first report came in, I was dispatched and the proper analysis was completed. As you know, two archodials can interpret the same set of features differently, so it was not that unusual.

Councilravenal: So, the outcome was?

Majore1074: The lead archy rewrote the report and nothing else occurred.

Councilravenal: A capture. So, what happened on Lark?

Majore1074: After the dig, a data breach in the form of a lecture was inserted into the Warp. Once the Council assembled the facts regarding this incident, I was sent to find the Truth.

Councilravenal: Who was responsible for the breach?

Majore1074: It originated with archodial-bragen1031, but zie did not insert it.

Councilravenal: These were surface readings?

Majore1074: Yes.

Councilravenal: And for the record, who inserted it?

Majore1074: Arion's wizened.

Councilravenal: A troublesome sort.

Majore1074: It appears so.

Councilravenal: Where on Lark?

Majore1074: The Glendom Valley.

Councilravenal: That planet has quite The Record. Keeps your type busy.

Majore1074: Yes. Several sites in this region had already been through a Phase Two when a new location was uncovered near an old river bed. It seemed clear that a strong stream once ran there and it was not long before they found the remnants of buildings. Then the fossils were discovered. That got everyone pretty excited.

Councilravenal: And that was because of the tharsonome readings?

Majore1074: Yes.

Councilravenal: Who was recording them?

Majore1074: Archodialbragen1031.

Councilravenal: Did you know that archodialbragen1031 had a previous… occupation?

Majore1074: After the pre-briefing. Zie talked about it later. A wager. A wratchet gatherer.

Councilravenal: Did you think there is anything odd about that?

Majore1074: About being wratchet gatherer?

Councilravenal: No. That zie became an archodial so late in zas phase.

Majore1074: Not really. I was not sent there to assess that.

Councilravenal: It was that wizened's work.

Majore1074: I did not know that.

Councilravenal: Zie got zam involved. Interested. You reported to the Hive. Seems like that would have come up. Did you know this archodialbragen1031 before the Genesis Project?

Majore1074: Not until Lark.

Councilravenal: And what is your opinion of zas competence?

Majore1074: Of course, I remained cautious around zam. Zie was very good. Perhaps zie brought something different to the profession. A perspective that did not always align with everyone else's. This wager interaction.

Councilravenal: Putting aside the breach, how did zie explain the readings?

Majore1074: Zie was confused. Zie demanded we do the tests over. Which I agreed to do.

Councilravenal: Which you did. So, did this… archy treat you with the proper respect? How did zie react to your conclusion?

Majorie1074: Different. I should have been sent there earlier. At first, zie disagreed with my findings, but eventually came around. We all know what happened.

Councilravenal: You say 'perhaps zie brought something different.' Obviously. The Warp was polluted. So, what should we do with archodialbragen1031?

Majore1074: That is not up to me. But zie did say some concerning things.

Councilravenal: We are aware. Such excavations often involve delicate matters, particularly where construction is involved. The Galaxial Warp is a wonderful gift to the Common Benefit, to the Hive, but misinformation can poison it. Can poison the Truth. That is why this is about so much more than a construction site. That is why you were involved. We must be sharper.

Majore1074: [a nod]

Councilravenal: Tharsonomes are not perfect.

Majore1074: [another nod]

Councilravenal: So, let's talk about what zie said.

Majore1074: Zie was leading a crew that had worked on several sites on Lark. Including the one in the Glendom Valley. I was sent there after the hot read.

Councilravenal: What did your probes tell you?

Majore1074: Zie was well-versed in both Rawnswawn and Sarkasian's works. To a certain extent all archies dabble in such thoughts at some point during their span. But I was unaware of the wizened's early influence.

Councilravenal: What else?

Majore1074: We know that zie engaged in flips. Who doesn't?

Councilravenal: And the black markets? Anything in depth?

Majore1074: Not really. I never saw that. The capture seemed an ordinary type venture. Once I re-calibrated the readings and informed zam and zas team, zie did not like it, but acquiesced.

Councilravenal: Yet told zas mentor, a major transgression. The wizened injected it into the Warp.

Majore1074: I think Bragen was as surprised as we were.

Councilravenal: Beside the point.

Majore1074: Yes.

Councilravenal: The Inducer recommended a remboot. What do you think?

Majore1074: I don't think that is my responsibility.

Councilravenal: But what would you do?

Majore1074: I would talk to zam again. Trace the memcore.

Councilravenal: Thank you. And good work.

Chapter 3

Bragen returned to the aerodrome and released the Silverstream to the waiting crew. Walking across the tarmac zie double-checked where zie hid the Mavwa's Gulch download, itching to open it. Zie noticed the Council starship docked near the gateway.

Briefs were usually mundane affairs involving the lead archodial and a Council rep. When excavated features were involved it became more complicated. Uncovering unknown artifacts meant the inclusion of a Warp Inducer and Council Coordinator. The Inducer was there to ensure that nothing was broadcast across the Warp that the Full Council had not approved. This was accomplished through the standard delay and flip mechanisms. Linatin was already in the Conference Room with Acendor, Acendoth, and Linweil. Bragen could feel the Inducer, but did not see zam. Zie did see Majore. Something was up. Everyone exchanged the galaxial greeting: palm up, circular wave.

"The Synthon of the age," Linweil offered.

Bragen nodded, zas eyes on Majore. "What's this?"

Linatin looked at the Dimensional. It displayed a panoramic view of Bricksite1. "The Council has brought new information from Wahlgahlen. We will be making a major announcement during the Show. Mythgarden Point has been linked to the Pioneer Expedition. Its historic news. What a discovery. Congratulations."

It took a moment for zam to process this. Through the Local, zie sensed their euphoria. And felt the probes. The Lost Pioneer Expedition involved the ancient Uhlman mission to found a colony on Dwarth. No such colony existed. It had departed Arion ten ages past. Somewhere between Thon and Dwarth it disappeared from the Warp. What happened to the craft and crew remained a mystery.

Bragen looked at each face, reading their thoughts. Each Synthon maintained close contact by using the Local. Zie gifted back their exuberance, yet at the same time shared zas uneasiness. Zie looked at Majore.

The Dimensional switched to an architectural rendering of the new capital. Inset within its multi-level buildings was an open space that included the excavated features.

Linweil pointed to the imprintation: '*Archodialbragen1031 made the Pioneer discovery.*'

"I would never have guessed, or imagined," Bragen admitted.

"Undoubtedly," Linweil agreed. "For this work, you've been elevated to Council Coordinator. No more digging in the dirt. Let's all sit down."

Everyone took a seat around the circular table.

"So, what about the readings?" Bragen asked. *No more dirt work?* Zie thought about that. "The tharsonome."

"As we suspected, they were off a bit," Acendoth answered. "Certainly Uhlman. That's been cleared up. Not your fault. The heat did it. But your excavation led us to the Pioneer."

"How?"

Acendoth continued. "The unknown material that

fell out of the cave. The metal. We think it is from Dwarth."

Bragen looked at Linweil. "They made it to Dwarth? Is there any evidence to support that? And here's a better question. Why did they leave?"

"We don't know. Early versions of what became the Warp were often misinterpreted. The important point is the age of the material and the artifacts track back to the Pioneer Expedition."

Bragen pushed back zas chair. That was a lot to unpack. Zie could not help but recall the transcript readout from the Genesis Project. *Tharsonomes are not perfect.* But again? And Cloyden's? Zie thought of the innumerable visor warnings zie had received over the past five years. This new promotion seemed like a reach. A failure. Which brought up more questions.

"That metal, or whatever it is. What data links it to Dwarth? And if it does tie back to that planet, the Record has to explain where it was found. Do we know?"

Digibits were rife with data concerning all the planets. As to Dwarth, Uhlman and Synthon excavations provided plenty of analysis regarding its elements. Certainly, individualized elements found within the artifact were common throughout the Prometheus. But this amalgamation?

Majore's thought wave penetrated them for the first time. "We have not ruled out Arion completely, but the consensus is it came from Dwarth. Both planets include the properties that show up in the readings."

"That's true of every planet and half our moons," Bragen replied, alarmed that this archy was involved in the conversation. "This material is unknown."

"Taken in context it all makes sense," Majore

replied.

As far as Bragen was concerned, it did not make sense. Zie had to be careful. It was important that zie kept zas thoughts small. They were telling zam that, as planned, the Pioneer Expedition *did* go to Dwarth, but for reasons unknown it ended up on Apollis. In other words, the shiny blue-black metal column that jutted out of the bottom of the cave came from Dwarth! "So... the Uhlman's were brick builders?"

"Not sure what you are getting at," Majore answered. "Colonizers use available materials."

There was an inevitability about the situation that did not bode well for zas future, despite what they were saying. It seemed eerily like what zie had experienced on Lark. Which meant zie was once again wrong. But what about the dirt blocks? Certainly, not inconceivable, but from the Pioneer Expedition? Uhlman? Zie found it hard to believe.

Uhlmans were not linked to such features. Additionally, nothing within zas memcore or The Record indicated they were linked to similar artifacts. What about the bones? Zie had to focus. If they wanted to, the Stellar Council could easily turn these additional tharsonome readings into justification for removing him from any future archodial activities. Instead, they were promoting zam.

"Of course," Majore said, "all features will be protected from the construction crews as the work progresses." Zas body was devoid of expression. Bragen was puzzled. *Why was this archy involved?* Zie had not seen zam since the Glendom Valley fiasco.

Bragen looked back at the Dimensional, forcing zamself to move on. "So Vatch is back on line."

"Zie is," Linweil answered. "But with certain strictures. It becomes a more complicated build site because of the preservation aspect. That is why Majore is here."

Bragen began to align the logistics of the situation in zas head, disconcerted with Majore's presence. "I can do that."

Acendor shook zas head. "You have some work left to do, but will soon be prepping for the coordination on Menomis. Majore will oversee the wrap-up here and write the report."

"And Romo?"

"Another archy can go to that moon. The Menomis oversight is a much more important to the Stellar Council."

Bragen was not so sure about that. Zie had spent the majority of zas career in the field. In the elements. Under the moons and suns. On zas knees in the dirt. Uncovering the next something.

All major excavations required that the lead archy write up the report that explained what had been found and what such features and artifacts meant, not only for a more inclusive history of the planet, but the galaxy. Zie always looked forward to the *write-up*, which gave zam a chance to assimilate everything zie had done, from discovery to artifactual reconstruction. Now Majore, along with tying this discovery to the Pioneer Expedition, was taking charge of the synthesis. What about the anomaly near the point? And Mavwa's Gulch? Zie had to be careful how zie thought about this.

Bragen could feel everyone's eyes on zam. Zie had to relent, but couldn't. "I can do the write-up. What's a few more moons?"

Linweil looked at the Dimensional. Bragen's image flashed across it with the news of zas discovery, promotion, and new assignment. "We understand your desire, but you're needed elsewhere. I appreciate how invested you are but this is bigger than anyone here. You know that. We have to get ready for the Show."

And there it was, a wave of info flowing through each Synthon in the room, linking the evening's festivities to individual roles and responsibilities. It was already two hours before the first moon. Radiwon, governor in waiting, would kick things off. Acendoth would talk about the history of Apollis. Acendor would recount the disappearance of the Pioneer Expedition. Bragen would then detail Bricksite1. The planet's governor was next in line, scheduled to say a few words before the Show wrapped up.

"Anything else?" Linweil asked Bragen.

"I guess not," zie answered, trying to control zas thoughts. Zie knew there was an Inducer close by, trying to read zam.

"It's a great day for the Prometheus. Let's meet back in an hour and shove off."

Strolling down the corridor toward zas quarters, all Bragen wanted to do was get in touch with Cloyden. Zie wanted to meet zam in the equipment room, but thought better of it. Once inside zas own quarters, zie flipped off the Warp.

They would know about this, but it really wasn't that unusual, especially after such an intense day. Once inside the confines of zas own abode Bragen fell into zas recliner and unbound the Recollect. It contained the scan that lay buried in the gulch where Mavwa had found the artifacts. When the excavation was complete, an icon was placed there to commemorate the site.

Leaning back in the recliner, Bragen opened the download. A variety of colors flashed across zas memcore. Reds, blues, greens, and yellows. Even black and white. Large chunks of information began to roar in. The colors disappeared, followed by a sheet of gray. After the download completed the archy rebooted the Warp. There were already two messages from Linweil and one from Majore. Linweil wanted some more insight on an odd tool fragment. Majore just wanted to talk. Zie answered Linweil and ignored Majore, then flipped off the Warp again and opened the scanned material.

****

Zie could tell the streams were ancient. Older than any device Bragen knew about. The files seemed to be in some kind of order, but zie had no idea where to start. Different representations of the same images began to rotate in and out. Something like a digibit. Then something like a sound. One after the other, the colors returned.

Red, blue, green, yellow, white, black. As zie observed each, a tingle went up the back of zas neck. There was an order to the colors. Nothing within zas memcore explained the why or the how. But zie knew. Files of some sort. Not readable digibits. Sounds. Music, attached to a jagged wave of multicolored lines. Clearly this particular stream was damaged, yet the sounds that came through were more like thoughts attached to broken slices of color. Zie flipped through the download. There was a lot there. Some appeared to be fragments, others too compartmentalized to easily unravel before the Show. They reminded zam of Interacts. Zie selected what appeared to be a short stream. No images. Just sounds.

Survivable... *[indecipherable]...* *land base.* *Elementals...* *[indecipherable]...* *no coordination...* *[indecipherable]...* *oxygen, nitrogen, carbon, hydrogen, phosphorus, sulfur...* *[indecipherable]...* *and a variety of mammals and marine life make it...* *[indecipherable]...* *damage to...* *[indecipherable]...* *heat...* *[indecipherable]...* *cannot...* *[indecipherable]...* *the plan is to salvage the...* *[indecipherable]...* *waiting...* *[indecipherable]...* *topographies [end of stream].*

Only when Bragen opened zas eyes did zie realize they had been closed. That *language. Fluid.* Not digibits. Zie flipped on the Warp. Two additional messages from Linweil. Both asked, "Where are you?"

Bragen bolted up. Zie was late. A bit dizzy, zie moved toward the door. Slower? Heavier? Walking down the corridor toward the aerodrome, zie knew the flips were tracked and might be mentioned.

They were waiting by the starship. With each step, zie tried to get control of the thoughts that pumped through zas head. Synthons? No. Uhlmans? Could those sounds come from Uhlmans? Zie dumped zas thoughts out the back of zas memcore.

Turquois was already replacing the red sky. It would soon turn green before swaths of yellow-green painted the horizon. The moons had begun their journey across the star-filled night. Linatin and Linweil stood next to the large ship's ramp with someone zie did not know. An Inducer. *The flips.*

Bragen walked briskly across the tarmac. "Sorry."

Linweil shrugged. "I guess you missed my call."

"Yeah, I kicked back and roamed a bit much, I am afraid. Time got away from me."

"A perfect archodial expression," Linweil responded. "So, you are ready?"

Bragen nodded. "Ready."

Linweil looked at the stranger. "This is Flarman. Zie is a Warp Inducer. Nothing to worry about. You know the formality." It was true. Inducers were rarely seen on Apollis. But their presence was always accounted for. No surprise.

Zie waved the palm of zas right hand in the circular fashion of the day.

"Congratulations," Flarman said.

"Thanks."

"Why so many flips?"

Bragen shrugged. "Nervous. I guess. Trying to get my thoughts in order."

"We should go," Linweil said. They were already late. "If we hurry, we might have time for a quick synthesis before the festivities." Linweil then stepped away, deferring to Bragen, who led them up the ramp and into the starship's spacious lobby. Bragen had traveled on them before, but always took a moment to size them up. This was no transit vessel.

"Get used to it, "Acendoth said, stepping up and slapping zam on the back. "You're a galaxial star now. Pun intended."

They were still greeting one another when a slight vibration ran up their boots and into their legs. The starship was on its way to Mythgarden Point. Soon they reset the conversation and concentrated on last minute additions and subtractions. Bragen felt Flarman's probe. To combat this, zie focused on the bricks. Zie brought forth images of the neat rows. Compacted soil formed into large blocks. Expertly arranged with corner coordinates. Zie methodically traversed each exposed row, expanding their size and granular detail. It was an old trick he'd learned in the homeland.

After what seemed no more than a few moments they disembarked on Mythgarden Point. Another starship and several hovercraft were parked on the grassy plains. An ocean breeze blew against their backs as they walked down the ramp toward the new grandstand that loomed over the excavation. Several dignitaries milled around on the stage. Bragen recognized the future governor, Radiwon, standing near the podium in deep thought. Radiwon had been the subject of several digibits after the colonization project was approved.

Soon, everyone was in their assigned place. Planetary communicators and other Inducers surrounded the dignitaries, including Bragen. Linweil thanked those who were there, with a particular nod toward Radiwon. The archy panned across the point and noted the beauty of the third hour of the second moon. There was no physical audience. Everyone in the galaxy participated through the Galaxial Warp. At the moment a view of the Aguila Sea, and white beaches blending into a series of waves lapping endlessly against the sands, streamed across the Flow. Then Radiwon and the other dignitaries appeared. The future governor explained that this was more than another colonial opening. Scans of the ruins flashed across the Prometheus.

"As most of you know," Radiwon began. "Apollis has always been out of our reach. Thirteen-hundred years ago the Solient Expedition, led by Mavwa, explored this planet, but zas findings dissuaded future exploration. Those findings, if nothing else, sparked countless inquiries, launched many careers, and more than a few unthoughts. But we are not here to discuss the old arguments of the past. At the time, it was determined that the expenditures needed to make colonization on Apollis a success were impossibly large. Too large.

"Now here we are. Recent technological advances have made lifeways on this planet more feasible. Bricksite1 is located on one of ten such colonies that will eventually be established here. Once again, we Move The Ball Forward. Today, Acendoth will begin the festivities by taking you on a brief historical journey regarding Apollis and some of its more alluring features. Later, we will explain why colonization here just got a lot more interesting."

For the next few minutes, Acendoth detailed some of the core truths about the planet. Only three were closer to the sun; Zech, Zule, and Uahn. All had been ruled uninhabitable ages ago. Zie made the point of noting the same was once said of Apollis. That was before technological breakthroughs in dome and perma-wall designs, along with the strengthening of the Warp. Since then, the Stellar Council had re-evaluated all possibilities concerning planetary colonization.

"...Millions of years ago it was a green planet. At one time Apollis was covered with lush vegetation, extensive tropical forests and a cyclical evaporative system that was conducive to a variety of fish, fowl, and mammals. This ecosystem was destroyed by the twin asteroids deemed Hammerhead1 and Hammerhead2, which led to an age of darkness and death. A gray-black radioactive belt of dust particles choked off the sun for an indeterminable length of time. The few species who lived through that cataclysm evolved and adapted. Survivors created habitats around the coasts or within the oceans.

"The crippling of the ozone layer made it almost impossible to survive within the interior but life near the sea still flourishes. That is why all ten of the new colonies will begin along shorelines and inlet bays. As life expands, so will our understanding of not only the Prometheus, but systems outside the galaxy. That is why we are here. Governor-in-waiting Radiwon will oversee these lifeways from this magnificent location, Mythgarden Point. We now know we were not the first to consider such possibilities. For more on this stunning discovery, I turn to Co-Council, Acendor of Lark."

Bragen could feel the thrum of the Warp as the two Councilors changed positions. As Acendor prepared zas thoughts, Bragen studied the excavation. Zie stared at the two courses of dirt bricks that ran under the perimeter wall near the room designated X12a, the main quadrant of the twelfth uncovered room. Where did those two courses go? There was no time to investigate. Majore would do it. Age data on the blocks was not available. It usually did not take that long. An image of the skull fragment flashed across zas memcore.

"In the base year 3150," Acendor began, "the Pioneer Expedition left Arion for Dwarth. Uhlmans were at the zenith of their exploratory activity during this period. By then they had activated lifeways on Thon and Menomis. The Pioneer mission was more logistically aggressive, engaging several transits and what we liken to our space haulers. The Record is a little unclear regarding the actual number of Uhlmans who participated in this mission but what has been preserved indicates that up to one-hundred were on the trip. As they made their approach to Dwarth they lost the connections that we now know as the Warp. Between one and two-thousand years ago the Flow was not as reliable, especially at such distances. We never knew what happened. The Pioneer Expedition was lost to history. Until today."

Acendor turned and looked at Bragen. "Five years ago, the Stellar Council appointed archodialbragen1031 to lead the Apollis field survey. This function included all ten lifeways, consisting of ensuring ancient fossils, artifacts, and intelligently constructed features were not destroyed by dozers and grinders. Zie was wrapping up the final survey, where ultimately it was decided to put the first colony, when zie and zas crew discovered this." Acendor extended his arm and open hand toward the ruins. "This my friends, Bricksite1, was built by the survivors of the Pioneer Expedition."

Bragen felt the Warp throbbing through the back of his neck, forcing him to *again* focus on one specific dirt block. Acendor's voice hovered at the back of his mind, faint, yet clear. "These fascinating features were once a part of some type of emergency base built to withstand the rigors of Apollis's tremendous heat. At this point we are unsure what type of disaster struck the expedition, or why they apparently left Dwarth and ended up here. As noted, before the asteroids struck, the grasslands ran further inland. A variety of life forms roamed these prairie coastlands. Their presence probably signaled to the newcomers the sustainability of this region. In addition to an array of artifacts and fossils from some of these animals, archodialbragen1031's team also recovered Uhlman bone fragments that date to the mission's time period.

"While all is not yet clear, enough evidence has been

collected to make this announcement. Over the next one-hundred moons, that's a quarter of a year for those not up on Apollis's calendar, another team will delve into the questions that remain and I can't wait to hear what they come up with. Apollis's main congressional hall is now being reconfigured to enclose these unbelievable ruins. I will now turn it over to the Synthon of the hour, archodialbragen1031."

Billions of Synthons ran through zam. It was an exhilarating feeling. Stamping down zas concerns, zie forced zamself into professional mode and began the prepared Council recitation. All the while, zie felt Flarman's probe, who no doubt was ready to initiate any required blocks. Somehow, Bragen got through it, giving the majority of the credit to the sharp-eyed sculptor and Cloyden's team. Towards the end, as had been agreed upon, zie talked about the upcoming hand-off to Majore and how much zie looked forward to starting zas new position on Menomis. With one caveat. Zie would enjoy a brief snapback on Arion before leaving for zas new assignment.

Afterwards, as zie took zas place between Linweil and Acendor, zie could not help but notice Cloyden's wide-eyed stare. Bragen's lead, near the back of grandstand with the rest of crew, had somehow managed to extend zas neck enough for Bragen to see zam. A common ploy by anyone trying to avoid the Local. Radiwon was front and center again. Bragen turned and listened to the governor-in-waiting wax on about the significance of the Apollis colonization. Radiwon managed to get in a plug for Vatch's New World Designs before reviewing the ten-year plan. All was available for download within the Prometheus Frame. As was always the case, the Hive had already approved this new information. The ever-growing mind was constantly being updated. The Flow, or One Thought, flashed the changes across the Prometheus.

When the festivities concluded, Bragen walked down the steps with several of the dignitaries and explained how the exposed row of block walls were excavated. A few bent down and ran their hands over the compacted bricks, marveling at how each seemed to be the exact size of the other. By then, the third moon had begun rising in the East. Radiwon was particularly fascinated with the excavated features.

"These blocks are perfectly symmetrical. Have you seen that anywhere else?"

"On Lark," Bragen answered.

"So, they are connected to the... Lark thing? Readings of some sort?"

"The features were never questioned," Bragen began, keeping zas thoughts in the professional, flat zone. "Back then, there was nothing else to compare them to. There is now. We have to study that. But you are right about the readings on Lark. There was an equipment malfunction."

An awkward silence followed. Majore spoke into it. "The corollaries are certainly worth investigating. That these features, with those Mavwa uncovered just to the east are tied to the Pioneer Expedition opens a new chapter into galaxial history. Worth its own commission."

The future governor cocked zas head further up, gazing into deep, black space. A million silver stars winked back. "I wonder what happened?"

Linatin interjected, "Mythgarden Point has given us

another clue, but we have no idea. I look forward to Archodialmarjore1074's complete analysis of this stupendous find."

Bragen strolled along the blocks, occasionally answering questions and adding some background. Once again, zie made sure that officials in charge of the lifeway were aware of Cloyden, Riverin, Shyden, and Loydback's efforts. Few officials were interested in what was involved in revealing the features. Most of an archy's day was spent on their knees with a spade or signaler, digging in the dirt. It was tedious and monotonous work. Being able to find what did not appear to be there was the reward all archodial's sought.

Finally, zie found zamself on the starship, heading back to the base. Bragen continued to accept congratulations on both the find and zas new assignment. Zie kept thinking back to Cloyden's stare. Zas lead's particular stance and the way zas neck arched, coupled with zas wide gaze, communicated something more than rapt attention. Over the centuries, all Synthons had developed a physical language removed from the One Thought. This language took different forms, based on interactions and relationships that evolved over time. Because of individual nuances, physical communication was unique to each Synthon and not easily picked up on by strangers.

When Bragen disembarked from the ship, zie nodded in appreciation to everyone and then removed to zas quarters. At least that is what zie intimated. But Bragen did not stop at zas door, instead continuing down the corridor to its end. Zie opened the doorway that led to some descending steps. Slowly, zie made zas way into the basement. There zie strolled amongst the pipes, blinking lights, and energy transfers to the back of the corridor. Several chairs sat haphazardly across the floor. Equipment rooms were built with three-pad perma walls reinforced with kulcat fibers. These walls ensured that any radon explosion or seep could be contained within the room. It was also one of the few places on Apollis where the Warp was completely disabled. This was different from a flip, which any seasoned Inducer could sense. In such spaces, archys and anyone who did not want their thoughts captured could blow off a little steam. Cloyden was waiting for zam.

Zas face was blank but zas body spoke the pseudo physical language that expressed both hesitancy and fear. Zie held an orange tag bag, the type used for field artifacts. Bragen immediately knew that Cloyden was experiencing similar misgivings.

"Here," zie said, handing zam the bag.

Bragen opened it. Inside was a tharsonome membrane. Zie knew where it had come from. "How did you get this?" But Bragen already saw zas assistant's thoughts. The skull fragment. The teeth. Teeth not associated with Uhlmans. The cave. Linatin.

Cloyden said, "I had a bad feeling about this from the beginning."

They had been through a lot together. Cloyden worked with zam on Lark. Was a member of the Genesis Project.

Bragen stared at the thin filament. "So, what do they have?"

"They have the original. This is a replicate. I made it before you and Vatch showed up. Just in case. Once Majore arrived, I made my decision."

The tharsonome membrane contained all the initial

readings.

"Why are you doing this?"

Cloyden shrugged. "I don't know. Thought you would want it as a parting gift."

"This could get you a remboot," Bragen warned.

"Or a clean scan."

Silence filled the void between them.

Finally, Bragen said, "Thank you."

"I better get back. Flarman will be roaming about."

Bragen gave a nod. Cloyden moved past zam and disappeared. The dull hum of the equipment room hung in the air. A question bloomed in zas head. *Is this why I became an archy?* Zie studied the membrane for a moment. A thin, slick, slice of replicated readouts. Dangerous stuff.

The Warp was a beautiful instrument. The collective thought. Seldom did zie think of it in any way but that, yet far from Arion, one became more relaxed. It was one of the perks of becoming an archy. Deep within protective layers of kulcat fibers zie allowed zamself another thought. The Warp went everywhere and into everything. Which brought up an image of the professor.

Bragen wanted to know more. Was the Mavwa download an Interact or something else? It seemed very old. Zie carefully placed the membrane back in the pouch then put it in zas pocket. Still within the equipment room, zie recalled zas last conversation with Professor Mador. It was after the hearing. A thought communique.

"Go to Apollis," the wizened said. That was the position the Stellar Council had offered. "You never know what might turn up there. They would love for you to take the remboot. Can't blame you if you did."

At the time, they were sitting among the old

professor's favorite possessions. Reems of digibits, artifacts, and fossils from all over the galaxy.

"To banishment," Bragen replied. Thinking back, zie wished zie was there now, sitting in that old chair across from zas mentor. Zie did not know how old the wizened was. Very old.

"The Record occasionally has good things to say about the banished. Get as far away from the Warp as you can."

So, zie did. Now Bragen had a new title and another distant assignment. Coordinator. On Menomis. But first zie would return to the homeland. To the greens and blues. To the clean and the orderly. To the heart of the Warp. As well as the professor. The packet in zas pocket suddenly felt heavier. A moment later Bragen bounded up the metal steps and into the corridor that led to zas room.

Chapter 4

Something odd and possibly illegal occurred on the flight back. Bragen dreamed. Once before such an oddity occurred, but an Inducer explained it away. Zie said it was a malfunction related to arrhythmia. A blood flow problem. That was zas boot-up year. At the time, zie was relieved, for dreams were considered voluntary acts. The Warp broadcast that flips and unthoughts led to dreams, yet under scrutiny, health concerns offered the subject a way out of a predicament.

Within that first *malfunction* Bragen found zamself in a boat of some sort. It floated across a large pond or lake. Behind and to zas side were several shiny metal buildings. Ahead loomed a mountain. As the boat neared the shore zie noticed several other crafts pushed up on the bank. A group of archys stood next to the crafts. All looked straight at zam. In a language Bragen did not know they repeated over and over, "Do not look left or right. Do not look in the windows." Immediately afterward a wall of tinted green windows appeared. Within one of them, something moved. A blur. The dream ended.

Later, zas assigned Core interpreter explained that arrhythmic boot-up glitches were not that unusual, especially during the new life phase.

As the passenger transport descended, Bragen stared out of the window into deep space. Deep space stared back. The last thing the Core interpreter told zam was, "But if it happens again, we will be in contact." That time had come. *They will know*. Was it zas heart again? Zie felt fine.

A soft tone alerted everyone to prepare for landing. The new dream was still there, hanging in the front of zas memcore. Bragen stood, feeling for Inducer probes. It was also possible that a Watcher may be searching zas thoughts.

Within this new dream, zie was not in a boat. Instead, it began with zam walking through a haze of smoke. Where was zie? Arion? Nothing seemed familiar. Or orderly. Just the opposite. No Warp. Zie heard popping sounds. Explosions. Ahead, the smoke cleared. Zie saw a jagged line of charred ruins. Was that a town or a village? Zie walked up a dirt road toward piles of rubble, crossing a stone bridge at one point, its intersecting side rails catching zas attention. The rails resembled tree branches. Each wrapped in intricate patterns of vines and leaves. The bridge ran over a dry creek bed. Once across, zie walked beyond a pile of rubble toward the smoking buildings. The road was pockmarked with craters. Disorder hung in the air like a damp mist. A swirling void, instead of the Warp, filled zam. A strange sensation. The smoke grew thicker. Zie snorted. At the end of the street fire blazed among several distant structures. An industrial plant of some kind. A mangled gate. Beyond the gate, blurs of movement.

Bragen wanted to get away. Zie turned and ran back toward the bridge. No Flow. No Warp. A floating feeling. Fresh air filled zas lungs. Then hot wind blew embers against zas neck. Something hit zas leg. A ripped piece of blue cloth. Clothing of some kind. Zie turned and pulled it off zas leg. Looked at it. The shape was odd.

"It's too small," zie said. Not a thought. A sound.

It was a smock. Very small. A large red inscription of some kind was emblazoned on the pocket. A letter. The letter M. *What is a letter?* Zie caught a movement out of the corner of zas eye. Something small. It came out of one of the burning buildings. Then another. And another. Small blurred shapes. They ran across the bridge and through a mangled gate. A moment later they were gone. Then zie woke up.

Moving slowly down the aisle with zas bag, Bragen bent and looked out the window. Deep space was gone. In its place zie saw the familiar skyline and a large stand of elderwoods. Zie had missed both. Buildings and trees. Blue sky. The structures glittered in the sun. But the dream remained. Zie could feel the cloth in zas hands. Thin and worn. Could see the red letter. That thought. *Letter.* What was a letter? How did zie know to call it that? *Strange.* Zie shook zas head. No charred ruins in front of zam. Only bustle and flow. After five years, the archy was home. The full strength of the Galaxial Warp soaked through zam, wiping away the emptiness of the dream.

Arion was very different from Apollis. The terminal was packed. Shoulder to shoulder, a teaming mass of Synthons pushed their way forward, each oblivious to the other. Bragen dropped into the crowd and began weaving zas way through the station. When zie passed through the massive gateway, the Flow was so strong zie had to tamp it down. The Warp was in full roar. A flood of information downloaded into the back part of zas brain: at the same time enervating and overwhelming.

The trick was to open different memcore vaults sequentially to ensure no overloads and no missed opportunities.

The Galaxial Warp was the webbing that tied everyone together. Despite its connectivity, the thousands of Synthons in the terminal ignored zam, as did the millions of minds throughout the Prometheus taking part in the Flow, each lost within their own individuality. No one looked zas way. Each kept their eyes straight ahead, moving into the future. Bragen did the same.

One-half hour later zie stood near the exit, studying the Dimensional that revealed the location and images of zas new quarters. It was good to be home. The outside air was crisp and sweet. Some of the elderwoods were already losing their leaves. Late fall. Zie hailed a rail splitter taxi.

Stepping into the craft, zie thumbed the transpo coin in zas pocket. The taxi floated up and drifted toward zas temporary quarters, located on the outskirts of Andrio, one of Arion's largest cities. It eventually picked up speed, shooting down broad, clean avenues, erasing any thought of the smoking ruins or strange garments.

Synthons moved along the same rail and flight paths in all manner of transport, including sky walks. Zas memory sifted through the Flow, organizing thoughts. The taxi stopped in front of a gleaming fifty-story skyscraper, zas home for the next ten moons. Bragen looked forward to the snapback, but had pressing business to attend to first.

The archodial could sense the wratchet-gatherers under zas boots. Wagers, generally hidden from view whenever possible, were underground, like everyone everywhere, busy Moving Toward the Future. Other Synthons, some in slick one-piece suits, some in team uniforms, passed zam on the walk, eyes glazed, fully engaged in the Flow. Bragen hopped out and ventured into the building.

Accommodations were basic and familiar. Bed. Chair. Desk. Typical Synthon. No need for a Dimensional. After putting away zas things zie sat down and engaged, no longer needing to tamp back. The full flow whirled through, each bit finding its proper place. First zie caught up on the latest Stellar Council news, which included a lot of information on the recently discovered Pioneer Expedition, then ran through what were called the gossip sections of the Warp, many of which zie had become familiar with on the way in. The room had a large picture window. Zas view of the city was a good one. Along with a lot of new skyscrapers zie picked out a new park. As usual, no one was in it. Work progressed. Everyone tasked with performing their Talent: Moving The Ball Forward. Filtering through some old archaeological news, Bragen noted that zie was only a few miles from East Andrio. Mador's home.

The phrases, "moving the ball forward," as well as, "moving toward the future," echoed in the back of zas memcore. Zie'd first heard it working as a wratchet gatherer deep underground. Wratchet gatherers, a part of the wager-force, worked the machines that bored the tunnels under all galaxial cities. Wagers of all stripes ensured that galaxial infrastructures remained invisible and proficient.

Early on, Bragen's innate talents were noticed, particularly when it came to mineral identification and stratigraphy. Zarn, zas longtime supervisor, was constantly talking about "moving the ball," and "expanding the future." Of course, this was common Warp talk, a part of the One Thought all Synthons exhorted and strove toward. Such practice was a sure way to move up in the standings. Zie enjoyed working with Zarn and zas machine-mates, and would still be there, perhaps with a position like Zarn's, if Mador had not come into zas life.

Bragen thought back to that other snapback. It was during a day-break. There zie was, sitting on a Brinslow Park bench in East Andrio, enjoying the morning. As usual it was empty. Synthons seldom lingered there. The future beckoned.

One day the wizened ambled over with a bag of bird feed and sat down. Very odd. After a bit of silence, their Locals linked, and they began to communicate. The stranger taught at University. Zas long, silver hair was braided in that particular way all professors of the wizened class did it up in. Once Mador found out zie was a wratchet-gatherer zie asked a number of questions about geology, soil compositions, and stratigraphy. At one point, the professor asked zam about zas interactions with archodials.

Bragen was very familiar with this class of wagers. Zarn often left it to zam to stop the boring operation when zie came across anything that looked out of place and to then get in touch with the archodial council. They often watched them work. Bragen found their jobs more than interesting, but had never contemplated becoming one until zie began to talk with the wizened. Mador eventually encouraged zam to query the Board of Talents about reassignment.

Over the next year they often met in an empty

Brinslow Park. The topic almost always turned to archaeology. Bragen began to utilize the Warp to find out as much as zie could about the profession. With Mador's help, zie eventually transitioned over, spending a lot of time with the old professor.

Years later on Lark, Bragen was stunned when tharsonome readings derived from the Genesis Project indicated a non-specific DNA was present in an excavated fossil. That discovery brought zam back to Mador's apartment and their late evening talks. There, sitting in overstuffed chairs in front of a roaring fire, digibits and digaforms everywhere, they discussed rayrakes, trench lines, and, occasionally, the possibility of life on distant stars and moons.

The setting was relaxed and casual, with no fear of leakage. The professor's den walls were padded with three stacks of perma-wall reinforced with Kulcat fibers harvested from Dwarth. They were used in the construction of several new buildings at University. Mador had managed to divert some to zas own purposes. Months had turned into years and then decades. Their conversations often included discussions concerning Rawnswawn's *Escaping Extinction* and Sarkasian's *Mawoan Myths and other Fables*. These conversations often skirted over to other controversial subjects, such as the illegality of dreams and the history of the Prometheus. Mador often criticized Sarkasian's theories, which in of itself, was controversial.

"Zas conclusions are not based on facts," the wizened would say. "They are based on beliefs." Mador had always argued that dreams, even myths, held keys to doors that need not be closed. Why not have an open discussion? This put Bragen's mentor into the Synthonic minority that often ventured into black-market thoughts. Hence the perma-walls.

"Understanding our essence has a connection to tales told," Mador often repeated. "Fables come from somewhere. Not from outside us. From within. I sometimes wonder if we do not listen because of what we might hear." Of course, the wizened was speaking in metaphorical terms, as thought-speech was not audible.

Bragen remembered one conversation regarding a black-market theory called Humotzero. This played into Mador's argument regarding keeping an open mind. Humotzero argued that Synthons and Uhlmans were a part of some unknown answer to a question that had yet to be formalized.

"What does it mean," Bragen once asked, "Humotzero?"

"A good one," the wizened answered before staring long and hard at zas student. "There are not enough questioners. Questions bring up answers that might be designated untruths. So, the questions are never asked. We need fewer locks and more keys."

"Doesn't a good question deserve an answer?" Bragen prodded.

"Yes," the wizened answered, zas golden eyes boring into zam. "But all answers are not equal, or easily derived. Perhaps you provide your own."

"The question or the answer?"

Mador looked away. "Both."

Everyone knew the Record, or histories. They were embedded at initialization and reinforced during each boot-up. There was no mention of Humotzero or anything beyond Uhlmans within a Synthon's memcore.

The wizened was constantly posing questions. Why

did Sarkasian mock Rawnswawn so? Of course, one had to be careful pursuing such a line. Warp Watchers and Inducers studied the Flow for such queries. Until the Genesis Project, Bragen considered most conversations with the professor to be little more than mind-play. Yet the initial tharsonome readings from the Glendom Valley made zam reconsider. The archy could not resist sharing some of what happened there with zas old mentor.

Even so, as lead archodial, Bragen was cognizant of Warp protocols. When zie did bring up Lark, zie crafted the information into a playful "what if" scenario. Later, Mador read between the lines.

Not long after, albeit in a subtle way, the wizened incorporated some of this information into a lecture on alien artifacts. Unless conscience flips or perma walls were involved, such lectures only lasted a moon or two before a Warp Watcher tagged it. Anything of concern was quickly removed from the stream until further review. Which meant they were erased forever.

Ten moons after Mador's lecture slipped into the Warp, it was taken off stream. A moon later the Stellar Council informed Bragen that zas Glendom Valley readings were inaccurate. That was six years ago. Bragen had not seen zas mentor since.

The day after zie settled into the East Andrio suite Bragen walked down to the same park bench and took a seat. As usual, it was empty. Zie sat for some time, admiring the few blue and green leaves that desperately clung to the elderwood's black branches. Soon they would lose their grip. Winter approached. The sun would hide behind clouds for one-hundred moons. Snow would fall. Bragen wondered how zie'd stood Apollis's heat for all those years.

Zie saw zam in the distance, gingerly coming down the steps of zas apartment. Mador's balcony overlooked the bench. The professor, now with a slight limp, casually walked across the street, zas eyes on the trees. As if the six years had been six hours, zie quietly took a seat and began to feed the birds.

"Sorry about the trouble," zie said.

Mador was not within the Warp. Bragen flipped. "No problem. No trouble."

"If you say so. How long are you back, Pioneer discoverer?"

Of course zie would know. Everyone interested in that sort of thing would.

"Ten moons of snapback and then off to Menomis."

"Oh." Mador looked toward the northeast, where that planet was situated at the moment. "Lead archy's are always on the clock."

"Not as an archy. A coordinator. The proctor class."

Mador turned and looked at zam for the first time. "You dig up archeological features linked to the Pioneer Expedition and get pushed sideways? You asked for that?"

"No. Still have the perma-walls in place?"

Mador's golden eyes studied him a full minute before replying. "Yes. Come up and we'll talk old times."

The Galaxial Warp was more than a communication device. Perhaps that was its original intent. That's what the Record said. A means to build the galaxial community. Interconnectedness. The One-thought. The Hive builder. Combining and weaving all minds into the One.

The Record noted that through this melding, a

higher order of Uhlmans evolved into Synthons. Within this evolutionary process came the secondary benefit, something collectively overseen by the Stellar Council and their acolytes, Watchers and Inducers. The ability of the Collective, through Inducers, to point out and eliminate black-market thoughts was critical to a smooth-running Warp. These same acolytes identified inaccuracies and eliminated Closemindedness. At least within the Warp.

Despite this oversight, individuals often avoided the Flow with flips. And perma-walls. But the costs for such violations escalated, depending on the frequency and subject matter. The Hive assimilated all, including the searches. At the Seers' direction, Inducers sought out the flips and tried to determine unusual patterns. Violations not determined to be premeditated included light reprimands and watch lists. Remboots and clean-waves, while rare, were reserved for the more egregious acts. More scrutiny was given to professionals as opposed to the wager class.

Of course, the less egregious, untethered thoughts were more common than any Synthon knew. Generally, investigators remained pretty casual. The majority of such thoughts were harmless. Most did so without intending to scatter nonsensical metadata across the galaxy. Far from Arion and the Warp, Bragen seldom worried about flips before the bones were found in the blueweed, but back home one had to be more careful. Hence the request to retreat to Mador's quarters.

When they started walking toward the building, they flipped the Warp back on. Bragen was more aware of the limp now, and noticed Mador taking deeper breaths as they made their way toward the entrance. In most cases, physicality did not matter. A Synthon's thoughts were its most distinguishing characteristic. True, a wizened's hair stood out, but by and large outward appearances were all the same. Blue skin, yellow eyes, silver hair.

Was zie three hundred or four hundred years old? What was the maximum, five-hundred? Bragen had known zam for ninety-nine. They continued with small thoughts in the elevator and the hallway that led to zas flat. A one room abode that remained just as Bragen remembered. An oddity. Cozy. Digibits and artifacts, deep chairs, and a fireplace. They settled into the chairs. The room brought back so many memories. As was their old custom, they continued to reminisce for an hour or so before once again making the added precaution of a flip. At that point Bragen reached into zas pocket.

"Something happened on Apollis." Zie showed zam the clear bag that held the tharsonome membrane. "These are from the fossils found in the cave below Mythgarden Point." Mador knew all about the lifeway and the subsequent discovery. As zie'd already noted, it was all over the Warp.

Bragen pulled it out of the bag and handed it to him. "You know what that is."

It was a statement. Mador gave zas old student a funny look before standing and turning toward a series of drawers that were built into the wall. After a couple of minutes zie pulled out an early model tharsonome and sat back down.

"It should work," zie said, more to zamself than Bragen. Then, "This is why you are a coordinator?"

"I guess you could say that." There was no reason to say anything else. Mador sat back down and stared at the membrane. At the same time, information began to flow from Bragen to the wizened. It started with the scorptor's discovery on Mythgarden Point. Then the image of the skull and the unusually large Uhlman teeth followed by a visual of the spiraled metal. It ended with a picture of the Show and the dirt-blocks.

Mador nodded. "There is always more to the story. Those teeth are not Uhlman."

The wizened flipped the tharsonome over and slipped the membrane into its slot, flipped it back over, turned it on, then sat back down. Together they reviewed Cloyden's readings. Non-definitive DNA readouts. Linweil had attributed Bragen's own readings to a tharsonome malfunction. Probably from Apollis's oppressive heat. On the surface, a plausible conclusion.

"Like Lark," Mador said.

Bragen nodded.

"So, we actually have three non-definitive readouts. Right? What you found in the Glendom Valley as a part of the Genesis Project. An error. Then Cloyden's. Then yours. What did they say about zas?"

"Nothing.

"Hmn. And yours was a malfunction." This was a statement, not a question.

"Yes," Bragen answered. "So, there is that. And Majore was involved. Zie took over the report."

Another long pause followed before Mador said anything. When zie did zie was looking up at several images that emanated from the walls. All were of University. "How strange."

Very, Bragen thought. More than a coincidence. Zas work had been questioned two times in zas career. Both times the same peer was involved. Zie wasn't quite sure how to express zas misgivings. "What do you think?"

Mador was still looking at images of the tree-lined trails that wound through the campus's glass buildings. "A loaded one. Was zie a rival?"

"No."

"You know zam well?"

"Just in the field."

"Academia can be a chum pit."

Certainly, there was competition within archodial circles. But zie found it hard to believe Majore might be involved in something underhanded. But zas appearance was odd. "Subterfuge? Why would zie do that?"

"Any number of reasons," Mador answered. "Perhaps something before the Genesis Investigation. Perhaps zas conclusions were not based on facts. Perhaps beliefs drove zam. Perhaps zie was encouraged."

"What beliefs?"

"That the only correct conclusion is the one that concurs with right thinking? With the One Thought? Who knows?"

Bragen contemplated this for a moment, then thought about Lark and Mavwa's Gulch. "The correct conclusion?"

A wizened's eyes were slightly different, depending on the way the light hit them, more gold than yellow. At times very much so. This was one of those times. "Correct conclusions lead to correct thinking, or so the Warp tells us."

Bragen thought about how to frame what zie was about to say. Before zie left Apollis, zie had run a second fragment from the downloads, which turned out to be just as puzzling as the first. The same sounds. Something like music, but a language. Something zie felt zie should know about, but did not. Zie wanted to know. That was why zie had come to Brinslow Park.

"Before I left, a ran a scan around the icon on Mavwa's Gulch. No one knows. Back at my quarters, I was able to open a few of them. Some are decayed. But I was able to understand, to a certain extent, what was on two of them. Fragments. Another resembled a table of contents, but the sequential inscriptions are undecipherable, or at least I could not decipher them. But I was able to identify a set of numbers running alongside the list. I want to open them. This first fragment is associated with the numerals one and eleven. The second ends with two and zero. There is something bizarre about both."

Bragen opened the first, then allowed Mador to enter zas memcore. The music. Then the colors. Seemingly a language. Not of their galaxy, but surprisingly, understandable. Mador flinched.

Survivable... [indecipherable]... landbase. Elementals... [indecipherable]... no coordination... [indecipherable]... oxygen, nitrogen, carbon, hydrogen, phosphorus, sulfur... indecipherable]... and a variety of mammals and marine life make it... [indecipherable]... damage to... [indecipherable]... heat... [indecipherable]... cannot... [indecipherable]... the plan is to salvage the... [indecipherable]... waiting... [indecipherable]... topographies [end of stream].

Bragen opened the second one: *"Now the cycle has been completed... [indecipherable]... several dwellings... [indecipherable]... no communication... [indecipherable]... we will soon move down below... [indecipherable]... into the sun... to the mountains... [indecipherable]... how much longer... [indecipherable]... chil... [indecipherable]... are...*

[end of fragment]..."

Bragen realized zas eyes had been closed. Zie looked at Mador. Zas mentor opened zas. The sound had mesmerized them.

Finally, Mador said, "Interesting."

"What is it?" Bragen asked, more interested in the sound than the message.

Looking toward the wall, the professor answered, "I do not know. But it is archaic. Ageless. Familiar."

Bragen shook zas head. "I did search the Warp."

"For the word *chil*," Mador guessed.

"Yes." A Watcher could have found this.

"And?"

"Nothing."

"Inducers will know by now," Mador said. "They'll send a lidscan."

Bragen had thought about that. Lidscans were automated snoopers. "I knew it would eventually end up in the metadata, but Watchers are involved in worthless searches all the time."

"True," Mador said. "So, what was the official determination regarding the tharsonomes?"

"Uhlman. Which confirmed their conclusions concerning the Pioneer Expedition."

"Which explains the walls."

"Yes."

A moment passed. The professor looked into zas eyes. "Those were not Uhlman teeth. Any archy would know that. I don't think it was the Pioneer Expedition."

"Neither do I. As old as they are, it is clear that an unknown talent went into the construction of those dwellings. I know of no Uhlman features like those we unearthed."

"And there is something else," the wizened added. "It has to do with the sound."

"What?" Bragen asked.

"The messages have nothing to do with the Warp."

"How could that be?"

They both knew the Record. An early version of the Warp had been in place for thousands years. As stated, that was when History began.

"I do not know," Mador answered. "But such communication has never been a part of the Warp. Interact, yes. An early version of that, but not the Flow."

The wizened was very interested, something Bragen was hoping for. "Should we open the rest now?"

Mador nodded. "We have to. There may not be another time. Other references must allude to—"

"*Chil*," Bragen broke in.

"Yes, as well as what, or who the creator was. But we may not find an answer. Still, it seems whoever left them knew we would be able to decipher what they contain."

There was no reason to say anything else. Bragen looked deeply into the wizened's golden eyes and opened the files. Strips of colors flashed by, at first one long stream, then compartmentalized groups. Reds, blues, yellows, and greens. One pattern was more ordered than the others. More sequential. About a third were irretrievable.

Together, they reviewed the sequential image first. It was probably a list that involved indecipherable inscriptions. Yet numbers they knew aligned with each, giving them a starting point. They picked one.

More colors. Blobs that began to pull away from each other. A moment later Bragen and Mador were inside a small, square room. A strange robed individual with a hood covering zas face stood on a dirt floor near a doorway. An orange glow surrounded its neck.

They noticed the walls were also dirt. Earth blocks. And a dirt ceiling held in place with wood beams. The hooded figure bowed. "Welcome."

It was a sound similar to the ones found in the fragments, more a melody than a thought. The orange glow brightened.

Bragen and Mador nodded. This was no Synthon. Nor, Bragen guessed, an Uhlman.

"Time is broken," the robed figure said. "The first step."

Synthonic Interactives used holographic imprints of categorized thoughts to teach all manner of Talents. They were also used to grow the Record. The past. All Synthons used them to upgrade their data banks. This was similar, yet strangely, more defined. Three dimensional. Synthonic versions were flatter, two-dimensional representations. And there was no Hive signature.

"Who are you?" Mador asked.

The stranger removed its hood, "Such a question provides us with information to best serve you." Zas eyes were much smaller, and neither yellow nor gold. They were blue. Its nose was also smaller, and its skin was brown. And something else about the skin. It had lines in it. Yet the most startling feature was below the nose. It had a mouth. That was where the strangely musical sound came from.

"You do not know me," it said. This was a statement. The orange glow brightened when it spoke. The ring resembled a collar. "We were before you."

The moving mouth revealed white teeth and a tongue. This vision so distracted Bragen zie found it hard to focus on what the being was saying. *The mouth was a means of communication.* Communication facilitated by the tongue within it. Zas memcore brought up an image of an ancient range arth using this organ to draw water out of a pond.

Its ears, on the other hand, were much larger than a Synthon's. It had yellow hair that contained streaks of gray. All Synthons began with light blue hair. As they aged it became silver. The yellow hair reminded zam of Lark's sea birds. Additionally, their host was about a foot taller, with well-proportioned arms, legs, and feet. Feet covered in some type of corded boot.

"Before me?" Bragen asked.

"Yes," the thing said.

Bragen pointed at zas own face. "Your nose is different. And of course, the mouth. How do you understand me?"

It pointed to the orange glow that wrapped around its neck. "Our mode of communication has been preset, anticipating that there would be various offshoots. Still, the roots are similar. We seem to have succeeded."

Bragen stared, too stunned to respond. Whether from an ancient Uhlman or a Synthon, all archodials were familiar with bone structure. Then there was the unthought, a vision of the Mawoan, with its tiny, useless teeth embedded into an imperceptible jaw structure that harked back to tree climbers. It was said such beings had large ears, sported lips, and ate jubal berries and insects from this orifice. This thing had a different appearance. An illegal appearance. A corruption of the Record!

Mador said, "You are not a Mawoan."

Bragen cringed. It was a statement, not a question. To mention such an unthought outside the protection of kulcat fibers, could get you a cleanscan. But they were not in the Warp. Mawoans were a part of those illegal thoughts, those whispered fables, that had been removed from the Warp. Thoughts that linked Synthons to mammalian tree climbers. Some black marketers even posited that Synthons' ancestors not only had mouths, but digestive systems, and most bizarre of all, like mammalians, procreated. This line of thinking was born out of Rawnswawn's flawed analysis.

Bragen found trace amounts of mitochondrial DNA in fossils found on Lark. Then Apollis. If the readings were true, procreation was more than an illegal thought. Yet all mention of such possibilities were disavowed by the scientific community as so much nonsense.

"Mawoan? No, we are not," the thing replied, its pale blue eyes studying Mador, seeming to see something within the wizened that caused its pupils to expand.

And something else. Something behind its blue eyes besides Mador's reflection. It was the same with the entire face. Synthons generally used body movements to emphasize certain words or to help them express a particular point. While the stranger communicated with its mouth, its facial musculature was also contributing to this flow. In conjunction with the sounds, the lined skin around its eyes and mouth were moving back and forth, evidently a part of the language.

"It is clear you do not know us," it continued.

Mador replied, "We are here to learn."

It motioned toward the door. "As we expected. Come. Let us start at the beginning."

Chapter 5

They followed the robed figure outside where they were greeted by a cloudless cerulean sky. The sound of waves crashing on a nearby shore filled the air. Dark brown structures, all made of earthen blocks, stretched west toward the edge of a cliff. Bragen knew that cliff. The Point. The roofs consisted of Highland Red Grass, thick and tall. Streams of smoke came out of pipes that reached above their red tips. Several stone paths lined with multicolored flowers ran between and around the buildings. To the east, the land descended through a valley of the same grasses. A faint outline of mountains hovered in a distant, maroon haze.

More robed strangers now came out of the other structures. Together, they removed their hoods. All had mouths. The skin tones were different; some were brown, but others lighter and darker. The same orange glow revolved around their necks. Each face was similar to the ones who greeted them, yet strangely, none were exactly the same. It was more than the skin. Each had different size noses, hair, eye color, and physical structures. *Defects?* Hair even grew out of two of these individuals' faces. And something else. Something zie could not pinpoint. Differences existed Bragen could not identify.

Zie looked toward the edge of the outcrop. "I know where we are."

"What do you call it?" The one who greeted them asked, quite curious.

Bragen looked at Mador, then zas hosts. "Mythgarden Point."

Another spoke, trying out the words, "Mythgarden Point." This one was taller, its flesh, pink. Its hair long and brown.

Bragen noticed that while it moved its mouth the same, the sound was different.

"And you call it?" Mador asked the one who greeted them.

"Sunbloom."

Yes, that was a different sound.

"Come," the taller one said. "We must get into the heart of this."

Together they all walked up a stone path that led between the buildings until they all stood beyond the last structure. Below, wave upon ocean wave slapped against the shore. The wind was strong, blowing back their hair. All stood in front of what appeared to be a circular amphitheater. Stone seating swirled around a blue-black column of twisted metal that loomed over them. It was capped with a clear octagonal object that reflected back the sun. A multitude of colors danced within its many sections. The column ran into the ground.

"Please sit," another yellow-haired one said. Bragen noticed this one's tone was different than the others. Lighter, with a higher pitch.

Bragen and Mador obliged, as did everyone else. Bragen thought it odd that zie could feel a stone bench that was not there, reminding zamself that they remained in the professor's perma-walled quarters, sitting in cozy chairs. A carving of a string of stars arching across the sky was etched in each of the benches.

"It is clear that much has changed," the one with the long brown hair and pink skin said, as much to zamself as to Bragen or Mador. "While you might find it hard to believe, we are a part of the same. You would not be here, you would not see us, if this were not so. You may find this puzzling, but that does not make it any less true. To some, we are known as the Carriers. That is not our name. We are Human, the same as you. This section of the Interactive is simply meant to give you a context from which you can understand what you are seeing."

"What is a Human?" Bragen asked. "You mean Humotzero?"

"We do not know Humotzero. There is no simple explanation as to what we, and you, are," said their host. "But the entirety of the segments is structured in such a way as to provide the answers you need. But not all at once. That cannot be. My name is Merwin."

"Humotzero," zie continued, "is a phrase from your age, not ours. Explaining who we are is tied to the historical thread that has brought us together. A thread that must be unwound. That you do not know us foretells the future. I, along with Arena, Golwina, and Feelwin, will lead this section. It would help to know who sent you."

"No one," Bragen answered. "We are here as a result of a deep earth scan that excavated the information from a site east of here. I am archodialbragen1031. This is wizenedmador454. We are not in possession of the original, only a facsimile, deposited in my memory, which I shared with the wizened."

There was a pause as their hosts digested this and contemplated what it meant for their discussion. Bragen noticed they were all staring at Mador. Zie immediately searched their thoughts. Of course, there was nothing there. The Warp was not there.

"As I understand," Feelwin began, turning zas attention to Bragen. "You do not have the Interactive as it was created, yet you have it none the less. You do not recognize the you in us, so this must be addressed. While it will not provide every answer you seek, by its end you will have come to some understanding."

Bragen exchanged another look with Mador. "The you in us?"

Mador looked back at Merwin. "We must be patient."

"How much of this history have you been able to translate?" Merwin asked.

"If you mean the scans, little," Bragen answered. "That I did at all was due to chance. There has not been time to do much."

Merwin nodded. "So, we use The Way."

Bragen tried to share a Local with Mador before zie realized that was an impossibility. *The Way.* Neither knew the term. Then the wizened gave a little jump. "The Way is how we got here."

"It is that. A mode of communicating across expanding evolutionary lines," Merwin answered, pointing to the orange glow that surrounded their necks. Zas eyes once again bored into Mador, as if searching for something. "You are familiar with this mode?"

Mador shook zas head. "We have no reference for what hangs around your necks. I am curious. Do you know the One Thought that emanates from the One-Mind, both of which flow through the Galaxial Warp?"

"We know of the One Thought and the One Mind,

but not as you say, the Galaxial Warp."

"You are disconnected," Mador said. "Or better put, never connected."

"And yet," the yellow haired one answered, "we understand each other. You know what an Interactive is. We are both familiar with the One Mind. I am sure we will find other commonalities. We walk the same path, whether you believe it or not. What of the Uhlman Wars?"

"We know of Uhlmans," Bragen began. "But what is war?"

Merwin looked at the others. They all looked back, but only at Mador. "The void is complete."

The archy looked at Mador, who faced the descending slope of red-tipped grasses. Something of import had passed between the mouthed beings and the wizened. They seemed to be waiting for zam to say something, but zie did not.

Instead, Bragen swept a hand in the opposite direction. "Is this your home?"

"No," another said, stepping forward. "I am Golwina." Zie also had yellow hair and pink skin. Golwina pointed toward the western sky. "We came from far way. The planet Lark."

"We know Lark," Bragen said, surprised. The same Lark? The commonalities meant something. This device was obviously an early Interact.

Golwina's mouth turned up on both sides, revealing white teeth. "That is more proof that we are of the same part. You say you do not know war. But you do know Uhlmans. How can this be so?"

Mador blinked, a dazed and distant look in zas eyes. "They are in the Record."

"I am Feelwin," the robed figure next to Golwina said. This one was shorter and rotund. More like Merwin in tone. Zas skin was black, zas nose flat, and zas hair red, which was in stark contrast to zas dark green eyes. "That is well. Knowing something of Uhlmans shortens the thread. What is your era?"

"Forty-five," Mador answered.

Feelwin looked at the others, and then back at the professor, "When we arrived here, the wars were coming to an end. Thirty-one five zero."

"A different age," Mador said.

They all stared at the wizened, waiting for more.

"You keep mentioning war," Bragen said, interrupting the impasse. "What is it?"

None of the robed figures moved. They continued to look at Mador, then one by one, looked toward the distant mountain range, the sound of waves slapping against the shore. Bragen thought of the small crevice in the cliff face that led to the cave. The orange glow moved down the strangers' necks and covered their chests before disappearing. They were making noises. Talking to each other. Bragen could not understand what they were saying.

When Feelwin looked back, the orange rings wrapped around their necks. "War is one people, or entity, committing violence upon another. What is your term for this?"

With each passing moment, Bragen became more confused. This entire endeavor was a horrible mistake. Somehow, the scan zie allowed into zas brain had corrupted zas memcore. Or was this another illegal dream zie could not get out of? Maybe, zie thought, zie *should* have a remboot.

"Synthons have no description for such activity," Mador replied. "It is an unknown."

Bragen looked at Feelwin. "Why would one... entity... do that to another?"

Again, Feelwin's face scrunched up in a way the archy did not understand. The expression evoked a feeling zie could not identify.

"To start on such complicated questions is probably a mistake," the Human said. "So let us start elsewhere." Zie pointed toward the multi-colored object that revolved around the metal column.

"Evolution moves the species forward. Eons ago, physical changes came slowly. With the manipulation of the double helix, the progressional process accelerated. You are proof of this. Yet something has been lost. Such is war."

Bragen pointed back toward the long line of block buildings. "This past you speak of, and everything around us, is not reality as we know it. Our past is not yours."

Golwina spoke again, first nodding, zas dark eyes barely open, zas mouth a little more than a slit. "That is your conception, not ours. There is purpose behind why you do not know who we are, a purpose that deceives reality. Such erasures may solve short-era goals, but the Interactives speak for themselves of what was and what will be."

Bragen counted seven robed figures, but sensed there were more elsewhere. Many more. Zie puzzled over the variations. Two seemed more like Golwina than the others. Zie took a deep breath, still convinced zas brain was damaged. It was like a dream, yet more tangible, from the sound of the waves to the movement of their mouths.

Finally, zie looked at Feelwin. "So, what is this context?"

When Feelwin started speaking, the swirling colors left the octagon, replaced with an opaque luminosity. "The Uhlman's term, the Carriers, is a pejorative. Long before our time it was decided that we were no longer needed. In the Long Ago, leaders were ambivalent, grudgingly willing to let the cycle take its course. Over time, that is what happened. As you attest.

"Acceleration begat acceleration, tyrants became less patient with the Old Ways. Once no longer needed to perpetuate the species, they sought our elimination. We resisted. From your reactions it does not appear that we were successful. Such information appears to confuse you. The only way to understand the past is to speak it. Prepare."

Once again, colors lit up the octagon. This time it began to spin. The splotches turned into distinct splashes of red, blue, green, yellow, white, and black, eventually becoming colorful lines. Bragen felt zas memcore being drawn into its whirling vortex. Zie grew dizzy. Heard voices, not thoughts. Singing voices. A multitude of individuals coalescing into one sound, singing the same message. That was when zie realized Golwina and Arena were females. Then the voices overwhelmed zam.

We are called by many names. Originators. Creators. In the Long Ago, our ancestors mastered the double helix. It led us into a future that sought the end of discord. The past that changed the future. Once accomplished, evolutionary changes that should have taken a million years occurred within a generation. It began with skin color. Multiple pigmentations were eliminated, leading to stronger societal cohesiveness. The same with eye and hair color.

In that Long Ago, Humans pointed toward the Common Benefit. Synthetically evolving neurological cells led to mechanical telepathy, an overarching governmental body that called themselves the Ruul, and a never-ending thirst to evolve. Bodies began to produce their own caloric intake, eliminating the need to ingest and excrete proteins and other consumables. The next goal was the most significant, reproduction of the species.

The Ruul argued that this archaic system was long overdue a progression, one that eliminated inequities and injustices inherent in a biological system that produced both males and females. One known to disprivilege the birthing person and half of the beings it produced. They began to call our offspring the products of conception.

The Ruul noted that the female birthing apparatus reduced achievement capacities for that sex, which in turn decreased their value in society, which led to inequities that bred natural conflicts of interest. In the midst of a genetic revolution the leaders declared the sex of an individual non binary, which allowed the Ruul to institute its New Thought laws. Out of these progressionals came the Uhlman, our so-called cousin.

Based on your time date, the synthetic evolution of which we refer began fifteen thousand years ago. The Uhlmans called this the Golden Age of Manipulation. We call it the Dark Age of Regression. This so-called Golden Age involved the advancement of synthetic intelligence within the Uhlman brain. Humans were left out of the progression.

James Bailey Blackshear

Yet Uhlmans still required male and female chromosomes to propagate, albeit the process had evolved to the point that their advanced genetic make-up required synthetic exo-wombs to carry their species to term. Gestation remained a backward notion they sought to eliminate.

Evolution continued. The goal became replacing male and females with a single androgenous species known as Mawo: for man-woman. An age later this came to pass. A single Mawoan began producing embryos that were transferred to the exo-womb through-ports. They argued this enhanced reproductive system equitably distributed the birth burden. While the majority of Mawoans birthed more Mawoans, a small percentage produced Human males and females.

These unwanted offspring were not telepathic, needed outside calories to survive, excreted their waste, and when mature, required mating with the opposite sex to produce offspring. The Uhlmans saw this as a regression.

Humans became a minority population. As the link between Uhlman and Mawoan grew closer, we fell further out of favor. With creators now a distant memory, we were delegated to menial, laborious tasks and did not participate in the normal order of galaxial society.

Humans, the Ruul declared, carried the defective gene of the Long Ago. In this Long Ago, dark times prevailed and old ways perverted the Prometheus. A species relegated to ingestion, excretion, and backward communication modes, our children became known as The Stain, relics of an inequitable past.

Through genetic acceleration, Mawoan and Uhlman began to merge into something new. Synthetic manipulations within the brain continued to re-engineer neural telepathy, which eliminated the need for mechanical enhancements. As higher order telepathic powers grew, speech diminished. Tongues receded, along with jawbones and teeth. Skin grew over the seam where lips once led to the mouth. The One Mind, One Thought, mentality bloomed, permeating the Prometheus.

The new Uhlmans made the decision to end us. Yet we are still here. Why? It has to do with a wave of unexplained miscarriages that began to sweep through the one-sex species. Over the generations, the cellular linkage between Human, Mawoan, and Uhlman frayed. This led to miscarriages. So numerous the progression was threatened.

The new Uhlmans required the forty-six chromosomes that were sourced back to Human somatic cells. Manipulated cells both the Mawoan and Uhlman inherited. Something went wrong. The problem was traced back to Human propagation. Twenty-three female chromosome cells and twenty-three male chromosome cells are required to create a Human. Evolutionary progression somehow perverted the admixture. To rectify this perversion, they reverted to extracting DNA from what they called the womb-nested products of conception. To do so, they began to take our born, and unborn children. We resisted.

In the name of the Common Benefit, they fed our offspring to the somatic cell farms. We fought back, but could not match them. As battles raged, they achieved the breakthrough they sought, developing a synthetic cloning string that allowed them to develop the next progression without need of our somatic cells.

You said you are unfamiliar with war. We have no concept of what life would be like without it. Long before the evolutionary leap, there was war. War between our own species. War throughout the Prometheus. Why? The answers are innumerable. It is beyond this Interact's capability to explain.

After the breakthrough, physiological mutation expanded. Only those who enter here can determine to what affect. Uhlmans argue the science is clear. They declare Humans have more in common with tree climbers and prairie grazers. To procreate became the First Abomination, to consume and excrete the Second. Yet our children are more than cells. We fought the extractions in numerous ways but in the end our only chance at survival was to escape.

Many plans and projects were put together, each mission independently devised to protect all others. This Interact is simply meant to provide context, and explain why we are here. We left our home in 3150. Moira will introduce you to the Core.

Another robed figure, this one smaller, stood.

"I am Moira. Please follow me." Zie walked toward the descending circular stone steps that wound down and around the metal column.

Bragen looked up before taking that first step. The octagonal sphere was no longer spinning. The sky was deep red, indicating the severe heat associated with the planet, yet there was no heat. The Hammerheads had yet to strike.

Moira walked down the steps. Mador and the others followed. Even though Bragen could not feel it, zie sensed the air was cooler. Down below, a bright light escaped an air vent. While there was no sound, zie could feel others were down there, waiting. After one more descending revolution, an arched entrance revealed a room. Moira turned. "Welcome."

Bragen stopped. That voice. The way the mouth moved and the face changed. So odd. Then zie remembered. *Female.* Zie looked back up the spiral staircase. *Like Golwina and Arena.*

A moment later they entered a brightly lit, squarely constructed room. A large crowd filled it, and soon had them surrounded. Each had a mouth. Each had different facial structures, hair colors, and body shapes. A soft orange glow surrounded their necks. Instead of robes they wore dark-colored, form fitting wraps of some kind. A series of tables positioned along the wall held various, unknown instruments. Topography and interstellar maps hung on the walls.

"This is our Core. With the exception of a few, everyone is here. Rooms adjacent to this one hold equipment we brought from Lark. We hope to use it later. Lab works. Agri and horti-forms. This planet has a lot of potential."

Mador looked at the ceiling. "Those buildings are your homes."

"For now," Moira said.

The professor glanced around. "So, if I am counting right, there are fifty of you... At least here."

Smiling, she shook her head. "No. There are sixty-three. The children are sleeping. Soon there will be sixty-seven. Not counting the scouts."

Bragen was suddenly appreciative of Mador's presence. While the Local was not working, they knew what each was thinking. *Four are pregnant.* What were scouts?

Everyone in the room was a myth, an unthought. Mammals with the arms and legs of a Synthon. But more. Even uteruses. Was it Interact or nightmare? A violation. The archy decided that as soon as zie woke, zie would contact a Watcher.

"Like the others, this segment has a specific end point," Moira said. "More context is accumulated with each."

Bragen looked at Mador. The professor stared at the individual with the pronounced bulge in their midsection. Bragen tried to visualize what that meant, but could not.

"It is somehow related," Mador whispered.

"To Rawnswawn," Bragen answered.

Mador shook zas head. "No. *Apogonos*."

Bragen searched zas memory. No thought came to mind.

Feelwin motioned toward the object of the wizened's fascination. "This is Arena. Our leader. My partner. Although we were hopeful, it is at least understandable why you do not know the Long Ago. What awaits you. It is disheartening."

Arena spoke. "And yet, you are here. A descendant. Which lights the way. We know our plight, and the challenges this planet gives us, but in some form neither of us understands, all is not lost. Amidst this confusion, it is our hope that these experiences will illuminate you. Make you the light. That is what is most important. As to this endeavor, the segments follow a numerical sequence. The second, as well as the others were developed during our last days on Lark. Others are anticipated. They are provided to ensure that you grasp our true nature. Only then will the future proceed."

"Apollis is not our home," Bragen said. "As to your reality, I cannot begin to fathom what you are talking about."

After looking back up the stairway, Arena glanced at Moira before returning her gaze to Bragen. Her eyes were green. After taking a deep breath, she said, "We prepared for such confusion. Other than following the Interacts, there is little I can provide you. Misla will guide you through the next sequence, where you should find some clarity."

More confused now, Bragen asked the wizened, "Who is Misla?"

Before Mador could speak, Feelwin said, "That you do not know means the Interacts are not in chronological form. It is up to you to reconfigure."

Bragen blinked. They were back in the apartment. Zie faced Mador, not Feelwin. Zas golden eyes looked back, but remained somewhere else. Instead of a room full of beings with teeth and tongues, they sat in soft chairs surrounded by digibits and artifacts. A room that seemed much smaller than when zie entered. A room where zie always felt free to express what ever thought came to mind. But now? It seemed dangerous. Several thoughts flashed through zas memory. Apogonos. The Long Ago. "Who is Misla?"

Mador did not reply, zas golden eyes focused elsewhere.

For the first time in zas life, Bragen noticed the professor did not have a mouth. *How odd.* Other thoughts, *no*, sounds, came back. *Humans.* Tall and short. Thin and wide. *Musical thoughts.* Glowing necks. Extended stomachs. Females. *War.*

The archy was no longer the Synthon who came into

the park. Mador remained still. Malfunctions again came to mind. Zie looked away from the professor. "That was not an Interact, was it?" Zas telepathic voice sounded different. Flatter.

"It was," Mador answered. "You know it was."

"I failed to tell you I had a dream earlier. It caused this."

"No. I am afraid reality is not static. You must accept that this is so before you can begin to understand... theirs."

"Mador. That would not be to our benefit."

"A benefit for one may not be for another. The future is not a straight line."

Bragen recalled standing in the cave, staring up at the strangely twisted metal. The image changed to the dry creek bed that ran through the heart of the Glendom Valley. Zie found bones there. Both the river bed and the cave brought Majore into zas life. An unpleasant sensation ran up zas spine. Arena said they were from Lark. The Glendom Valley was on Lark.

"What can we do but report?" Bragen said, as much a statement as a question.

Mador stood and stretched. Zie walked to the small door that led to the balcony and peeled back the flap, revealing Brinslow Park. "Sometimes it is best not to think too much. The Warp, even within these walls, might hear."

The Warp might hear. Bragen had almost forgotten it. How could that be? Zie turned in zas chair to get a better look at the wizened. "So, what do we do? As soon as we leave our thoughts might leak."

"A pronouncement comes to mind," Mador began, pulling on the longest of zas silver braids. "If you let them," zie said, "they will take the I out of you and replace it with the We that only They control. Every discordant note will be replaced with a thrum. Everyone will bleat the same answer to the old question and the people will lose their voice.'"

Bragen remained sitting, staring up at Mador, who stood near the balcony, studying the birds that flitted through the tree-tops. After a long pause, zie turned and stared at Bragen. "The Hive eradicated it from the Warp," zie said, reading the archy's Local. Zas golden eyes emitted an iridescent glow. "An unthought."

Bragen searched zas memcore for something relevant about the line, or the term, "It was there? When?"

"Before you," the wizened answered. "We must focus on the most important aspect of what we just experienced. They were wrong, weren't they?"

"The... Humans?"

"No. Not the Humans. Perhaps *wrong* is not the right word," Mador clarified. "The unthought is a part of a larger reality. They deceive."

Bragen stood. The professor seemed to know more. Something lurked behind those eyes. Zie seemed to be saying something that deep down, Bragen had always wondered about. The tharsonome readings were correct. "There is danger, Mador. There is danger in what you say."

"Perhaps it was always so. We look the other way. But there comes a time," the professor said, as if this was enough.

Bragen walked to the patio. "The readings on Apollis. And in the Glendom Valley. They were neither Uhlman nor Mawoan, were they?"

89

Mador nodded. "They were not."

"And they knew. Majore. The Council. They knew. Didn't they? Why hide it?"

Mador looked down at the park bench where they used to meet. "Sometimes the Truth is too horrifying to admit."

Bragen saw a lidscan trolling down the lane in their direction. It was not that uncommon to see one, but at this moment, in this place?

Mador flinched. Zie saw it too: stepped back and closed the patio door. Together they reinstalled the loose perma-flap and sealed it over the doorway. They moved to the interior of the room and stood there, staring back toward where the park and street were. Lidscans were automated vehicles controlled by the Watch. The Watch, and its Inducers, utilized them to trace down thought origination points considered counterproductive to the Flow. Watchers reported their location to Inducers. Inducers sent out lidscans to catch the trace. Once identified the owners were subject to a variety of reintroduction programs, which included remboots and cleanwaves.

Mador placed zas hands on Bragen's shoulders and stared into zas eyes. "You have to go."

"Surely it is not looking for us?"

"Not us. You. You searched the Warp for the phrase *chil*. They will connect that to Apollis rather easily. And then the rest."

Bragen watched zas mentor. Beyond clear pools of gold zie saw something ageless. A clarity. "I have nowhere to go. And if I did, you would have to go too."

"No," Mador answered, extracting the membrane from the tharsonome. They both looked at it. Zie placed it in Bragen's hand and closed zas fingers over it.

"Take this. Get rid of it. They will be looking for you, not me. Once found they will want to facilitate a probe. We can't have that. I know a place. And I can stall."

The archodial trusted the wizened but did not like what zie was suggesting. Running. Hiding. "What about you? About your memcore?"

"Its old and full of what they already consider damaged ideas. They know all about me. It's different with you or so they think. Go down the hall to the drop. Take it to the basement. If you can get to the subroutes it will be much harder to detect you."

That was true. Bragen knew the infrastructure footprint from zas previous occupation. But digital viewers were down there.

"Go one stage below the subroute," Mador said, reading zas mind. The auxiliary tunnels below the basement had few such devices.

Of course. The wager routes. These tunnels carried the pipes, wires, and pneumatics that ran the city.

"Down the Red Line," Mador continued. "There is a hub center, I believe it is zero one twenty. Get there if you can. Ask for Maice. Zie can show you a place. Tell zam I sent you. Zie can make all the inferences zie wants. The important point is zie knows me and should help. Find a place to enter the next Interact."

It seemed a lifetime since Bragen had first met zam. An old professor walking through a park on a summer afternoon. There was a blue sky. Zie carried a bag of birdseed. That was when zas life began. Now zie placed zas own hands on Mador's shoulders. They looked at each other a moment longer. Then Bragen left.

Chapter 6

Bragen darted out the door and down the hall. From there zie found the drop and took it to the subroute. Oblivious, a few Synthons stood in the bay waiting for the tram. Head down, zie did as Mador instructed, turning right and moving toward the end of the landing. The exit sign read *zero-one-twenty*. Zie opened the door and descended the steps into a basement. Zie swung around the handrail and stopped in front of three additional doors. The one to the left was painted yellow. The center, green. The right, red. *Redline.* Bragen walked through this one into a dimly lit room.

The wires and tubes running over zas head reminded zam of the decades spent in similar tunnels, laboring alongside team-members building the future. Zas memcore reorganized these familiar images, correlating them to the equipment room on Apollis. Like that space, the Warp was faint. Zie thought of Cloyden and the membrane, familiar vibrations moving up through zas boots and into zas legs. The lights up ahead grew brighter. The coordinator den.

Bragen walked into the circular room that resembled the hub of a wheel. Several multi-colored doors led to other hallways that ran under the basement and the tram-lines. Two Synthons who had been staring at a Dimensional turned and looked at zam. The one in the gray jumpsuit, the supervisor, took a step in zas direction.

"Are you lost?"

Bragen felt the probe and shook zas head. "I am looking for Maice."

"I am Maice," the other one said. Zie wore a green jumpsuit.

The supervisor looked at Maice. "Who is it?"

"I do not know," Maice answered.

"Sorry. Mador gave me directions," Bragen said. Zie had to be careful of the Local. The room was filled with the low rumble of large machines.

"This is a work-space," said the gray jump-suited one. "What brings you here? And who is Mador?"

It had happened so quickly. One moment zie was in the wizened's study. The next underneath a tram station. "I met zam at University."

"At University?" Maice asked. A bit apprehensive, zie stepped toward Bragen. Clearly zie was concerned Bragen could get zam in trouble. "This is no classroom. Why would zie send you down here?"

"I might know," the supervisor answered, placing zas hands on zas hips and facing zas assistant. "Are you meeting with that old wizened again?" There was an edge to the question. It was clear the supervisor had no use for Mador.

"Not in a while," Maice answered. Zie looked at Bragen. "What do you want?"

Bragen kept zas eyes on the gray jump-suited one. Zie felt the Local. Probing. Zas old boss, Zarn, didn't like disruptions either. Bragen knew zie had to say something that would ease the situation. "I am an archodial. I used to be a wratchet-gatherer. Bored tunnels all under Andrio. Even East Andrio. Then I changed careers. Met

Mador at University. Zie was my wizened. I am in the process of developing a digibit on the relationship that exists between wagers and archodials. Mador suggested I visit zero two one and talk to Maice, as well as you. I should have sent a message request instead of just wandering down here. I will leave. I apologize."

Bragen turned and started toward the hallway. A lot of what zie said was true. Yet not everything. A rewind sent up to a Watcher might catch the inaccuracies.

"A digibit?" The supervisor asked.

Digibits on wagers were rare. If mentioned at all they received a line or two on topics concerning glittering new buildings, revolutionary modes of transport, or thought maps that channeled work toward the Common Benefit. Or team standings. All such bits flowed throughout the Prometheus. Bragen stopped, but kept zas eyes on the exit. It was important that zie draw this Synthon's thoughts away from the deception.

"Yes. There is a slot reserved for next week's *Arion Transport*. I am just about finished with it, but clearly, I violated a protocol and I will leave you to it. Again, I apologize."

"I am zas supervisor. Your full representation?"

"Archodialbragen2031." The name was right but the numbers were not. Again, a studied Local might reveal this, which would activate the notification system.

The supervisor made the sign. "I am WagerWren13067. Glad to meet you. I guess it would be ok for Maice to show you around a bit. When would you want to connect with me?"

Bragen looked at Maice, whose eyes grew wide with suspicion and fear. "Thank you, Wren. If Maice can maybe give me the breakdown sequence of priorities concerning what happens after the tunnel is bored, I will get back to you in about an hour. Is that ok?"

Wren looked at Maice. This was an obvious violation of wager etiquette, but if it offered a chance for zas crew, as well as zamself, to illustrate just how important zas team was to the Common Benefit, it was worth it. A digibit! After a pause, zie looked at Maice. "Well, what do you think? Can you show zam around? Show zam the sequencing?"

Maice deferred to zas boss, not sure what zie was getting into. Zie looked back at the Dimensional. "Router 1 will be on the fly in one minute."

"I can handle," Wren said, already gravitating back toward the control board.

Maice slowly approached Bragen. "So, Mador sent you?"

Bragen nodded, taking one look at Wren before looking at the other doors. "Zie did. Could we?"

Wren was no longer paying attention, but Maice caught the tension in Bragen's request. For a moment zie hesitated, then pointed toward the green door. "So, tell me what you are looking for."

Bragen waited until they were through the opening and several feet into the next pipe and electric-grid filled corridor before responding.

"I am not creating a digibit."

Maice looked back toward the controller den. Wren was focused on the Dimensional. "Of course not. So, what is it? What kind of unthought are you involving me in? How do you know Mador? Or do you?"

"I was just with zam in zas quarters when a lidscan approached. We could be in trouble. Zie told me to leave, and that you would help."

Maice gazed at zam a long time, the alarm still there. This meant the Watch was involved. "With what?"

"You might not want to know."

"Lidscans are everywhere," Maice said, a hard edge to zas thoughts.

"Mador said you knew of a place."

"Where we sometimes talk?"

"Maybe. Where the Warp has a… harder time."

"So, this lidscan is after you?"

"Maybe."

Maice looked up, toward where Brinslow Park was located. "What about Mador? Are they there now?"

"Probably. I am not sure."

The wager stopped. "I have to know what I am getting myself into. Otherwise, we turn around."

"Are you sure?" Bragen asked.

"Yes."

Bragen nodded, looking back in wager's direction. "Ok."

When they started walking again, Bragen told zam about zas time as an archy on Apollis, as well as the faulty tharsonome readings. Zie also told zam about the tharsonome membrane. Nothing about the Interacts. Just enough detail for zam to understand why zie could be in trouble and why zie needed a space disconnected from the Warp.

"I will be gone before you know it. You can tell Wren you left me in a breakroom or something and when you came back I was gone. Make up something. An emergency. Tell zam I will be back before your shift ends, whenever that is."

"I know there is something missing from your explanation. But maybe that is a good thing," Maice reasoned. "I can't ignore Mador's trust. I guess this has something to do with our old talks. I knew it was risky to think so freely. Such freedom is not worth it. I worried about the wizened getting zamself in trouble someday. Guess I should have been more worried."

Maice stopped next to a door marked *storage*. "In here." Zie opened it. Bragen walked in. The wager followed then shut the door.

It was little more than a large closet. Tools, maps of the tunnel system and a rectangular box hung on the wall. Three folding chairs stood in one corner.

Maice pointed at the rectangular box. "The Warp has no access here. The actuator is wave and fire proofed for safety. Every once in a while, Mador and a few others would drop by after hours and we'd talk. So, this is what you want?"

Bragen looked around. "Yes."

The wager paused, a million questions in zas eyes. "Ok. No more thoughts. You have an hour. When you leave, stop at that bend in the corridor. You'll notice a yellow light to your right. That's a directional. Look up and you'll see a ladder. Pull it down. Up above is a hatch that will lead you into an old escape tube. Take it. It ties to another closet, which opens up next to the main plaza. That's all I can do."

"Thank you."

Maice looked at zam a moment more, then turned and left, closing the door behind zam.

The room was immediately darker. Bragen pulled one of the chairs away from the wall, opened it, and sat down. After taking a deep breath, zie bent forward and looked through zas memory for the Interacts. Zie had trouble focusing. Zas last image of Mador kept getting in the way. Finally, they came into view. Bragen thought about what Feelwin said. *The wrong chronology.* Zie looked at the list and picked one.

Once again zie was in a brightly lit room. Not alone. In front of him stood a being, this one smaller than Arena, Golwina, or Feelwin. Smaller, but the same. It too had a mouth. It curved up on the ends, revealing perfectly white teeth. Dressed differently. A blue material. A smock. An orange glow surrounded its neck.

"Hello, I am Misla."

The same musicality. More a song than a thought. *Misla.* Bragen nodded. The right chronology? Zie had no idea.

"So, you do not know us," it stated.

Bragen was mesmerized by this smaller version of a Human. So mesmerized zie had a hard time replying. More Golwina than Feelwin. Definitely shorter than both. But more than just smaller. Here was a fresher version of a Human. This one was involved in some type of reverse biological process. Then it dawned on zam why it, or she, was more like Arena than Feelwin. Definitely female. Just like the range arths, steedfells, and horned grazers. One of each gender. Zie looked away.

They were the only ones in the sparse room. A few chairs and a table, some maps, and a type of Dimensional hung on the wall. The maps indicated a very large mountain range, interspersed with numerous valleys. Several rivers ran out of the valleys towards flatter land.

Misla motioned to one of the chairs. "Perhaps you should sit down."

Bragen pulled one up and sat. For a moment zie thought of zas real self, sitting in another chair in a dark closet.

"I am here to take you to my home," Misla said. This one's hair was yellow with hints of brown. Small, bright, hazel eyes. Almost green. When she communicated her mouth moved, emitting the musical tones that still stunned zam. Made zam dizzy.

Bragen forced zamself to organize zas thoughts. Was this a child? The same being that was denigrated in Mawoan Myths and Other Fables? What had Sarkasian said? *There is a difference between extinct species and species that never existed. The extinct species, such as a bull mouth rutter, left fossils and other evidence of its time in the Prometheus.* The Fables noted the species that never existed, Mawoans, like the baby bull mouth, kept their offspring within a womb until term. Then birthed it. *The mythical womb.* Why? Sarkasian continued: *There is no biological evidence of such creatures in the Prometheus. Anecdotal tales have perverted the Warp and led to wrong thoughts and wayward ideas.*

Bragen remained mesmerized by the smaller version's features. Something softer than those zie met in the previous encounter. And something different about her eyes. A spark, or light, seemed to flicker behind the irises. With no Warp to access, Bragen searched zas memcore's files. While this exercise proved fruitless, zie did realize something. She was looking at zam with something else, something more than her eyes. As if some inner substance zie could not begin to comprehend hid behind the sparks. It reminded zam of a look Mador sometimes gave zam.

The room began to spin. Bragen closed zas eyes and held onto the chair. What was happening? Something was coming loose inside zam. Was this what Inducers called false imagining? The spinning slowed, then stopped.

"Where are we?" Bragen asked, opening zas eyes and studying the room.

Misla stood, her smile growing. "Good. I can see you have caught your breath. Now we can begin." She spread her arms and opened her hands. "This is not my home. This is just the construct created to introduce you to me before we venture to my village. In a moment I will show you Sagev Sal, which you might know of. That is why we start here and not in Ollepas. If I am unknown to you, as seems to be the case, such a place might give you the geographical context from which you can orient. As you know by now," she continued. "I am a part of you. Long ago—"

"You are a girl," Bragen interrupted. It was as much a question as a statement.

"Yes." She smiled, cocking her head to one side. "I am twelve."

"Twelve?"

"Twelve-years-old."

Bragen searched zas memcore, again longing for the Warp. The number meant nothing to zam. Zie thought of baby gracks. "Young?"

"That is what my father and mother remind me of every day."

Father. *Mother.* The tharsonome readings. *Mitochondrial DNA was inherited from the mother.*

"You have a mother?"

A trilling of some sort gurgled out of the girl's throat. "Yes. Everyone does."

Bragen looked around the room. What a preposterous thought.

"Everyone?"

"This is a question?"

"And a father?" By the time the thought had left zam zie pictured Feelwin and Arena. Of course.

Misla stared, the strange gurgling sound was gone, but her mouth still curled up on both ends. She turned and looked at the maps on the far wall. "Forgive me. This Interact is to provide you the proper context to understand who we are and where we came from. We should continue. So, let's go to Ollepas. Please follow."

Bragen followed her across the brightly lit room. She opened a door that had not been there a moment earlier. A bright-blue, cloudless sky greeted them. They were in a town. Not large and not small. A lot of single-story buildings and roads surrounded them. Machine noises in the distance. A strange, egg-shaped vehicle floated by. There was a window in it. Someone turned and looked at them as it passed. A flock of rookers flew over. In the distance, Humans walked down one of the streets. *Other humans.* Clad in multi-colored garb. No robes. Tunics and smocks. Only Misla wore the orange ring around her neck.

She walked over to a similarly shaped turquois colored vehicle that hovered near them. She touched its side and a door that had not been there a second earlier opened. She hopped in.

"Come on," she said, her voice high pitched with excitement.

Bragen looked around. The buildings spread in all directions. Zie noticed a large tower in the distance. All Interacts were information devices so whatever that was, it was important. Zie stepped into the vehicle. The door shut and then disappeared. The craft hovered about two feet off the ground for a few seconds, then began to float away. It followed the road just beneath it. Zie saw no controls.

"This is Sagev Sal," she said, answering zas question. "Do you know it?"

Bragen studied the buildings as they floated through a series of hilly avenues. Another tower came into sight and then it was behind them. Zie noticed the strange apparatus on top.

"What is that?" zie asked.

"A goldrum," Misla answered. "A part of the Watch."

Was there a correlation? "I saw another in the other direction. What are they watching for?"

"The Uhlmans," Misla said, her tone now flat.

The craft hummed along, passing buildings and other vehicles. When they approached an intersection, it slowed, let a similar vessel pass, then moved on. Those within the other craft ignored them. Misla seemed to think Bragen might recognize something but that was not the case. Many of the buildings were decorated with a series of squiggly dark lines. After a while there were fewer of these structures and the land began to open up. Bragen looked west, beyond the remaining rooftops, toward a distant line of snow-covered peaks. They looked familiar.

"What are those mountains?"

"The Sagev Sal, just like the town. In the old language, it means the Truth is in the Blood."

The Truth is in the Blood. Bragen looked behind zam, wondering what language she was referring to. The town was behind them now, and growing smaller. Ahead was a rolling prairie. Soon they were flying very fast over a blurred series of hills. They remained over a path of some sort, the craft's shadow running across an indention in the soil that was obviously an old land route. To the west the mountains grew taller.

They flew north over an expanding green prairieland. Misla began to talk of its history. "When the first colonials arrived, they noticed how the sun reflected off the mountains each morning, casting a red hue over their peaks. In the old language, Sagev means blood."

"There is something strange about this place. Strange, but familiar." Zie said this, as much to zamself, as Misla. Zie knew nothing of Sagev.

The vehicle began to slow. They crossed over a river. Zie saw its rapids rippling around rocks as it headed east away from the mountains.

"That is the Ollepas," Misla proudly informed him, pointing to the silver ribbon of water. "We will follow it home."

The topography changed, beginning to roll again, but this time conifers and ragged outcrops jutted up, becoming thicker as they grew closer to a series of ragged snow-topped peaks.

"What does Ollepas mean?" Bragen asked.

"It's a type of finscale. They're native to this region. They spawn each year in river valleys like the one we are going to. They make a fine meal."

Bragen studied her. *Meal*. She was obviously enjoying her part in this project. No time to ask about Uhlmans. Zie looked at her small body and wondered. "You… eat them?"

Misla turned and faced zam, her mouth once again exposing a row of white teeth, as well as part of a tongue. There was that trilling, gurgling sound again. It came right out of her mouth! The ring around her neck glowed bright orange. "Of course," she finally answered. "Do you not know what a meal is? Does that mean you do not eat?"

Bragen looked up. The mountains were closer. "I do not," zie said, recalling the digital sight of a range arth eating prairie grass. Such a thought.

The trees began to thin and then the rolling hills fell into a large valley. The river turned south and so did they. Green and yellow grasses swooped up the edges of both sides of the bowl-like vale, disappearing into a line of trees that ran up the mountains as far as they could see. Bragen could feel her eyes. Out of habit zie searched for her thoughts, but of course, they were not there. She was not a Synthon. Yet her face spoke a language of its own. A language zie did not know. The eyes, the brows, the mouth, all seemed to communicate, a part of a larger expression, one that moved beyond thought. What was that?

Several steedfells ran below them, their manes bouncing behind them like white waves as they galloped across the meadow. Misla squealed. Bragen jumped, but quickly realized there was nothing unpleasant about this burst of noise. The orange ring glowed.

They remained above the river, following it down the center of the valley. Zie saw more steedfells and a herd of horned grazers. Off to the left a field of figures were bent over rows of upturned dirt. Humans? Beyond the field were pine trees, mountain peaks, blue sky, puffy white clouds. Above it all hawks of some kind floated lazily in the sky. Beyond the valley loomed a hump-backed mountain, a large cleft cutting across its spine. A file opened in zas memory. It did not include the route, but it did recognize the precipitous drop, the deep blue sky, the hawks, and most of all, the hump-backed mountain. Bragen knew where they were.

A series of low, flat buildings came into view. They were plastered white and had red roofs and smokestacks. Behind the buildings, more mountains. Valley's end. Slowing, Bragen noticed that the stream had turned again, now moving west toward the Sal Sagev Range.

Misla, now standing in the craft, pointed at the river. "It runs through Ollepas."

Their vehicle was almost at a stop now, very near the village. Something else caught zas attention. A large group of individuals, similar in size to zas host, scattered across a close-cropped field. They were running back and forth, chasing a ball. Misla pointed.

"Those are my friends," she said, her voice an octave higher than before. The vehicle had stopped. A door appeared. She opened it and jumped into, for her, waist high grass. She looked back. "Let's go!"

Bragen got out. The air was crisp and cool. The grass came to zas thighs. Zie followed the girl toward the others, who moved in their direction. At the same time zie kept an eye on the nearby structures. Moving after her, zie could barely feel zas feet. The ground seemed to vibrate up through zas boots as the images came back. Instead of a river there was a riverbed. It was the same valley without the buildings. The same imposing mountains. Of course it was the one with the deep cleft that tied it all together. *Heretic's Cliff.* Zie was in the Glendom Valley.

"Come on," Misla shouted. She stopped and waved back at zam; her lips curled up. The others ran toward them, making the same squealing and trilling sounds.

In a moment Bragen and Misla were surrounded. *Children.* Various sizes. Different skin hues. Different hair lengths and colors. Those rings around their necks. They wore the same smock. *Why had the Interact done this?*

Smiling, Misla looked at zam. "I wish I could draw your face."

Bragen studied each head. So many colors. Zie looked at Misla. *What is drawing?* Shaking zas head, zie asked, "Why this place? Why are we here?" Several rookers floated high above their heads, tilting their wings back and forth as they lazily spiraled toward them. *I remember that.*

"To learn," Misla answered, as if it was a silly question.

Bragen looked down at the others, who were looking up at zam, their mouths curled up on the ends. "What are they doing?"

A thin, red-headed one, his light skin tone dotted with small brown spots, held up a blue ball that was twice as big as his head. "Playing. It is between lessons. My name is Bilabo. Catch." He tossed zam the ball.

Bragen caught it, a new thought coming into zas memcore as zie did. *Boy. Where did that thought come from?* "Playing?"

"Yes," the boy answered, his dark blue eyes searching Bragen's face. "Two-spot. Ever play it?"

"No," Bragen answered, looking at the ball. No one seemed to notice zas bafflement. Zie threw it back.

Bragen looked from one to another, amazed at the differences. No uniformity. Dressed in a variety of colors, some with long, straight hair, others with short curly locks. A few were almost as tall as Bragen. Others barely came to zas waist. Some were thin. Others bulky. Some were darker, some did not seem as healthy. Several had something smudged around the little slits they called mouths. Dirt?

"Where are…"

"Our parents are over there," Misla answered, pointing to the village.

Parents? Once again, zie was surprised. *I know what it means.* How? Had Mador told zam? Zie felt dizzy, the reality in front of zam hard to process. A high-pitched horn sounded.

Misla took Bragen's hand. "Come along. I am glad you got to meet my friends. It's time to meet the others."

The children were all around zam. Zie let Misla lead zam out of the circle and toward the buildings, marveling at how much smaller her fingers were. They followed a crushed rock path that led to a small white bridge that ran over a gurgling blue-green stream.

As they crossed over, Bragen noticed the entire structure appeared to be of one piece. Like the dream, the cross and hand rails resembled tree branches, complete with knots and what appeared to be tree bark. Intricately carved vines and leaves wound around the rails.

The buildings on the other side of the river were aligned around a green space. Their walls were covered with some type of white paint or other protectant. Red and yellow flowers filled the beds that surrounded each foundation. The doors, with rounded tops, were blue. The roofs were covered with a red clay substance. Not surprised at this point, archodial Bragen noticed the building's dimensions seemed to match the footings zie had dug out of this very soil so long ago. Along with fossils. Zas memcore recalled being on zas knees, carefully drawing the tip of the spade around newly exposed bones. Zie looked at the children, then back at the village.

One of the buildings was larger than the rest. And different. Its red roof was pitched, not flat. A twisted column of blue-black metal protruded out of the roof's peak. It was capped with a clear, octagonal object similar to the one zie'd seen at Mythgarden Point. One of the double doors opened. A larger figure stepped out. Dressed in a single, close-fitting tunic-like garment, Feelwin opened his arms. The same Human zie had met in the other Interact. Yet he was not the same.

"Welcome to Ollepas," Feelwin said.

The children had followed them. Misla still held zas hand. Someone else touched zas arm. Others lightly touched zas back.

"Look at them," Feelwin said, a slight upturn to his mouth. "This is why you are here."

Yet, Bragen couldn't take zas eyes off of Feelwin. It was the same Human, but without the lines in his face. And there was no gray in his hair. Finally, the archy turned and looked at them. They looked back. All sharing something with zam. What was it? Energy? Their own Local?

Bragen could not remember ever being surrounded by such physical presence. A presence that somehow reminded zam of the Warp, yet this co-mingling was neither the Local nor the Warp. Such an interaction within the Prometheus would send alerts to the Watchers.

Forcing back zas curiosity, zie said, "While this is all very strange and interesting, I do not see the purpose. As you say, the context." Zie nodded at Misla and the other children. "They are why I am here?"

"And the *purpose* of these Interacts," Feelwin answered. "Come inside."

Somewhat reluctantly, all the children but Misla began to back away. Still holding zas hand, she led zam up the steps. Feelwin held the door.

"I have to go now," she said.

Bragen could see inside. There was someone else there, but otherwise the building seemed empty. Zie looked back. The children were walking across the field toward another building. Like a soft breeze, a hollow feeling passed through zam. Misla squeezed zas hand.

"It is ok," she said.

As she spoke, the ring around her neck faded, then turned a brighter orange. She looked up at zam. Bragen bent down. Those hazel-colored eyes seemed to suck something out of zam. Her mouth turned up. Bragen knew this was something pleasant, like a language, but could not relate it to anything zie knew.

"Where will you go now?" Zie asked.

"Back to school. I will be with my friends there."

"What do you do there?"

"Learn."

Bragen knew the word, but only within an animal context. How a rooker learned to fly. A baby sly-tail's first venture out of its ground hole. How forest and desert animals adapted to their individual environments. That was what Misla was talking about, but probably something more. What?

Still bent over, zie asked, "So, what could you teach me that you have learned?"

Misla reached over and placed her arms around zas neck and whispered, "Not to be afraid."

A tingle went down zas back. For some reason zie thought of the Warp again, and the towers zie'd seen in Sal Sagev. And Mador. What had happened to Mador? How could such a little thing come up with such a reply? During zas time at University zie had experienced many types of Interacts. Of course, those were much more sophisticated. Yet, in another sense, they were not as real as what zie was experiencing at that moment. Something about the archaic expressions jumped out and shook zas senses.

Staring at Misla, Bragen felt compelled to do something very strange. Standing up, zie touched her cheek with a finger. Something burned inside zas chest. Zie stepped back. The girl pointed at Feelwin.

"This is my father. With mother, they will finish this section."

"I thought you and your friends were the reason I am here."

"We are!" Misla squealed. The ring glowed an even brighter orange. "But there is more you should know."

Misla hopped off the porch and caught up with the other children. All were waving their hands now and talking at the same time. Zie could not make out what they were saying. A moment later they turned as one and ran toward the oblong building on the opposite side of the greenspace. A moment later they filed through a door and disappeared. Everyone.

Chapter 7

Bragen looked back at Feelwin. "You are going to explain now," zie said, as much to zamself as the Human.

"Come," Feelwin said, guiding zam into the building. The metallic column that protruded out of the roof was centered in the middle of the room, seemingly coming right out of the floor. Bragen thought of the cave. Arena stood next to it. The same Arena zie encountered on Apollis. Yet different. The lines were also gone from her skin. Another smoother version, her light hair almost yellow. No gray.

"There is little we can help you with," Arena said. "It is all within you, or will be," she continued, turning toward the twisted column. It hummed.

Bragen felt a vibration on zas skin. Arena was dressed in the same one-piece tunic that Feelwin wore, yet there were physiological differences between the two. Zie studied her a moment, trying to assemble the proper question. Both seemed to have shed the skin they wore on Apollis. For some reason, when zie looked at Arena zie thought of range arths dropping their offspring.

"You birthed Misla?" Zie asked.

"I did," she answered, her lips curling up. "And her sisters Zawlwa and Tewla."

Bragen pondered the first part of what she said and ignored the second part. So, a birth-person was a reality.

At least in the Interact, or wherever zie was. Zie looked at Feelwin. "Could you have…"

Feelwin emitted a similar, yet lower, trilling sound. "I could not."

"Misla said you are her… parents?"

"We are," Arena answered.

Bragen looked behind them and into the room. A large mural depicting a star-filled night covered the wall. Benches were scattered around. A meeting place of some sort. Working on Apollis meant zie was often working at night, out of the heat. Most archys were familiar with many of the configurations that lit the sky, no matter the planet. That zie recognized many of them meant one of two things. Either they were keen students of the Prometheus or, like Bragen, from it. They had already told as much in the other Interact.

The building was of some import, the room an obvious collection point. The mural dominated it. One depiction caught zas eye. An unknown constellation was placed between the Five Fingered Hand and the Raring Steedfell. Yet it looked familiar. Then zie placed it. Similar arcs were scratched into the surface of the Human's bench on Mythgarden Point.

It meant something. What?

"You know our galaxy," Bragen said. "But this one, what is that?"

"The Horn," Arena said.

Zie had never heard that name. "Your home?"

"In a way. As it is yours," Arena replied. "But that is for another Interact."

Frustrated, Bragen shook zas head. "All the answers seem to wait within another Interact. I have never seen that… place. You say it resides within the Prometheus.

How could that be?"

"Sometimes the truth hides in plain sight," Feelwin said. "Everything cannot be opened at once. That is why we created them the way we did. To provide a more gradual context."

"That is your answer to everything. Context."

"Yes," Feelwin said. "It is very important that you are here."

"Interacts are planned information portals," Bragen continued. "Yet I have not been able to process much of anything since I began opening them. All, including this," zie said, pointing toward the map, "are riddles. I can't see the point."

"Sometimes sight is not enough," Arena said.

The constellation Arena called The Horn blinked, causing zam to jump. Once again zie searched zas memcore. *Nothing.*

"You say we have common ancestors," Bragen said, looking at the small arc of stars. Misla's face flashed up. "How is that possible. Look at me."

"We can only present the reality we know," Arena said. "You bring another, one of several eventualities that we have prepared for. Now our realities come together, creating something new. In a future we can only anticipate, the Ruul, or something like it, will find this place. With you, we are preparing for that time. This Interact is a part of that preparation. It seems our future is not your past but in the midst of this anomaly we find hope. Whether you agree or not changes little."

Bragen couldn't begin to conceive of what she was talking about. "Why would they come here? To this valley? What do they want with you?"

"Uhlmans deem us to be irrelevant. Irrelevant, but a

threat. Our existence is a contradiction to their Truth. So, we must be ended. Thus, this war."

"Not logical," Bragen said as much to zamself as zas hosts. The all-encompassing Truth that flowed within the Galaxial Warp contained no reference for what these Humans spoke of. *Ended*?

"Once eliminated," Arena continued, "there will be no record. Literally and figuratively, we will not exist. You are confirmation of their wishes. Yet our Interacts are not prey to their erasures. We are not a part of their Flow. Thus, they have not seen what you see, nor have they the ability to do so, unless they find it within you. That is the only way they can see what you know. Only then will they see their future was built on a foundation of lies."

"And *they* are?"

"The Uhlmans or what comes after."

"You mean like me? A Synthon?"

"We do not know that name. At present, the Ruul, or what follows, are genetically engineering the next progressional leap. It must lead to you. The you in me. Their Truth controls the past but not the future. They seek that as well, yet you provide us hope that another Truth prevails.

"They believe we are a resource. But babies are more than the embryonic products of conception. Their cells are not the property of others to be used for the Common Benefit. Our children are the best part of us. The best part of you. They will not erase them."

"I have no such part."

"If that were so, you would not be here. You could not be here. While your ignorance of us is confirmation of their accomplishments, it also foretells of our ultimate triumph. Somewhere deep inside you, the Long Ago remains, left by a cohort. Like a grackle follows a trail of seeds, you have followed a path to the Truth. A Truth prepared long ago."

Bragen looked around. Zie stood in the room, but at the same time, sat in another. A work closet, bent over a chair. Or was what zie was experiencing a destructive contagion that was gradually eating away zas memcore?

Bragen studied Arena's face. "Tell me again why you have created this. Give me the essence. Do you believe this Record will preserve your culture? Your ability to procreate? What is it that you are trying to preserve?"

"Life," Arena answered. Her mouth curled up. An older version of Misla.

Bragen scrutinized the language on their faces. *Life?* Life was a certainty. But that was not what she was talking about. It was something else. Something no Synthon could conceive of. Why was that? What life?

"If somehow we are connected," Bragen began, "I do not see how, what does that mean? How could I help you? That does not seem possible. You are... not with me. You are from... some other place. Some other time."

"The Truth has little to do with time," Feelwin replied. "This is not about you or us. It is about the Truth. This Interact expresses this Truth through you. A reality you must grasp in your own time. In our time, Uhlmans believe our children are inconsequential mistakes that hinder the Common Benefit. You must determine why this is important. Only then will you know what to do."

Bragen looked back at the constellations on the wall. "We have no concept of war. That there is no violence in my homeland should hearten you."

"Battlegrounds are fought on many fronts," Feelwin replied. "Subjugation is one. Without the sacred there is no peace. Just void. The Ruul says otherwise. They state that only through science can there truly be peace. The Common Benefit. They call us the Carriers. Our children the Stain.

"Such mandates are generations old, going back to the Mawoans. It is ironic that not long after the first Mawoans, when the men-women began to propagate, science failed. Sadly, only for a while. They came after our born and unborn to solve their puzzle. The Ruul expounds upon these manipulations as the pathway to a future free of animal burdens. The somatic cell farms are on every planet we inhabit. Soon, we will be gone, but not from you."

Bragen's memcore raced through a sea of blank spots. While hinted at in the *Fables* and back-room whispering sessions, they had never been more than that. *Whispers.* The Warp was unavailable within an Interact. No way to search. What about the dream? The small blue smock with the torn pocket? The steedfells. The river. Was it all a part of the same malfunction? *Without the sacred there is no peace. Just void.*

Feelwin put his arm around Arena. "This Interact is complete."

Bragen continued to look at the mural. She called it *The Horn.* Zie had too many questions to leave.

"It can't be," Bragen said. "We haven't talked about anything really."

"We talked about what was most important," Arena said.

Bragen nodded at the arc of stars, "Where is it?"

Both Arena and Feelwin made that trilling sound.

"I assume that means you know," Bragen said. "What galaxy?"

"Not the purpose of this Interact," Feelwin said.

"What about the Light," Bragen demanded. "I don't understand the symbolism."

"No symbolism," Arena said, lips still curled up, exposing her teeth.

"But I have no idea what you are talking about," zie said.

As the last words came out of zas mouth, Bragen opened zas eyes. Zie was back in the equipment closet, stooped over the metal chair. A bit dizzy. The stars that covered the wall were gone. Feelwin and Arena were gone. Instead, tools and maps came into view. Red and blue lines ran down the center of the maps. Zie stood.

No symbolism. The musical lilt of her voice lingered in zas memcore. Bragen stood. Still dizzy, zie placed zas hand against the wall. The tools and maps were a foot away, but that was not what zie saw. It was Misla, looking up at zam with the curl at the edges of her mouth. And the others. *Children.* The sound they made when they ran across that field. What was that? *Laughing*, zie realized. They were laughing.

Bragen looked at zas hands, wondering if this was the end. Was zie mad? Corrupted? All the while, zie could feel her small fingers tightening around zas palm. *Do not be afraid.* It was there, all of it. Lodged in zas memcore forever. Something a flip would never hide. Where was Mador? What comes next?

Bragen knew that once zie left the bowels of the subroute, the Warp would find zam. A flip would only delay the inevitable. Taking a deep breath, zie walked out the door. The thrum and hum of the underground tunnel reverberated around zam. Zie quickly made zas way to the corridor. Around the corner were the stairs that led to the coordinator den. A yellow light painted the top of zas head.

Bragen looked up and saw the lowest rung of the ladder and pulled on it. After a moment of hesitation, it squeaked and gave way. Zie put zas boot on the lowest rung and began to climb. A minute later zie was in a dark, cobweb filled vertical tube. Climbing up, zie soon found the bottom of the trap door. With both hands zie pried its rusty lever loose and pushed up. A moment later, just as Maice had said, Bragen was in another closet. Light streamed in from the gap at the top of the door. Zie opened it and walked into the sunlight.

The main entrance to the East Andrio Transit Station was packed with Synthons. All fifteen gates had lines, some winding back into the street. Dressed in the typical colors that distinguished their status, each individual, lost in the Warp, compliantly waited their turn to enter the station. Similarly dressed teams filed out of the building, on their way to the future. Some carried bags, others, shiny flat hand-sized Dimensionals. Everyone looked straight ahead. Few were cognizant of the other Synthons. Focused on the destination, they followed the Warp's constant flow, information streaming in and out of their brains. New knowledge pushed old knowledge to the back of their memcores. Progress was made.

Bragen turned to zas right and followed the sidewalk toward Brinslow Park, looking for lidscans. The street was filled with the usual trams and sidecars, but none of the vehicles that concerned zam. Zie knew Inducers were on it, searching thought waves for zas ident. It was only a matter of time before a location alert signaled everyone.

Flips were a double-edged sword. While preventing access for a short period of time, broken thought patterns eventually set up low level alerts that were sent to the nearest Inducer. Thus, zie had to be careful with this capability.

Once in the park, zie flipped. Head down, Bragen walked past the bench where zie often met Mador. A group of grackles scattered. Zie gave a furtive glance toward the balcony. Two green clad Synthons were up there. Bragen's heart sank. Zie kept walking. At the end of the park zie exited a small gate, crossed the street, and hailed a rail-splitter. The transpo-coin in zas pocket buzzed and the door appeared. Once inside, Bragen removed the flip. Zie had no idea what to do. Then zie saw the lake.

"Take me to Rezcom Lake," zie thought.

The craft acknowledged zas order and silently began to move through the busy streets of East Andrio. The sidewalks and businesses were packed with Synthons going about their workday, as were the millions who filled the skyscrapers that loomed above zas head. As if it was zas very life-blood, the Warp pumped within zas cortex and flowed through zas memcore. News of West Andrio, Wezestra, and far away Chinwie popped up. Information on Lark, Dwarth, and Menomis. Experiments. Studies. Conversations. Questions. Answers. All there. All accessible. All flowing toward the creation of a Common Benefit. *That phrase.* Bragen forced zamself to listen. To take it in. To absorb, yet not participate.

The rail splitter slowed as it approached zas old haunt, Rezcom Lake, part of West Andrio's rural zone.

A minute later it landed. A body of water surrounded by a small forest. A couple of boats tied to a pier. A few tables near the landing zone. Bragen had been there several times to escape the crowds. Zie got out, releasing the flip, knowing zas location would eventually seep into the Warp. The rail-splitter left.

Bragen walked down to the rock-strewn beach. The water was yellow-green and clear. A school of finscale skittered off, leaving a ripple in the water. Other than a couple of Synthons walking near the pier, no one was there. The work period was in the middle of the prime day shift. Few were on break. Even so, few would venture to such a place. Idling was frowned upon in the homeland. Yet that had never bothered zam. Zie looked across to the western shore. A thick pine forest ran up the mountain, its dark green shadows painting the water below.

After a moment zie pulled the replicate membrane out of zas pocket. It fit in the palm of zas hand. Seemingly so insignificant. Zie looked across the lake. Smooth as glass now. Bragen whipped zas arm back and threw the clear rectangular object as far as zie could. Thirty yards away it skipped twice before sinking beneath the yellow-green surface.

Bragen sat down, still at a loss. Zie was no match for the combined efforts of Inducers and Watchers. The Watch. Feelwin had used the term, associating it with the towers around Sal Sagev. It meant something different to the Humans.

Zie sat there, watching the water ripple away from the spot where the membrane sank. Was zie a criminal now? Forget the remboot. Zie was past that. Would zie just be put back in the wager class and be forgotten? Or would they dismantle zam?

Without much thought zie took off zas boots and socks and put zas feet in the water. It was cool. Zie searched back. Zie had visited this same park thirty-three times. Not once had zie put zas feet in the water. The cool felt good. *What an odd thing to do*. For some reason it reminded zam of Ollepas. Which did not make a lot of sense. But what did at this point? The finscales were back, albeit remaining several feet away, seeming to study zas toes.

Bragen leaned back. The sun was straight overhead, a bright, clear yellow ball of light. Closing zas eyes, zie tried to wipe it all away. Another sun, this one on Apollis, intruded. That blast furnace could kill you, just as it had much of that planet. But the Humans had lived there. When? Obviously when the planet was alive. Or at least more alive than it was in zas time. Zie imaged Mavwa's Gulch. The red sands. The icon. What had happened to Mavwa? Bragen searched the Warp. There it was.

A thousand years ago archodialmavwa led the first survey to *distant* Apollis. After several years onsite, the mission was closed out and all fossils and artifacts were returned to Arion. The most significant finds were uncovered at what became known as Mavwa's Gulch. That was all zie could find. Nothing more existed. At least not that way.

Bragen took another tact. Closing zas eyes zie completed a two-word search, "retired archodials." Retired was a euphemism for pulled from service. The variety of explanations as to why this was so was never mentioned, but such open-ended lists provided endless guessing games to all manner of professions, including the wager castes.

Bragen found zam. Archodialmavwa was "retired" to Menomis a couple of months after finding the ruins. *Menomis.* Zas new assignment. Zie looked up. Cupping zas hand over zas eyes, zie saw two hawks floating lazily overhead. What happened to Mavwa? Clearly there was a pattern of some sort. Was it similar to what happened to zam in the Glendom Valley and Mythgarden Point? The common denominator on both those jobs was Majore.

Bragen thought of all zas years as an archodial. How much zie had enjoyed zas life uncovering bones and old ruins. Now what? Zie could feel Misla's fingers in zas palm. Everything seemed to be funneling toward a certain inevitable conclusion that zie had no control over. Was there more to Majore? Twice now that archy had shown up on zas sites. In both, Bragen's readings were determined to have been flawed.

Zie lay still on zas back, staring up at the sky. After sucking air into zas nose, zie closed zas eyes again. Zas feet remained in the water. Zie opened the download from Mavwa's Gulch and ran down the sequential list of inscriptions, then sat up. Zie shut down the Interacts and stared at the dock.

Chapter 8

Majore clicked on the Silverstream's auto route and punched up Dalimath's coordinates. Once the craft was out of Lark's atmosphere zie reviewed the briefing called ArionBreakout1. The Flow was private, restricted to planetary Seers, Inducers, and Majore's team.

The lidscan traced archodialbragen to a block of East Andrio apartments, one of which housed the wizened. This Synthon was already linked to the archy, so a preliminary scan started there. No one was in the apartment so the search expanded to the neighborhood. An hour later a lidscanner picked up the trace.

The professor was back in zas building. Majore alerted Mulendur, zas Inducer, who quickly arrived at zas apartment. Zie did not knock. The door was rammed open. The wizened stood in the middle of the room, a black-market messenger in zas hand. Smoke surrounded the device. A moment later it was gone. All that remained was a large red welt on the wizened's palm.

The Inducer sent a quick block into Mador's memcore, freezing zas mind's ability to maneuver. Mulendur searched, but zas probe came up zips. Somehow, the professor had initiated a short memory erasure. The apartment search proved more fruitful. The walls were covered with kulcat fibers, a sure indication of unthoughts and black-marketing. Once the fibers were pulled down, a large hole was found in one of the walls.

It contained a long piece of metal. Thin with jagged edges. One side bore an indecipherable inscription. Majore ordered Mulendur to take the wizened to Wahlgahlen and the metal to Dalimath.

On the trip over Majore scanned Mador's history. The trace revealed an unusual number of flips, long voids outside the Warp, and evidence of occasional dark meetings. By the time zie arrived at Wahlgahlen it was confirmed that the metal was Ariztex. It was an old sheathing material. A thousand years ago, rockets used it as a protective cladding. It was no longer in production, mined, or stored anywhere. The inscription was also translated into thought. *Apogonos*. No one knew what it meant. Everything was shipped to Dalimath. These discoveries, coupled with the wizened's use of a black-market messenger elevated the investigation to breakout status.

As always, the Hive watched through the Third Eye. Majore could feel them in zas thoughts. Once at Wahlgahlen, the professor's extracted conversations regarding Synthons, Prometheus archeology, and odd digibits was sure to provide new leads. It was the same with the illegal acquisition of kulcat fibers.

Majore was not an archodial. Few within the Prometheus knew this. Zie was a Benefactor. Benefactors oversaw high level wager activities, including excavations. Archys spent their lives searching for artifacts and fossils. Benefactors were not concerned with understanding the past or artifacts. Majore's true role involved oversight. Sondaman, Dwarth's Seer, once noted that, "Truth in the wrong mind is little more than a lie. This is how infection spreads." Majore and other Benefactors focused on disabling such infections before they damaged the Warp.

Using a Black Hole transit, the Benefactor quickly descended into Arion's atmosphere. Moments later zie walked into the Wahlgahlen facility. All blue glass and green beams, while its corridors were devoid of traffic, its rooms were filled with Synthons. They huddled around Dimensionals and Warp penetrators, or stood transfixed over their recessed desks, focused on select priorities. The Flow was tangible here, as much a presence as the Synthons it ran through.

****

Mador was in the fifth floor Wake Room. A room that took up an entire wing. Zie sat in a large, armless chair. A soft bracket wrapped around zas head, making it impossible for zam to move. Zie had not seen it, but zie knew it was a cleanwave chair. Zie could feel the probe rummaging around in zas brain. Zas head was shaved. Zas silver braids gone. Small suction cups pressed against zas temples and the back of zas head. A fix had been put into zas pupils, which prevented zam from closing zas eyes. An emptiness grew in zas chest but it was the intruder in zas head that bothered zam. Mador could feel them searching, copying, hunting.

The wizened dared not think of the place they looked for. Such thoughts left trails. *Let them find it.* The effort left a nagging throb at the back of zas skull. *My shield.* Zie refocused attention on the pain in zas hand, a result of the device incinerating. The head bracket prevented zam from moving. This fix prevented zam from blinking. All zie could see was an olive-green wall.

The report noted zie was harvested on Thon and processed to Enray. But that report had been manipulated by Mador long ago. Zie purposely selected that model.

The majority of Synthons were wagers of some sort, working toward the Common Benefit. Transportation. Infrastructure. Planetary mining. The service sector. That was zas track. But not zas span.

Instead, zas past included advancing from historian to anthrogenecist. This promotion afforded zam the chance to travel the Prometheus. The Galaxial Warp bound each mind to its purpose. Cloaked as a professor, zie worked toward the position of wizened. Wizeneds trained the archodials and anthrogenecists responsible for helping advance colonial expansion.

Once achieved, University contacts kept zam within a particular aspect of the Flow without garnering suspicion. Over time, different smatterings of conversations and distant discoveries indicated a language no one understood. A language zie knew. Had they found the metal sheet? The door in the olive-green wall opened. Zie closed zas shield.

Three Synthons walked in and stared into zas eyes. Or were they? Mador could see them all, but something was off. There did seem to be differences. Differences not related to standard caste demarcations like eye shadings, tunic colors, and buttons. Upper-types carried themselves differently. Not exactly straight. A certain bent to their shoulders and necks. The language of superiority. One stood out. The same silver hair and blue skin, the same penetrating eyes, but something else. It leaned forward. Mador cavalierly tried to run a trace. *Blocked.* Not surprised, zie waited.

****

Majore stood between Linatin, who had gone to Apollis in the guise of Council Coordinator, and the Guide. Barnam would take over once they were done.

They set aside what was found in the apartment to focus on the Interact. The search of zas memcore was quite fruitful. Even extraordinary. Through Bragen, this one had met *women*. Carriers. Majore wondered about the *scouts*. Zie closed off those thoughts to focus on the priority.

This one did not seem like the typical blackmarketer. Majore was not there to extract every illegal thought from the wizened's stubborn head, that was the Guide's job. Zie was interested in something deeper. Whatever came of this encounter, Barnam would later dig between the temporal lobe and the brain stem for additional information. An emulsion would follow.

Archodialbragen1031 was the priority. The Mavwa's Gulch extraction should have been recovered long ago. Now the Planning Board for all colonization efforts would have to reevaluate everything, including construction. Data from old technologies had been used to affirm Mythgarden Point's viability. That data did not indicate the presence of Interacts. Devices from the earlier era were not capable of deep scans. Prompted by the cave-in, Bragen returned to the ravine with better scanners and found the files.

As inconceivable as it sounded, this inexcusable mistake could splinter the Warp and destroy the One Thought. The same archy, oddly enough, had found similar evidence on Lark. That first excavation led to Bragen's semi-banishment to Apollis. In something of a troublesome pattern, this wizened was involved in both.

The result was a contagion that now involved lidscanners and an East Andrio Inducer. Disinformation blocks were in place and monitoring had begun. To slow the spread, the Warp around Arion had been reduced, thus, much of the work ahead must take place within a weakened Flow.

Who was this wizened? Mador's memcore retained information concerning origination of the ruins and who the escapees were, but there was more to learn. And what about Bragen? What had zie learned since leaving the wizened's apartment? What conversations had taken place between the two after leaving the Interact? It was clear the professor was hiding something. What?

Majore studied zas golden eyes. *Who was Misla*? They knew Mador heard the name when zie was within the Interact, but zie did not appear to know who she was. The other Interacts surely contained that answer. Had the archodial shared more? Majore studied zas face. This interview was different. Previous subjects contained a certain look in their eye, a sense of their own doom. Such knowledge usually led to the answer before the Benefactor asked the question. Mador's eyes reflected back a serene, endless quality.

"You have yourself in quite a fix," Majore said.

"Who are you?" Mador asked, pretending not to know.

"My name is Majore. Like you, I know Bragen. We are trying to find him. You think you know me?"

Mador wanted to shake zas head, but could not. Instead zie tried to block zas thoughts. Zie felt something different in the probe. This was more than an Inducer. Zie recognized something very old. The pain grew worse. *Good.*

"My friend has alluded you," Mador said.

Majore paused, assessing the brashness. "For the moment."

"Zie knows something you do not."

There was no greater threat to the Truth than such a statement. Perhaps zie had underestimated the wizened. "Who *are* you?"

Mador stared straight at zam, but did not see zam. The creases around zas eyes deepened, a clear sign of intense pain. Majore ran the probe deeper. There was nothing there zie did not already know. "What is Apogonos?"

Mador could not move zas head, but was able to shrug zas shoulders. "I do not know."

Maybe. But zie knew *of it.* The defiance was extraordinary. Something lurked behind the eyes. More like golden mirrors than a window into zas thoughts, they reflected back Majore's own questions. What now? Events were overtaking zas ability to remain in control of the situation. Perhaps zie should just give zam to Barnam and focus on the contagion.

"You are spreading the Infection," Majore said.

"Am I?"

"You are trying to."

"Am I?" Mador repeated. "But perhaps the opposite is true. Perhaps you are the infection and the one you are looking for is the antidote."

"And who gave zam this antidote?"

"Some cures originate from the disease."

Majore probed again. Nothing. "Untruths."

"Untruths?" Mador asked. "Reality hides under them."

"What reality?"

Eyes bulging, the wizened started to respond, but did not.

Majore leaned over, having caught the thought. *The past is not over.*

The Benefactor looked up at Linatin. *This is a wizened?* Zie stared back at the old Synthon, shaved and immobile, water running out of the edges of zas eyes, probes rummaging around in zas brain.

"The lidscanner traced Bragen to the apartment you live in," Majore said. "No one was there when we arrived. You walked in an hour later. Where did you take zam?"

"Nowhere."

Again, the truth. After a long pause the Benefactor sighed, then looked at the Guide. It was spreading. For a moment zie wondered if the wizened had planned zas own capture.

"You were talking to someone when we found you."

"Yes."

"Why not just tell us." Majore looked at the professor's burned hand, but searched zas memory. A shield. Linatin also found it. It was quite unique. "What do you mean, the past is not over?"

Silence. Golden mirrors reflected back zas own face.

Majore looked at Barnam. "Go ahead. I am needed elsewhere." Zie turned and walked toward the door.

****

Mador could not turn zas head. Zie knew zie shared something with the questioner. Something old. Their footsteps trailed away. "There is only one Truth."

They had stopped. Mador knew zas time was coming to an end. Scanning back, zie reviewed several hidden conversations from zas University days, the ones that concerned the links between Synthons and mammalians. All spoken with students and colleagues as pure conjecture, meant to ameliorate the demands of everyday life. Or so they thought. Yet what zie had in common with the questioner, was more than conjecture.

The footsteps started again. Majore was not going to take the bait. Too bad. Zie sought a more prolonged conversation. Any delay meant more time for Bragen. A door opened. Barnam came back into zas line of vision, tightening the straps around zas head. Mador thought about zas days in the park first, then drove deeper back, focusing on the interior rotation of the Black Hole. This brought zam focus. The pain grew worse. A river of light ran through zas memcore. Zas last thought was of the pedestal. It was wrapped in the golden roots and vines that grew out of the stone. Then it was over.

****

As they strode through the corridor that led to the tarmac, Linatin contacted the Inducers, seeking a new report. There was news. A wave location indicated Bragen's whereabouts. Majore was out the door, focusing on the pattern. Zie shaded zas eyes against the brilliantly bright day. While chatter between a lidscan and the Watchers noted that the target was no longer at the ping, there was data worth investigating. As zie jumped into the Silverstream, Linatin sent zam the coordinates. A moment later Majore was in the sky and shooting toward Rezcom Lake.

Two lidscans were there, hovering a foot off the beach. A rail-splitter sat nearby, as did another Silverstream. Mulendur's insignia was on the craft. The Inducer stood near it, bent and looking at the ground. A part of Majore's team, Mulendur turned and watched zas leader crawl out of the Silverstream.

"The archy sat right here," Mulendur said, nodding at the imprints in the sand. "The rail-splitter's script notes zie boarded it twenty-three hours ago at East

Andrio Station 234 and came here. That station is next to the wizened's apartment. But zie left it here. Everyone at the substation has been scanned. All were zips."

"What about the infrastructure tunnels?"

"We are doing that now."

"What about around here? Any subroutes?"

"Not for a mile. You take this path toward the city to get to them."

"You know he was a wratchet-gatherer."

"Yes. How did that happen?"

Majore ignored the question, thinking about the path. Mulendur's thoughts were out there. Yes, personnel were at that substation as well. No need to ask. The Benefactor turned and looked beyond the lake. A forest running up a mountain. Zie looked down at the prints.

"Have we traced this yet?"

"The lidscans just got back. No other tracks."

There was a clear indentation in the sand. Bragen's boot. But others. Odd. Just offshore a couple of finscales got Majore's attention. Zie watched them a moment, perplexed that the Inducer had yet to find the straight line. Zie noticed the indention in the water. The Benefactor bent to get a closer look. The finscale scattered, leaving plumes of sand in their wake. When the water cleared Majore became certain of it. Toes. A left and right foot. Bragen had taken off zas boots, which made no sense. A skater on the run had taken off their boots.

Majore stood and turned around. Zie studied the walk-path. *We need the full Warp.* Much easier to pick up a thought-trail that way. A thought-trail could lead to the straight line. On the other hand, the Benefactor knew unlocking the Warp made the Prometheus more susceptible to contagion. If it were to spread, misinformation flags would go up, which would only lead to blank spotting and confusion. But that did not mean some sharp-minded Synthon who caught a whiff would not act beforehand. Thoughts could be frozen. Thoughts could be downloaded. A messy after action that involved more lidscans and interrogations. Such activities always made the Hive uneasy. Where was the archy?

Once again, zie pulled up the brief. It detailed Bragen's time at University, and zas physical visits to Brinslow Park. Most Synthons found their relaxation within the Warp. Why go there? Few used such places. Of course, it involved this wizened. Where was zas student? The subroute was the obvious answer, but there was no trace.

Majore scoured every detail concerning this latest pattern. Zie looked back across the water, then to the dock. A boat was moored there. What else? If zie hadn't already, Bragen would soon detect that there was something wrong with the Warp. Then what? Majore studied the dock, analyzing all the information they had gleaned from recent events. Linatin's face came into view.

"Mador's memcore has been extracted and we are setting up the deep scan. Information?"

Majore studied the lake's perimeter. Noted the park benches. The pine trees. The mountains in the distance. "Not really. Mulendur is searching the tunnels beneath the station that is adjacent to the wizened's domicile. Zie has lidscans and some Synthons searching every subroute between here and the apartment. As of yet there is no thought-trail. The deep scan should help. Is that ready to go?"

"Almost. The preliminary indicates what you already knew. This professor is unique. There is a block somewhere. We will find it."

It was up to Majore to ensure Mador's autop followed protocols. Time was paramount. The longer this episode continued the more rumbling there would be about a reduced Warp. Was Bragen opening more Interacts?

"So, the wizened is gone?" Majore asked.

"All but the memcore is emulsified."

Majore noticed more movement in the water. Not finscales. Tadpoles. Amphibians. They formed their progeny within unshelled eggs that were deposited in water. Unlike finscales, they eventually crawled out and lived on land. And they had skin, not scales. And their bodies were constantly changing. Unlike tadpoles, the adults were carnivorous. An image of Barnam leaning over the memcore flashed up.

"Good," zie said to Linatin. "One outbreak has ended."

While hesitant to leave, Majore knew Mulendur was more than competent. "Look at those toes," zie told zam. At that moment the tadpoles skittered north, just below the lake's surface.

"Oh," Mulendur said, looking into the water. "I should have caught that."

Majore remained focused on the amphibians' mastery of the lake. The water had cleared. Like Bragen, the tadpoles were gone. Time to move. If the Inducer was able to find the straight line Majore would come back. Mador's secrets were about to be cracked open. The archy was a different story.

On the way back to Wahlgahlen the Benefactor entered zas own mind, the older one, not the Synthon model. Zas original memory predated the Warp, or what became the Warp. Zie opened the history chamber that contained zas time on Lark and reviewed several ancient downloads. Zie searched the coastal belts, looking for a connection, but came up zips. Many of the last briganders operated there before they were eliminated.

The Benefactor found it quite ironic that the very abominations the Uhlmans sought to erase saved them. Once determined that they needed those products of conception to advance the progression, procurement centers and somatic cell farms followed. As a matter of course, solving the mitochondrial riddle led to chromosome genderization. As is always the case, there was deep resistance to progress.

Which led to the Uhlman Wars. With victory, physical anomalies were eliminated. Wombless regeneration was perfected, evolution accelerated, and the species was freed of physical inequities. The One Thought followed; its deeper message articulated by the Seers. With victory there was no room for unthoughts. No room for the Stain. Such progress led to the Common Benefit.

Majore scanned zas old self, paying particular attention to events on Lark. Zie turned away from the coasts, instead paying greater attention to the interior. In the center of the planet's western hemisphere a northern mountain range rippled across the continent. These mountains were cut with numerous rivers and valleys. Many of the Carriers made their stand there. Extractions and exterminations followed. Evidence related to the

Apollis fiasco indicated not all were eliminated. A craft had escaped the Glendom Valley.

Mavwa found the wreckage, but not the Interacts. Of course, it had nothing to do with the Pioneer Expedition. Majore was sent there to inspect the site before the perfunctory seal was put in place. By then data had been collected and shipped. Burn scars ran up the sides of the gulch, indicating some type of powerful explosion. The consensus was no one survived the crash. In hindsight Mavwa was given too much leeway regarding the final report. This led to some problems, yet in the end, the Truth remained intact.

Which led the Benefactor back to the Glendom Valley. And Bragen. And the inevitability of coincidence. The Warp was made of Synthonic patterns and flows. Watchers and Inducers, working through the Hive, controlled both. Misinformation was rare and remained contained. Yet now the pattern was bending away from that same Truth. The determination as to what had gone on in that gulch was rushed. *Mistake one.* Survivors had created a colony. *Mistake two.* The Interacts had somehow been missed. *Mistake three.*

Majore reviewed the file Bragen shared with the professor. The Benefactor knew of the orange rings, old translation modes, but still found them innovative. No such modes were legal within the Warp. A Carrier deception. It was clear that Golwina, Moira, and Arena were a part of the clan of terrorists who withheld the products of conception from the Common Benefit.

Archodialbragen1031 and zas mentor threatened the future. Threatened the Truth. Females were the greatest threat to that Truth. Only breeders transported the mitochondrial line to the next generation. Their elimination erased the Stain. Which led to equitability. Which led to harmony.

Majore's old self pulled forth archives that noted the Glendom Valley sect originated on the East Coast. At some point they escaped to the interior. They were known to exist somewhere within the Sal Sagev Range. Only one name did not correlate with the old lists. Who was Misla?

Barnam awaited Majore at the double doors of the Processing Center. The Guide quickly led zam to the Wake Room, where the gray memcore sat on a long white table. A red beam connected all that remained of Mador to the large Dimensional that floated above their heads.

Barnam pointed at the screen. Several images of dark rooms and blurry faces flashed by. "Clearly there are others we need to locate. Some of these conversations go deeper than the usual conspiracy chum we put out there. The old coot was on to something. And spreading it."

"The Long Ago," Majore said, as much to zamself as the Guide.

"Surely archodialbragen1031 is not of this level," Barnam said. "We have broken through all the blocks except this last one."

Majore pointed at the screen. Several images flashed by. Zie stopped on one of Bragen sitting across from the wizened. The images advanced. Numerous clandestine conversation files flashed by before the Benefactor stopped it again. It was an image of a thin piece of metal. Something was inscribed on it. "That is the metal found in the apartment. Anything else?"

"Not yet."

The object held a place of secret prominence within the wizened's memory. It was there, but it was not. Just the object. Not anything that explained where it had come from. *Apogonos.* What was that? For the next hour Majore scoured other pathways and storage units. No clues surfaced regarding this mystery. Zie did find other low-level whisperers, including a logistics professor and several wagers.

The melding of the two classes was unusual. Zie returned to the Dimensional and enhanced the image. A purple sheen began to emerge from behind the web of red and blue veins. Zie enlarged it again. A shimmery, veil-like shadow hung between the hippocampus and neocortex. The shimmer reminded zam of the glint in the wizened's eyes. Zie looked at Barnam.

"Did I do something wrong?" the Guide asked, taken aback by the Benefactor's stare.

Majore knew this veil. It was like zas own, the one that hid zas true self. Which meant Mador was not a Synthon. Zie looked back at the Dimensional and followed the red line from the image on the screen to actual extraction, which sat on the table like a forlorn amphibian. *Tadpoles skittering across the water.*

"I see a lake in your thoughts," the Guide said.

"Rezcom," Majore answered. Zie connected with Mulendur.

"Yes?" the Inducer asked.

"Anything at the subroute?"

"I am standing outside it now. Just finished up. Zie was not here."

"I thought not," Majore replied. "Check the park again. The dock. The boats."

"The boats?" Mulendur asked.

Majore looked back at Mador's memcore. *Who was this?* Zie could hear the professor's thought: *Zie knows something you do not.*

"Yes. The boats. See if any are missing." Zie stared at what was left of the so-called professor. Amphibian. *Metamorphosis.*

Chapter 9

Flip on, Bragen walked down the dock and stepped into the boat. It wobbled from side to side until zie sat down. The same transpo-coin that woke the rail-splitter brought this craft to life. A moment later the archy was gliding across Rezcom Lake's glass-like surface, moving toward the far shore.

In the minutes it took for zam to cross zie thought about those flips. Bragen had executed several since leaving Mador's apartment. Why hadn't lidscans been tracking zam between those moments? They traced zam to the apartment. Why not the lake? What about the Inducers? Where were they? Had Mador managed to throw them off the trail with some clever divergence? Was it something else? Zie dared not search the Warp for clues.

The northern shore grew closer. Mountain pines loomed down, casting shadows in the water. The beach was strewn with boulders, some as large as the boat. Bragen slowed the craft, then maneuvered around several large stones. There was no dock. Zie was able to get the boat's nose on solid ground before hopping out. As soon as zie left, the engine stopped. Looking back, zie calculated that zie had traveled two and a third miles.

Where to hide the boat? Away from the shore, the land ascended, becoming very steep. Bragen fruitlessly looked for a cave or crevice of some kind. Nothing.

There was a large pile of boulders. If zie could manage to get the boat out of the water, perhaps zie could hide it behind them. It was small and lightweight, but too heavy to pull out. Leaning over the bow zie studied the hull. Toward the back was an octagonal plug.

Bragen pushed the craft back into the lake and hopped in. Using zas hands, zie paddled out a little further, then activated the transpo-coin. The engine started. As it backed away from the shore zie kept zas eyes on the instrument panel. Zie had to get the boat into waters deep enough to submerge it. Once the depth reading indicated five feet zie killed the power source. Getting down on zas knees, zie tried to pull the plug out. It would not budge.

Bragen sucked in zas nostrils. Far above, several hawks made lazy circles in a deep blue sky. What now? Zie turned to the steering compartment and felt under the dash, finding a small door. It would not open. Sitting down, zie placed both feet between the handle and pulled backwards with all zas power. The latch broke and zie fell backward, hitting zas head on the deck. When zie looked back, the door was open. Running zas hand into the cavity, zie found several tools. One was a wrench.

Sweating now, Bragen turned and fit the wrench over the plug. After a couple of tugs, it began to move. Several revolutions later it unthreaded from the floor and water began to spout up. The depth gauge indicated zie should be able to stand up, but for the first time in zas life Bragen wished zie'd learned to swim. Holding tightly to the end rail, zie slid over the side. After a moment of uncertainty zas boots found the soft bottom. The water was up to zas chin. Zie hopped forward several steps before finding zas footing and walking to the shore.

Soaked, zie turned and watch the boat sink. After it sank bubbles continued to gush up for several minutes. Bragen sat down and took off zas boots. Zie turned them upside down and let the water run out, then wrung out zas socks. The bubbles subsided. Bragen put the socks and boots on, and waited until there was no sign of the boat. Standing, zie ascended the steep shore and penetrated the tree line.

The forest grew thick. The air cooler. Shadows covered the ground. *Where was zie going?* Bragen stopped and looked down. No boat. No bubbles. No trace. Zie gazed across the lake. No movement. At least none that zie could see. No lidscans. No Inducers.

Far beyond the park the East Andrio skyline jutted above the treetops. A dark outline of rectangles and squares that ran in each direction as far as zie could see. For a moment zie pondered just how many hundreds of thousands of Synthons were within and below those buildings, progressing toward the future. *What future? How do I fit into it?*

Bragen sat down and caught zas breath. Despite the coolness, sweat ran down zas neck and back. That had not happened since zas first days on Apollis. That damnable sun. Zie lay zas head back and touched the mountain. Sucking air into zas nose, zie closed zas eyes. The list flashed up. Zie studied the script, trying to make some sense of it. The numbers beside each hinted at some type of organizing principle, but zie had already failed deciphering it. The first took zam to Mythgarden Point. Humans called it Sunbloom.

The second led to the place Misla called Ollepas. In that one, younger versions of Feelwin and Arena lived in the Sal Sagev Mountains. That is what Misla called them. On Lark. That valley. Heretic's Cleft. Which was the older Interact? Bragen scanned the inscriptions, settling on the last one.

A moment later zie stood on the edge of an outcrop, a sea wind in zas face. Down below the waves crashed against a white beach. Zie turned around. A being, another Human, stood between two steedfells. One red colored, the other yellow. Based on characteristics zie had filed away, it appeared to be a male. A *he*. General commonalities appeared the same. The same nose, mouth, and ears. Much larger ears than a Synthon's. Straw-colored hair tumbled down his shoulders. Broad shoulders. A similar growth grew under his chin. This hair ran in front of his ears, across his temples, on top of his head. Clad in some type of leather, he also wore a chain-ring around his neck. A neck that glowed bright orange.

"Welcome to Sunbloom," he said. The sound was the same, musical in nature. "I am Landerwin."

The archy stared. The Human's hazel eyes bore into zam with an intense inquisitiveness. The experience was akin to being probed, but Bragen knew zie was not. The steady roar of an ocean filled the silence. The sea breeze blew the Human's long hair back. Landerwin turned away, gazing down the slope. "It begins."

Bragen followed zas greeter's eyes beyond the steedfells and the field of Highland Red Grass that fell toward a distant valley. In that distance a ragged line of purple mountains beckoned. A golden glow backlit the peaks, hinting that morning was on the way. The red-colored steedfell snorted at zam. Zie looked back. In zas five years on Apollis, zie'd found a few fossilized remains of this extinct species. Zie pictured the skulls, and the protrusions that rose between its long, pointed ears. But like on zas approach to Opellas, here they were. It stamped a hoof.

"I am Bragen," the archy thought. "I know this place, but not by Sunbloom."

Landerwin studied zas face. "What do you call it?"

"Mythgarden Point."

"I have never heard it called that," he said. "Maybe my parents will know it. We are glad you are here."

That word. *Parents*. Bragen knew it. Zie looked behind zam. Beyond the Point the Aguila Sea's blue-green horizon met a light pink sky. The third moon was about gone. Zie turned and looked east again. The rim of the sun, almost as red as the grass, was visible now. *Odd*. The heat was not there. The Hammerheads had not hit yet.

"That term, parent," Bragen said. "You mean those who created you."

Landerwin's mouth turned up, revealing his teeth. "That is one way to put it."

"Where are they?"

"I am here to take you to them."

The site was familiar, yet different. The red grass came to zas knees. Zie walked in a circle, listening to the waves crash on the beach. Zie bent down, feeling the earth, searching.

Landerwin studied zam. "You might not know the name, but as we hoped, you know this place. You know us."

Bragen stood, wondering about the *we*. Zie continued to run zas boot along the top of the soil. Nothing. Zie looked back at Landerwin, "There were buildings here. I think your species built them. Where are they?"

"Species," Landerwin repeated, as he studied the thought. After a minute or so he blinked. He had no idea what a *species* was. "Everything that was above ground was moved before I was born."

Bragen studied the soil. The archy in zam began to pick up the almost imperceptible undulations. Upon further study, zie noticed some different colorations. But no sign of dirt bricks. They were gone, or hidden. "That must have been quite an undertaking."

"My mother said it was."

Landerwin's eyes felt like lasers, but it was his mouth that caught Bragen's attention. It remained curled up on each edge, reminding zam of someone else.

"Your mother?" Bragen repeated, more a question than a statement.

"Misla," he said, his mouth once again exposing perfectly white teeth. "You should know her."

Bragen nodded. Zie knew a Misla, but surely not this one. At least not yet. "And your father?"

"Reenquo was his given name. Do you know it?"

Bragen shook zas head. "I do not."

"Come. Mother is waiting." Landerwin walked forward and handed zam the braided rope that was looped around the red-haired steedfell's neck. "There is much to learn."

Bragen looked at the animal's dark red mane, about to ask where they were going, but felt it best to wait. Perhaps this was some type of false image, a Watcher's trick to spill some name. "I am sure there is," zie said, studying the tiny horns that protruded out of the top of the animal's head. Just as interesting were its ears. The

145

fossils provided nothing on these long-pointed marvels. "What do you want me to do?"

Landerwin looked at zam a moment longer, that odd trill coming out of his throat. "What I do." The Human turned and swung his right leg over the yellow-haired steedfell. A moment later he sat squarely on its back. "That," he said.

Bragen was not so sure. It did not look easy. In fact, it looked dangerous. Zas memcore flashed no images of such an exercise. Gripping its long red mane in zas left hand, zie attempted to swing zas right leg over the animal's back. It jumped forward, causing zam to lose zas balance and fall into the tall grass.

Landerwin emitted that trilling sound again, only louder. "If you are scared, you'll scare her. Be assertive."

Bragen stood and dusted zamself off. Scared? What was that? Certainly, a weakness of some sort. *Her*? Zie looked at zas host. Zie seemed to be enjoying himself.

"You have never ridden a steedfell?"

"We do not ride animals," Bragen answered, once again grabbing a handful of mane. "No such beast exists in my world." One of its large green eyes glanced back at zam. Bragen swung zas leg up again. This time zie managed to get it over, as well as ending up in an upright position on its quivering back.

"Good," Landerwin said, the orange ring glowing. He flicked the rope that looped around his own steedfell's neck. It started to move toward the valley. "This way. We have a journey of some length."

Bragen watched zas guide. Zie listened to the waves. I can hear that, zie thought. Is that how Humans hear each other? Do the musical tones require larger ears? Zie inspected Landerwin's ears. Half-covered with hair, they were much larger than zas own. Bragen's side orifices were about the size of zas fingertips. Humans' were as big as zas entire finger. Zie looked down the valley. The sea breeze bent the grass tips eastward. Zie felt the steedfell between zas legs. The animal's backside was not that uncomfortable. In fact, sitting up straight and looking toward Landerwin, zie felt a sense of... something. Higher up than afoot, zie could see further down the slope.

"Do this," Landerwin prompted, nudging his own animal in the flanks. "We have two destinations. We can't wait for the first moon."

Bragen, shading zas eyes with both hands, looked beyond the valley. Deep, red, and ominous, the sun was climbing over those distant mountains. It was strange to be so exposed. No visor to warn zam. No shield to block the heat. The air was pleasant. Nothing was changing as the sun rose. As Landerwin directed, zie nudged the steedfell. It walked forward. Soon zie was next to the Human. In tandem and at a rhythmic gate, the animals walked through the red tipped grass sea toward the valley.

Bragen rocked along, trying to mimic the easy manner of zas guide, who seemed to be a part of his steedfell. Landerwin called the one zie rode Sky and Bragen's Moon. Naming steedfells was just another oddity the archy had a hard time understanding. Zie almost asked zas host if they could talk. Instead, zie began to wonder about Mador.

Over the next hour, Landerwin described the approaching topography and explained that one of his obligations was to create a map in Bragen's head.

"Couldn't this Interactive just pull one up?"

147

"You have to make it," Landerwin said.

Bragen thought a moment. "It seems a waste of time. Premaps embedded within memcores are much more efficient."

"A guide does not have all the answers you seek," Landerwin said. "I do not understand how you would learn the way if it is just given to you. How would you remember?"

"I would not have to," Bragen answered. "It would always be there."

Landerwin gave zam a sideways glance, but did not say anything. The wind changed direction, coming from the mountains, bending the grasses in the opposite direction.

"What if I am an imposter?" Bragen asked, changing the subject. "What if I reveal this place to the Uhlmans?"

"Perhaps that is a part of the plan," Landerwin replied, his mouth curled up on each end. "As my father says, the future cannot be fooled. On the last day before forever, He will lead them back to yesterday where all tomorrows will be reborn."

Bragen puzzled over this. "These Interacts are little more than one riddle after another. Who is *he*?"

Landerwin shrugged. "It is from the Long Ago, yet speaks of tomorrow. What is a riddle?"

The archy had never thought about what a riddle was. Everyone just knew. Zas memcore drew a blank.

"You do not know?" Landerwin prodded.

Bragen shrugged. "The answer to a puzzle that reveals a surprising meaning."

"Why surprising?"

Their capacity is sublevel. Bragen jumped, wishing zie had flipped before expressing that thought. But the

Local did not work within an Interact. There was no flow. Landerwin still stared at zam but did not look insulted. Just the opposite. His face was open. Interested.

Certainly, a lot had changed in the centuries since this archaic device. What the other Humans had called The Way, was buried in Mavwa's Gulch. Modern Interacts were training mechanisms created by Hive personnel and available throughout the Warp. All Synthons used them. Modern versions gave directions and answered questions on specific subjects. These were different. More intuitive. More… zie could not think of a proper thought.

Landerwin, oblivious to Bragen's confusion, looked down the valley, and began a discourse on their surroundings. He pointed out specific plants, named them, and did the same with rocks, gave the elevation of the distant mountains, and finally a bit about his life on Sunbloom. "That was my first real home. I was five when we moved away. I remember how they dismantled the beams and threw most of the earthen bricks into the ocean. We took everything we could and buried the rest."

After reaching the bottom of the swale the land began to rise. In due course the red-tipped grasses receded, exposing hard baked earth. The steedfells navigated around more red and yellow rocks and larger swaths of orange-colored sand. As the last wisps of grass disappeared, a dry riverbed came into view. Bragen noticed a faint, eroded trail leading into the ravine. Another led up the other side. By then the sun was directly overhead. It was warm, but nothing like what zie experienced in zas own time. Once out of the river bed, an isolated peak came into view. Behind it loomed the larger mountain range. The same hint of a trail led them toward this jutting finger of rock and sand.

An hour later found them in this lone peak's shadow, just above another ravine. Much wider and deeper than the first, Landerwin stared into it. "We landed here," he said. "As you can see, this environment is not as rich as where I met you."

"They landed here?"

"We landed here."

"You remember?"

"A little, but again, most of my first memories are of Sunbloom."

"So, before here, where?"

"I was born on Lark."

"Born," Bragen repeated, more to zamself than Landerwin. Zie looked from zas host to the sky, then into the ravine. Mavwa's Gulch. Zie looked up. The cone-like peak's shadow touched the lip of the ravine. Beyond, the larger mountain loomed.

"Born," Landerwin repeated, pointing to the ring around his neck, "Even with this facilitator you make the word sound strange."

"It is not a word Synthons know," Bragen said. Zie had no idea how to explain. Besides, the Interact was for zam, not the Human.

"We were all born somewhere," Landerwin replied.

"You say *we* as if you mean me," Bragen said, staring into the ravine.

"As my mother likes to say, I am the me in you."

That did not correlate in any sensical way, but Bragen remained silent.

"Our start came here," Landerwin continued. "But Sunbloom was our first real home. I was not much taller than the grass tips when we left it," Landerwin said. "I know this route well."

"But this is an Interact. All could have been laid out within it. I do not see the point in getting on this... animal."

Moon snorted. Landerwin's steedfell shook her ears.

Bragen shifted on its back. "It seems to know what I said."

Landerwin said, "No. Just your manner. Feelwin says we all have our roles. I am performing mine."

"Feelwin." Bragen shifted on the animal, thinking. "Feelwin helped make Misla?"

"Something like that. With my grandam."

"Which according to the Old Way is how children happened."

"Yes. But *happened* is not the right way to explain me."

"A male and a female," Bragen said. "Like a steedfell."

After a pause, Landerwin nodded. "Yes. Like a steedfell."

They sat their horses in the ravine, the sun over their heads.

"Those mountains. That range. That is your new home?"

"My home, yes. For most of my life," Landerwin replied. "I was raised there."

"Raised," Bragen pondered. Zie knew it to mean to lift something over your head or off the floor. But that is not what Landerwin meant. "And your first home. Not here. What you call Sunbloom. Was it just the location?"

Landerwin looked beyond the cone-topped peak. "Knowledge of the Long Ago traveled with us. It has served my parents, my grands, and the others well. We moved to Sunbloom for a number of reasons. Better climate. Fertile soils. The hunting was good. Yet, an intercept precipitated we establish ourselves elsewhere. A ship approached. A ship that could do us harm. Sunbloom was in the open. Vulnerable. I remember the rush to discard everything. I was not much help. What I most recall are great plumes of dust. They did similar work here, in Wasenah Rift. Every visible feature was dismantled and taken away in carts. We did not want them to find anything."

Bragen looked up and down the ravine. Nothing looked as it had when zas hovercraft scanned the icon. *Wasenah Rift.* Zas memcore pulled up a particular curve along a series of benches and an oblong boulder shot through with striated black and white lines. Zie studied the edge of the ravine, looking both ways. Zie saw it fifty meters down the gulch, perched on the lip of the ridge. Directly below the rock, the river bed had one particularly flat section, free of stones and pebbles. It was too smooth. "What is that?"

"A place of preparation," Landerwin replied. "This deep space intruder was looking for us. By the time it landed they only found what we wanted them to find. All signs of our early days were gone. In its place were the remnants of failure. A crash site sprinkled with a few burned artifacts and fossils. They even burned dark scars on the walls of this ravine, creating evidence similar to a great explosion. They hunted. We believe they concluded, as we wished, that there were no survivors. Everyone seemed to have been incinerated. We were deep in the mountains. They scanned the range, but never knew us. After about a month, they left with a few trinkets and bones. The day after they left, preparations began."

"Preparations? For what?"

Landerwin made the trilling sound. "For you."

Bragen stared at the dirt. "You mean the Interacts?"

"Yes. The Way was meant for you."

The archy's memcore brought up the image of zas Silverstream hovering over this very spot. "That is impossible."

"I cannot comment on that. I was seldom a part of those conversations, but heard snippets. They talked about Wasenah Rift and how The Way unlocks time. I never understood what they were talking about until recently. Your questions must wait."

But the questions could not wait. Sweat ran down Bragen's back and stuck to zas shirt. "How do you know they were placed here for me?"

Landerwin shrugged. "You are here."

"You said they could not find you. That they do not know you. You mean Humans?"

Landerwin shook his head. "While they were looking for us, that is not what I meant. They could not see us. We are not linked to what they consider the higher order thinking. As a result, they cannot see our thoughts. I am not the one to explain these things."

"Seldom is anything explained," Bragen said. But zie thought zie might understand. Humans did not possess a Local. They were not a part of the Warp. The archy pointed to the odd flat spot in the ravine. "This is a place of preparation? That is where the Interacts will go?"

Nodding, Landerwin said, "Yesterday will become tomorrow. In your time, you perceive the opposite. We will plant them here, beneath strong shields. Encased in zara tubes and protected by ceramalic, it will be buried under several feet of rock and dirt. Some will even come from another ravine to ensure there is a proper appearance."

Bragen wanted time to think about this, to search the Warp for information on such a puzzle. But that was impossible. All zie could do was hope the 'elders' would be more forthcoming. Zie looked toward the mountain range. "How far?"

"If you keep asking questions, dark will fall before we reach home. I was instructed to take you on a specific route to Aromla, only providing the most basic of answers."

The archy stretched. Zas's steedfell snuffled and shifted under zas weight, its back muscles twitching under Bragen's legs. Zie looked from the ravine to Landerwin and then above the gulch's rim to the isolated peak. The mountain range remained a hazy outline. Zie looked down. Mavwa's team had collected those artifacts, finding only what the Humans wanted them to find. Even so, the bones told an unanticipated truth.

Bragen understood why they left them. It gave the hunters enough answers to file away their remaining questions. The answers included the Humans escape ended in disaster. But Mavwa's written report contained too much detail. Rawnswawn linked it to zas analysis. Despite the blank-spotting, whisps of the truth slipped into the Warp. Mador did the same when Bragen informed zam of that first discovery on Lark. And all was erased. How many times had that happened?

Landerwin nudged his steedfell and led it up and out of the ravine.

Bragen, more confident now, nudged zas own. Once

on top, zie pointed toward the mountains. "Aromla?"

Landerwin smiled, the ring around his neck glowing bright orange. "Yes."

The steedfells followed a slight indention in the soil. An hour later the climb became more pronounced. Bragen paid attention to everything. They passed by a series of sandy hills and broken cliff faces.

"How long have you lived there?"

Landerwin looked up the path, even steeper now. "Almost two decades. Look."

A plateau sat at the feet of the range. Bragen squinted. It looked like there might be a wall or something on top. Zie looked at zas guide. "Up there?"

Landerwin nodded. "Another hour."

As they grew closer, the almost imperceptible trail became a well-worn path. An hour later, they sat their horses at the bottom of a sheer cliff face. Several robed figures came out from behind a half wall and moved toward them. Greeting Landerwin, they pulled back their hoods.

One stepped forward. Zas white hair was longer, seemingly woven around zas waist. Even so, it was his skin, not the hair, that set zam apart. It too was white. Pure white. Just as striking were zas opaque eyes, which bored into Bragen with stark intensity. The man bowed zas head, then stepped back.

Bragen was mesmerized. Zie could see blue veins running across zas cheeks. Landerwin hopped off of Sky and motioned for zam to do the same. Bragen slid off, slowly running zas palm across Moon's broad neck.

"Thank you," zie told the animal. Moon's green eyes studied zam a moment. It snorted. Someone grabbed the reins. They were both led away. Landerwin was moving toward the cliff face. So did the crowd, gently nudging zam in that direction. Zie looked back. The white skinned one was hanging back, watching. Synthons did not get that close to one another.

Bragen could feel something, a warmth, coming off their bodies. Not oppressive heat. Something pleasant. Males and females. The same, yet different. Like the children of Opellas. Different skin tones, body shapes, and hair colors.

Their orange rings brightening, in unison they said, "Welcome to Aromla. All is prepared."

Bragen did not respond. What could zie say? Behind the half wall was a rather wide lane that ran up the cliff face. Zie turned again and looked for the white-skinned individual. He was gone.

Chapter 10

The stone path was cut into the side of the plateau and ascended the mountain. They all walked up. As they approached the top, the path ended in front of a metal gate built in the middle of a larger stone wall. The gate opened. More robed figures were inside. These Humans stood on either side of a clearly delineated route that cut through the middle of a courtyard. Zie saw several curved benches along the edges of what looked like a parapet. They reminded zam of the benches zie had seen on Mythgarden Point. They too, had some sort of markings on them.

Landerwin had not spoken since they had started up the path. Bragen decided zie would hold zas thoughts, not as comfortable amongst so many of the strange beings.

Zie force zamself to once again consider the possibility that it was the arrythmia. A dream. The plaza. The robed figures. Their mouths. Mavwa's Gulch. A mammalian species that mimicked Synthons. Or was it the other way around? Procreation. War. Such a concept. As inconceivable as children. Birthing. Zas tharsonome told zam otherwise. More than once. Majore was involved both times, convincing zam that zas eyes did not see what they saw. To question the Stellar Council was to propagate an unthought, which brought unwanted scrutiny, or worse.

Landerwin guided zam through the crowd toward the end of the courtyard. Here, the rock face of the mountain stretched into the clouds. Yet there was an opening. An archway was carved into the face, the entrance into a large cave. Others were waiting inside. Including the smaller species. Children. A variety of voices echoed against the walls. High and low octaves. An individual musicality lacing it all into one sound. Excitement. *What was excitement? Where did that word come from?* An electric hum filled the air.

As they moved deeper into the cave Bragen saw a multicolored strobe spinning on a column of twisted dark metal. Pulsing lights of red and blue, green and yellow, beat in cadence with zas heart. A woman stepped out of the crowd and held out her hand. The multicolored lights ran across her face. Something about the skin on her face told zam she was older than Landerwin. It looked rougher, and contained a few creases. Something about her eyes and nose reminded zam of the guide. Was this zas mother?

"Welcome," she said, breaking into a smile. More lines appeared around her eyes and mouth. Hazel eyes.

Bragen nodded. "Misla?"

"No," she said. "Zawlwa."

Bragen knew that name. From where?

"I am Misla's sister," she said.

When zie visited Ollepas, Arena had said something to that effect.

"What is a sister?"

"Her sibling," Zawlwa said. "We have the same parents."

"Oh." Another strange thought. Siblings, sisters, and parents. What could make such a world?

Landerwin reached over and wrapped zas arms around the female. "Are they ready?"

"Yes," Zawlwa said.

They walked deeper into the cave.

When they entered the cavern, the globe spun faster. The colors blended. A bright white light emanated from its center, painting the walls and ceilings with constantly moving silver dots. Bragen noticed the buildings, or structures of some type, high up on the walls. They were fastened or carved into the sides of the massive chasm. Human faces appeared in windows. Others stood on open balconies looking down. Several clear-bottomed catwalks connected one side of the cave to the other. Broader bridges ran over their heads, intersecting and overlapping. Above it all, the octagonal ball whirled and hummed, its metal base swirling into the cave's floor.

Landerwin noticed Bragen's fascination with the twisting pole. "Our magatonom."

"I have seen one," Bragen said.

Along with Zawlwa and several others, Misla's son led them to a platform that sat on the cave's floor near the magatonom. Landerwin stepped onto it and motioned for Bragen to follow. "Do you know its purpose?"

"No."

Bragen stepped onto the platform.

"It extracts power from the heart of the planet," Landerwin said. "Once captured it is tamed to do our bidding."

A moment later the platform began to float. Bragen reached out zas hand and struck an invisible rail. Everyone on the platform made the trilling sound.

"We embrace the heart," Zawlwa added. "Do you know what that means?"

Bragen just stared at her, afraid if zie moved zie would fall off the platform.

"You must trust the Truth."

They ascended above the bridges and through a rectangular opening that Bragen had thought was the cave's ceiling. Instead, it was another floor.

More rooms. Brilliantly lit. Other Humans walked toward zam. Some looked familiar. One in particular. Very similar to Zawlwa. Her light-colored hair was flecked with white. When her hazel eyes locked onto zas, she stepped forward and smiled, opening cracks in her skin. Despite this aberration, Bragen was sure this time. Here was the child zie had encountered in Opellas.

"Misla?"

"Bragen," she said, that same musical quality floating out of her mouth, the orange ring glowing around her neck.

"This is an Interact," the archy stated, as much to zamself as the image in front of zam. "What you call The Way. Each is a separate entity, meant to provide context. If that is so, how do you know my name?"

"It is true each is a self-contained interaction, but once activated, they remain accessible. Over the last forty years, the one we met in has been watched many times. What we learned was incorporated into this one. Which means we are better prepared for your return."

None of it made sense. Zie looked at her. *Her.* "What has happened to you?"

For a moment, Misla hesitated. She looked to her left.

Bragen followed her gaze. An even more ruined looking Human stared back. Still, zas memcore recognized Feelwin. Was it the sun? The planet?

Feelwin's robe swallowed him. His eyes were sunken and watery. His flesh hung limp on zas face, as if it might fall off. There was no hair on zas head. Even so, zas mouth was curled up, exposing a row of perfect white teeth.

Bragen searched for a correlation. One of Mador's lectures popped up. It was on the petrified forests of Dwarth. Students encircled the wizened. The Dimensional lit a hologram above their heads. It showed a dissected elderwood. Five feet in circumference. Mador pointed to the series of concentric circles within the cut. "Each represents the seasonal cycle. This tree's life was broad in scope. The rings indicate it lived a long life, yet you must remember a young sapling's appearance is much different than that of a mature elderwood."

Feelwin's physical body, Bragen realized, like the tree, changed with age. Instead of rings, lines etched zas skin, like a range arth past its prime. Similar lines ran across Misla's face, yet not to the same extent. Humans, Bragen realized, did not last long.

The father stepped forward, a long stick helping zas balance. "You look like you have seen a ghost."

"Another term I do not know. What I see is a more worn you. Like a gyro that has been used too long," Bragen said, studying zam. "Is this why Synthons do not know you? Is this why you no longer exist?"

"I still exist," Feelwin answered. "In Misla, Zawlwa, and Tewla. In Landerwin and my other children. Most importantly for this moment, in you, as you exist in me. This is not why you do not know us."

While there was no Galaxial Warp, the musicality that flowed through Feelwin's orange ring and into

Bragen's memcore highlighted that there was more than one mode of communication. Bragen sensed another language behind those dark watery eyes. Stronger than the One Thought. Something ageless and true.

"The unknowing you expressed at Ollepas was disturbing, but it informed us. As did Mador's presence."

Mador's presence? In the Interact? Bragen was about to ask about this when the crowd parted and a woman holding a small blue bundle walked through and up to Misla. She was smiling. "I am Tinda," she said. "This is Marabella."

The blue bundle moved. A tiny hand slipped out. Its pink fingers wiggled back and forth. A strange, mummering came from within the bundle. Tinda pulled the blanket back, revealing Marabella's small, pink, wrinkled head. In an odd way the lines that creased it reminded Bragen of Feelwin. Yet this seemed the opposite of age. A new, more desperate sound came from its mouth.

Alarmed, Bragen stepped back. "What is wrong?"

Everyone made that trilling sound. Once again, zie realized what this was. *Laughter*. Something good. Zie stared at the wiggling bundle.

Misla told him, "She is hungry." To Tinda, she said, "Show Bragen."

Tinda pulled back her robe and turned the baby toward her exposed breast. Mirabella began to suckle.

"The Uhlmans who did away with the Mawoans were just as determined to do away with her," Misla said. "This was a part of what they called The Progression. Yet plans were disrupted by misbirths and deaths. Science remained certain the admixture was perfect, yet genetic malfunctions began to occur within second and third generation evolutionaries. Despite the science, these progressional Uhlmans lack the same twenty-three somatic cells both Human males and females possess. Their solution involved taking what they called the products of conception, born and unborn, to their somatic cell farms. Science, they declared, led the way. The tissues of both genders were needed to create the perfected evolutionary leap. So began the Uhlman Wars, because we refused them our babies."

Bragen had heard much of this already. Zie was more interested in Marabella. The baby suckled Tinda's breast. Its cheeks drew in and out. Like breathing. It was something mammalians did. Sustenance. Long ago fables talked of this, but here was a new phrase. *Babies*.

"And they come from inside you?" Zie asked Tinda.

"Yes." She smiled.

"And your own body feeds them," Bragen said, as much to zamself as Tinda. It seemed similar to what zas own body did to itself.

Again, she nodded. Of course, zie was familiar with mammalian biology. It made sense that Humans with similar organs would have a similar process. Zie looked at Feelwin. "This occurs through breeding. Correct?"

"In a manner," Tinda answered. She noticed that Bragen remained focused on Feelwin. She turned and looked behind her. Out of the crowd stepped a smooth faced, red-bearded man. "This is Slewmwa," she said. "Together we made Marabella. Do you understand?"

Bragen nodded. "I do. To some extent."

Misla walked up to her daughter. Tinda slipped the baby into her arms. "I am her grandam," she said. "This was left out of you."

Bragen studied Marabella's small, pink face. Her

eyelids opened, revealing dark blue eyes. *This was not in zam.* No record. Zie looked up at Misla, beginning to understand. *This is why I am here. Marabella. Wasenah Rift. Aromla.*

"Follow me," Misla said.

Bragen took another moment to digest zas surroundings. The Humans. The baby. The cave. Zie could almost feel the neurons firing in zas head, rewiring zas memcore. Zie looked at the Truth the Warp left out. Its small pink hands were moving, reaching. According to all zie knew, this was nothing more than an unthought.

Bragen started to follow Misla out of the room but heard something. Something painful. A bleating noise. Zie turned around, finding nothing. Tinda was gone, as was the baby.

"She has gone to the nursery. Perhaps you can tour it later."

Still too stunned to understand it all, the archy continued to follow Misla. They walked through another arched doorway into what looked like a study. One window ran the length of its northern wall, revealing a yellow sky full of stars. It seemed very high up. A large stone desk was centered against the wall near this window.

Bragen studied Misla's face. "Who is Reenquo?"

She paused, turning her gaze from the window and focusing on zam. "My other."

"Your other?"

"That part of me that brought the future."

Bragen thought about this. "You mean Landerwin."

"Yes.

"Where is he? The... father."

Misla blinked. "He died."

Bragen felt an odd tingle in zas chest, but did not know why. Whatever died was, it seemed very final. "He is not here, in Aromla?"

She placed her hand on her chest. "He is here. We must continue. You came to Sunbloom forty years ago," Misla said, her hazel eyes looking deep into zas own. "But our journey to Opellas took place before that."

It was clear she was not going to talk about Reenquo. "You were not at Mythgarden Point," Bragen said. "What you call Sunbloom."

"I was here, making preparations. But in your time, that was very long ago. Ages." She looked out the window, casting her gaze below, then motioning for zam to do the same.

"Not that way," Misla said, a light trill to her voice. She pointed north, "Look." She gazed beyond the tops of the distant peaks at the constellations that were beginning to blink.

Bragen thought about the mural Misla's parents had shown him on Opellas. "We know them well."

"What do you call it?" she asked.

"Which one? On the right is the Raring Steedfell. On the left is the Five-Fingered Hand."

"And the one between?"

Bragen looked again. Nothing. "On the wall, back in Opellas, I saw something else. I do not see it now. Where?"

"You are in my time, archodialbragen1031."

Puzzled, the archy looked again. "Synthons know the stars. We know the constellations. We should be able to see what you see." Zie searched the space between the two. Zie scanned the rest of the sky. There was The Ram. The Long Brow. Familiar and charted. The Warp was full of details about those constellations, as well as the Raring Steedfell and The Hand. She kept staring at a specific spot.

Bragen thought of the etchings on the benches. "It is not there."

Misla leaned out, continuing to stare at the same location. "Yet there it is. They left it out of you."

Bragen could not accept it. "This proves I *am* in a dream.""

"You think I am a dream?"

Bragen looked at her. The yellow-gray hair. The skin lines. The hazel eyes of the little girl who grabbed zas finger.

"The Horn has always been there," Misla said. "And always will be. Like us, you just have to look."

Zie looked again. "The Horn?"

"Yes," she said. "It is always calling us home. Even you Bragen." Misla looked down. Bragen peered over the window frame. Far below, three elongated ships sat on a broad launching pad. An arc of stars was depicted on each nose cone. The Horn.

"You are leaving?"

She nodded. "Soon. Preparations are almost complete."

"There?" Zie asked, looking back at the sky.

"Yes," she answered. "You should say it out loud."

Zie could not. It was not there.

The ring around her neck glowed bright orange. "Thoughts do not contain the same intentionality."

"Intentionality?"

"Meaning."

Bragen reviewed this. Thought to thought. Mind to mind. Was this riddle, this meaning, wired into all

Synthon memcores? Was the musicality that came out of a Human's mouth highlighting some meaning?

"The Horn," zie thought, listening for a sound. There was none.

"I felt it," Misla said, her lips curling up. "The connection will come. We have much to discuss. Come." She walked over to the desk. The granite top was smooth and level, just like the room's walls. Several cylinders, some encased in black and red tubes, were stacked on top of it, as were an assortment of rectangular and oblong instruments. One emanated a dull, orange glow.

Misla picked up one of the cylinders and pointed it toward an alcove that jutted out of the far wall. More cylinders were stacked within a series of recessed shelves. "This is the only one we will leave."

The girl who was no longer a girl, so different from the child zie had flown into the Opellas Valley with, tapped the end of the cylinder against her hand. An oblong roll of material fell into her palm, which she quickly unfurled on the desk. It was composed of several layers. The top one was covered with two columns of the same indecipherable script that ran across the Interact's legend.

"This is The Way. Much has occurred since your last visit."

"Landerwin explained that term is interchangeable with Interact."

"My son has trouble containing himself sometimes."

"Why The Way?"

Misla looked up. "It will guide you into the future." Instead of explaining, she returned her gaze to the desk, placing several small, rectangular objects on each side of the scroll to hold it down. She picked up the glowing instrument. It painted an orange fan over their heads. "Like the balance of those that follow," she said, "this… Interactive… began after you and Mador came to Sunbloom. I was here, making preparations for the new settlement. Certainly, our earlier meeting helped to shape this one. Look."

Bragen pulled zas eyes from Misla and looked at the thin, flat material. She ran the oblong instrument over it. Through an orange haze zie was able to read the last string of sentences.

Landerwin awaits. That moment will be memorialized with the rest. As my father reminds me, the Truth is not burdened by the constraint of time. Like the purple fliguan, it may lay dormant for long periods, but its beauty remains, waiting for the sun.

Misla put down the strange tool and motioned for zam to follow. "Time is getting short. Here," she said, moving over to the alcove. The ends of several cylinders were visible. "This will be enclosed. If you have trouble finding it, look up here."

Bragen followed her gaze. All zie saw were more stones. They ran above the alcove. "Here," she said, reaching up and putting a finger on a small black rock. She moved it, following an arc of similar stones to a larger, rust colored one. "The wall will be constructed below this one." She grabbed the rust colored one and twisted it. "Do that and it will open. Only you will know."

Bragen studied the rocks. It was harder to pick them out once she moved away. Still a nightmare. Zie walked back to the large window and peered down at the ships. Each looked as if it could launch at any time. *They expect me to return. To what? How*? Zie noticed a small ledge below the opening. It ran south, around the mountain. "This was meant for someone else," zie said "I am really just a wager. This was meant for Mador. They will just cart me off."

"Mador has done more than you know. Truth cannot remain in the past. Neither Mador's nor yours."

Bragen recalled the wizened sitting on the park bench, a quizzical look in zas eye. "Mador is gone."

Misla thought about this. "So is Reenquo. So am I. So is my father. Despite this... we live in you. Nothing can change that."

Small jets of steam floated lazily out from under the rocket's undercarriage. "Whatever happened to Mador will happen to me. You do not know them."

She joined zam at the window. "I may not know your world, but I know such forces. They proclaim Truth is their highest priority. Instead, it is what they fear the most. They call our greatest gift an abomination. They believe our elimination is the gift. It is not."

Bragen studied the three nose cones. The rockets, long and slim, stood like giant sentinels pointing toward the stars. Zie returned to the desk. "I will never make it back. They are looking for my thoughts. I'll be arrested as soon as I get close to a transport. Look at us. We are not the same."

The ring around Misla's neck glowed deep orange. "Inside we are. As intended, more now than before. Words are more than thoughts. They fear this connection. They fear the change. The change you will make."

Bragen stared at her, thinking. "When I get on a transport, the Watchers will notify the Inducers. The

Inducers will send lidscans. They will find my thoughts and then they will find me."

"Perhaps not."

"How can you know?"

"I am not in your future, but your path has changed, as has everyone's you have touched. And will touch. Including Marabella. It may be hard to see, but it is right in front of you. This interaction is coming to an end."

Bragen whirled around, wanting to soak it all in. The cave. The alcove. The rockets. The *words*. Opellas. Wasenah Rift. *Marabella*. An emptiness filled zas chest. An uncontrollable sensation zas memcore could not express. Zas time at Opellas flashed up. A little girl held zas finger. *Those words*. Zie identified the emptiness. "I am afraid."

Misla cocked her head to one side and studied zas face, then placed two fingers of her right hand on zas forehead. She quickly moved them to zas chest, "Do not be. Tomorrow is coming."

"Tomorrow? I don't know the way back."

"Radom will show you," she said.

Bragen shook zas head. "Another riddle."

Misla smiled. "More a parable. Do you know parables?"

Bragen searched zas memcore. *Nothing*.

"It is a gift."

Bragen was completely lost. "From who? Where is Mador?"

"In your tomorrow. Goodbye archodialbragen1031."

Chapter 11

Majore was an Uhlman. Zie knew Humans. In the last years of the war, zie became a Benefactor. This involved a unique genetic sequencing pattern that elevated zam above the masses. Benefactors oversaw Inducers and Watchers. In overall control of the Warp, they served the Hive in a variety of ways. Majore focused on preventing breakouts and closing entry points. Through Black Hole transits, zie and Linatin, of the same ilk, traveled the Prometheus securing the Flow, ordering remboots, cleanscans, and in rare instances, emulsions.

From the Hive, Seers watched all, initiating alterations, blank-walling, and new thought patterns. A billion such thoughts flowed through Hive rings, connecting everyone to the One Thought, aligning all to the Prometheus. Each Benefactor's ultimate goal was to Move the Ball Forward, maintaining a universe free of discord and unthoughts.

Despite best efforts, traces of the Long Ago remained lodged in the recesses of Synthon memcores. A genetic anomaly. Even the Seers had a hard time controlling dreams. Dreams of vaulted thoughts. Vaulted because they often led to leaks. This was why the Watcher class were always looking for abnormal neuronic firings. If warranted, such dreamers were interviewed, informed they were practicing unthoughts, and sent away with a higher level of scrutiny. Yet the most egregious cases were sent to Benefactors. Benefactors looked for malevolent intent. Possible contagions.

The wratchet-gatherer was a contagion.

Majore was on the way back to Rezcom Lake when Linatin's face flashed up. "The Hive has located a Misla."

Majore slowed the Silverstream. "On Apollis?"

"No, on Lark. On the West Coast."

"The West Coast?" Zie immediately thought of the terrorists.

"Look," Linatin directed. A blurred image of a young woman moving out of range illuminated the craft's Dimensional. "This is from the vaults. Another old Interact. Taken on the outskirts of Seaport. In the last weeks of the war, she led raids on several somatic cell farms. Pre and post birth males and females were removed from the extraction centers. After the war, the Seers blank-walled her. She was a brigander. And a prolific writer."

White streams of light flashed by the hovercraft. Arion was moments away. Was this what Bragen had learned? Those last weeks of the war were the worst. Briganders commanded the resistance. Once removed, order was established. The Warp gained control. All thoughts became One Thought.

Misla. Majore made a connection in zas head. *Stainspreader.*

Arion's Flow was still in a weakened state. "Send it all through the Dimensional."

The city's skyline came into focus, layers of blue, painting the horizon. The Silverstream burned through the barrier and descended to the lake. As zie prepared to land, Majore reviewed two separate concerns, the wizened and this Misla. Both were connected to Bragen. As soon as zie landed the Inducer approached the craft.

Zas thought arrived before the door appeared. "A boat is missing."

Majore nodded. *Amphibians.* Zie spotted two hovercraft in the distance, slowly moving over the water. Most of the lake was surrounded by pine trees. While not far from the city, this area was intentionally secluded. Once considered a respite. A mountain ran up the far side. What lay beyond it? Still in the craft, zie checked. A river valley populated with several wager buildings. "It will take some time, but we need to scan the region. We need lidscans and more hovercraft."

Mulendur nodded. The order was immediate.

Majore got out of the Silverstream and watched the Inducer's thoughts as zie ran through each detail of the hunt. During the brief, they walked toward the water. The Benefactor imaged Bragen sitting on the shore, in this very spot, with zas feet in the water. What did the wratchet-gatherer know?

A boat was moored to the wooden dock. A bench was built into the end of that structure. It faced the mountain. Majore walked out and sat down, staring at the other end of lake. Yet zie did not see it or the mountain. Zie saw briganders. Smoke. Burning soma farms. Vacant product bins. Humans were an obstinate bunch. Their elimination was such a boon to society. Yet... Something had slipped. The image of the purple-sheened wall that shielded a part of the wizened's life flashed up. Then those eyes.... Numerous files flashed up. Zie opened another.

*Report #2, Seaport, Lark: Second season-3128.
Three attacks. One successful. Somafarm105 breached
on the third day of the new moon. These Carriers are
seasoned terrorists. Several hosts removed prior to
tissue transitions. This includes the wombnested
products of conception, taken from the farms via
portable incubation modules. In addition, ten male and
thirteen female post-natals were freed. Range three
months to two years. Their leader is a woman. The Ruul
has designated her the Stainspreader. Her given name is
Misla. The terrorists call her Lifegiver. She originated in
the east, a part of the Carriers who fled to the mountains
that divide the continent. Constant surveillance in that
vast region has proven fruitless, yet this current series of
raids indicate that at least one sect has moved west, and
live along the coast.*

*Report #7, West Coast, Lark: Fourth season, 3133.
Operations complete. Clean up phase in process.
Reconnaissance continues. The carrier sect located east
of the Wild Mountains eradicated. Current evidence
indicates they are the ones who have been operating
near Seaport for the last several years. As of yet, there is
no proof that Stainspreader is among the captured or
deceased. Genetic signatures continue.*

Majore sat on the bench, thinking. Additional
hovercrafts flew over the park. A lidscan, less useful
within the weakened Warp, operated over the tree-lined
shore. *Report #7* originated over a thousand years ago,
near the end of the conflict. Not long after, peace spread
across the galaxy, the Warp bloomed, and the Hive
cemented its control.

Stainspreader. Uhlmans gave her that name. A
name vaulted and forgotten. The Carriers were gone.

Erased from The Record. Only the Seers were privy to those erasures. Which seems to have been a mistake. *Zie knows something you do not.* Majore watched the lidscan fly north over the distant shore, yet zas thoughts were on the wizened, strapped in the chair. What unthoughts hid behind those golden eyes. That veil? What had zie shared with Bragen? Just as important, what had the wratchet-gatherer shared with zam?

The Benefactor stood and stretched. Below, the water bubbled. Finscales darted away. Zie should have known her. Misla. Stainspreader. *The Lifegiver.* An abomination! Majore inhaled deeply and brought up another old Interact. It began with another blurred image, this time with a time stamp, 3135. In the distance zie heard the collective hum of hovercrafts as they combed the forest. Zie opened the file.

The blur turned into the face of a serious young woman, her hazel eyes burning. Her mouth a hard line. *That cursed innovation,* the orange ring, glowed around her neck, "We leave this for friend or foe. There is no signature required. Such parting requires a gift."

She stood on a rampart of some type. In the distance, a particularly unique mountain loomed: a rising outcrop with a deep rift across its middle. It looked as if a giant axe cut across its spine, leaving a great cleft. *Target!* Majore's memcore found it. That particular mountain was known as Heretic's Cleft. It was located in Sal Sagevs. That was a Carrier term, but it stuck, and was used in all the files. Possibly the Humans' last sanctuary. Data noted it shadowed the Glendom Valley. *Another mistake.*

The Benefactor studied the image. Others stood on each side of the woman. Each held a product of conception. Little ones. *The Stain*. The leader's long yellow hair blew behind her. All were draped in dark leather wraps with studded snaps. The babies were naked, revealing parts no Synthon could imagine. They made sounds with their mouths. Screeching like the animals they were. Their small hands and feet moved up and down. Majore noted that several of these Humans were in the Interact Bragen brought back from Apollis. The woman was not.

"My name is Misla. We came here with purpose and leave with purpose. Perhaps having found this, you understand. Perhaps not. Despite our leaving, we remain in you. Like our offspring, we live on." The image blurred. Froze. Ended.

Majore looked up. Far overhead, several hawks drifted in a circle. What was the purpose of such a short message? It was an insult. But something more. What? At least the connection was clear now. Terrorists from the Glendom Valley had fled to Mavwa's Gulch. Still staring at the hawks, a slight vibration alerted zam to the Hive.

"I am going in," zie told the Inducer, walking back to the Silverstream. Bragen was close, but the Seers beckoned. A visit zie should have instigated on zas own.

"Got it," the Inducer said. There was no need for further explanation.

While most of the Record was vaulted, Benefactors knew this history. Terrorists had long been linked to the Sal Sagevs. Heretic's Cleft rose above that range like a hump-backed trigadorous. The numerous valleys that ran out of those peaks provided good hiding spots. The land was vast. In spots, the topography almost impassable. The Uhlmans knew they were there. Somewhere.

These were the ones who made it to Apollis. Ultimately, a failed attempt. Majore had visited the site, talked with Mavwa. All who made it to that planet died in some type of explosion. Or did they? Majore slipped into the craft, wishing for a stronger Warp.

Once into the Black Hole transit, zie made for Dwarth, as good a place as any. That planet's climate was somewhere between Apollis and Lark's. Far from Arion, the Flow was much stronger there. Penetrating the atmosphere, the Galaxial Warp rippled through zas cerebral cortex and down zas spine. Night had descended when the Silverstream glided into Dalimath and landed at the Stellar Council headquarters.

Alerted, various Synthons greeted zas arrival. A suite was already prepared. With little to no acknowledgement, Majore withdrew into the room and lay on the bed. The Hive, center of the Galaxial Warp and governor of the Flow, came into view. Concentric rings of light met zas closed eyes. Brighter dots, each planet's Seer, hung onto these rings. All thoughts from the galaxy flowed through its center. Every Synthon thought, every communication, was observed as it passed through the rings. In the process, they redirected or closed thoughts, opened new ideas, encouraged commonality, and provoked the masses to move forward.

Feeling their probes, zie said, "I haven't opened everything."

They knew this and zie knew they knew it, yet it was the best way to start. After a momentary pause, their silver orbs brightened.

"If I had known," zie began.

"There was no reason before now," Fladnag

interrupted. Zie was the Arion Seer.

Like dust particles caught in a shaft of sunlight, Majore watched billions of Synthon thoughts flow through the rings' center. Each iridescent particle gave and absorbed information as it passed.

Together, they reviewed the entire package. One by one, they opened the old reports. Each event occurred before the Heretic's Cleft Interact. All concerned the Stainspreader, from cohorts to raids and possible hideouts. Yet the name Misla was absent from all. The next item was different. A material of some kind. Flat and thin. Inscriptions were embedded on it. They looked Human, but Majore was not sure. Zie was versed in the digital languages, and had viewed imprimaturs on functional objects, but never on such material. The hieroglyphs reminded zam of the etchings found on the metal skin found in Mador's apartment. Zie could not read them.

"That is paper," Lark's Seer said. Zas name was Tibboh. "Also vaulted. A device of some kind. Intentional or not, it cannot be deciphered. Such materials seldom last more than a few centuries."

"It becomes dust, or something like dust," Neiklot, Dwarth's Seer corrected, "unless they protect it. Most often, they used hermetically sealed tubes. Look at this last bit."

A typical archaic digital appeared, replacing the image of the paper.

"This is a translation of something she wrote," Neiklot said. "Since it was digital script, we were able to translate it. Read."

Majore read what Misla had written:

Greetings from the coast. I hope this finds you and

father well. It was a blessing to receive your missive. It appears our time here must end, so we are now making preparations to return. While we have had some success, there is still much to do. Unfortunately, there are not enough of us, and we do not have the capabilities to do more. I long to see your smiling faces. You know how difficult it will be to leave Reenquo. We talked of such possibilities many times. The caravan plans to leave before the snows.

I understand your concerns. I know they were heartfelt and what you thought to be in my best interest. I could not do otherwise. Nor could those who came with me. Including Reenquo. Together we stood in the face of these genocidal emissaries, their righteous indignation, their science, their accusations, their violence. In the face of this moral oblivion, we spoke the truth. They cloak their universality in virtuous phrases, the same that beguiled our ancestors and the Mawoans. They do not beguile us. Find solace in that we have saved many and look forward to seeing everyone soon. You were right. Life on Lark is no longer tenable. I have a surprise. It must wait until I see your eyes.

Love, Misla.

Like flickering fireflies, thoughts flew through the Ring. Some burned red and blue. Special Watchers picked out unthoughts. All vaulting was left to the Seers.

"What is paper made of?" Majore asked, just as interested in the devise as what it communicated.

"Cellulose," Fladnag answered. "An interesting material but there is no time to explain."

The communique indicated Misla was returning to the Sal Sagevs. Which meant she had gone to Apollis.

"Who was Reenquo?"

Neiklot answered. "One of the briganders. We believe it was a male. Possibly a conjugal partner."

Majore stared at the illegible scrawlings that swept across the paper. Rawnswawn got a lot wrong, yet zas meanderings were close enough to the old reality to ignite a slew of illegal dreams, flips, and unthoughts. The Warp's domination was tied to its strength, its ability to flush Right Thinking through every Synthon's memcore, yet this amazing conduit was also a weakness.

Two major breakouts occurred under archodialbragen1031. Zas association with Mador, clearly a different species, was not a coincidence. Was it a part of some larger plan? Did this connection make the current circumstances inevitable? Or was it just the inevitability of coincidence? Did the wratchet-gatherer know what *Apogonos* meant?

Majore felt each Seer's probe.

"For reasons you have always known about and helped maintain," Neiklot began, ignoring zas thought question. "Carriers have been vaulted. They do not exist. But you knew. This terrorist has been vaulted from you and everyone but the Seers. If it is not within the Warp, it does not exist. We only reveal this ghost now because the wratchet-gatherer has been woven into the Long Ago, and has become a part of a larger pattern. Vaults have deep purpose, yet occasionally must be opened for the Common Benefit. Discarded artifacts from another age do not."

They do not know what it means.

"Irrelevant," Tibboh interjected. "Yet there is something else. Barnam made a retrieval."

"Yes?"

"The Guide found a partial thought-line. Just as

important, the wizened contained a non-functioning signal."

Majore paused, recalling the shimmering purple wall. Few Synthons had the capability to hide files. Only Benefactors could signal. *The Fallen*? Majore quickly shielded such thoughts. *That could not be true.*

Barnam flashed up the partial. The wizened stood in a small square room with an earthen floor. Clearly Apollis. Several of the robed Humans stood near a large interstellar map that hung on the dirt wall. They were all looking at a specific constellation.

"Where?" Majore asked the Guide.

"Lodged in a side pocket of the frontal lobe," Barnam answered.

Majore nodded. A hurried burial.

The image activated. Mador was pointing a clear, cylindrical device at Feelwin, whose neck ring was glowing. "This is not what you think. I do not know if it will work." The wizened bent, as if in pain, "I am—"

In mid-thought, the professor turned. Feelwin stared at the device. Majore checked the Inducer's log. The correlator indicated this was happening at the same time Mulendur was ramming the door. Mador stared at the device. A black-market messenger. It was cracked and smoking. Then it was gone.

Majore connected with Oblib first, but all the Seers were probing zam. There was more to learn about the wizened. Much more. "The emulsion?" Zie asked.

As one, their thoughts returned to Barnam.

"It is done," the Guide said.

Majore flashed back to that last moment in the Wake Room. The imposter was immobile. Probes ran out of the top of zas head. Zas eyes were propped open. *The past is not over.*

The Seers thrummed.

"What was that?" Fladnag asked.

"It slipped out of zam just before I left," Majore answered. "It makes more sense now."

The image returned. Feelwin was focused on Mador's hand. Other Humans stood in the background. This had to be *The Fallen*. A lost Benefactor. Zie could no longer hide the inevitable thoughts.

"How long have you known?" Majore asked.

"Two centuries," Thon's Seer answered.

"That is the formal answer," Tibboh corrected.

"It occurred much earlier, but as to when, we do not know. Of course, it is vaulted," Fladnag interjected.

"I have seen that communicator," Majore said. The image was frozen. It showed the last wisps of smoke leaving the wizened's hand.

All the Seers answered, "It is quite common. Each has its own code. We cannot translate the image. As to whether the Humans could, we doubt it."

Majore studied the professor's image. The eyes and hair of a wizened. The face of a Synthon. Yet an imposter. "Perhaps the message was not meant for Humans."

Silence.

"Bragen," Fladnag finally thought.

"Yes," Majore said. Perhaps the message was for Bragen.

"There is nothing left," Barnam assured them.

Any remaining answers were emulsified. Majore thought about that. A Benefactor, living outside of time, had given all away. For what? Zie reigned in zas thoughts. *Careful.* An image of Rezom Lake flashed up.

"It is all connected," Fladnag said.

"On purpose it seems. A thousand-year-old trace," Neiklot added.

"More than that," Tibboh said.

Majore tried to puzzle it out. "So, this imposter affected…"

"We do not know," Oblib said. "Apollis meant little until now."

"The escape was a failure. They are extinct. They never happened," Fladnag said.

"That is the Record. These Interacts are a revelation. The wratchet-gatherer must be found," Oblib demanded.

Long before Apollis's colonization was approved, a year-long anthro-scope of the planet took place. All potential lifeways were scouted. If such a species had survived, the Mythgarden Point project, along with all the other colonies projected for that planet, would have been cancelled. Bragen would have been sent elsewhere.

"No Human heart beat there," Fladnag said.

All thoughts agreed.

"Why didn't we perform the geomorph scan at the old crash site?" Neiklot asked.

"Mavwa's stored archodial report seemed sufficient," Majore admitted. "A mistake." Of course. A target to blame.

"Archodialbragen1031 did not rely on it," Tibboh said.

"It was the cave-in," Linatin offered.

"This does not solve anything," Neiklot said. "None of the other Interacts hint at what is going on in this one."

They simultaneously reviewed the same questions. Had Mador altered something with that device? If so, why wasn't it reflected in the other records? One moment changes all moments.

"The Humans shielded it," Oblib said, then added, "somewhere."

"Or destroyed the thoughts born from it," Neiklot added.

"Humans do not have that capability," Majore said.

"So, they hid them," Tibboh concluded.

"On Apollis," Neiklot said.

The Warp was still being reduced on Arion, which meant normal operations were strangled. The orbs dimmed. Incandescent sparks ran through the rings like a raging river. The Seers turned their focus to Rezcom Lake.

"We need zas memcore," Oblib said. There was no need to mention the wratchet-gatherer's name.

"Report," Majore said.

Mulendur's face flashed up, pine trees in the background. They switched to the Inducer's sight-line and studied the forest.

"I am on the eastern shore. Nothing yet. Zie must be close."

"Perhaps," Neiklot said. "Do we know when zie got there?"

"Yes," Majore answered, "three hours ago."

"Then there is much to consider," Neiklot said.

Not used to communicating with the Hive, Mulendur focused on Majore. "If we opened the Warp, we could catch a trace."

"And open the Prometheus to infection," Neiklot interjected. "No."

"Send in more hovercraft," Fladnag ordered.

"We have six here now. And three lidscanners." Mulendur looked up. The Seers saw several craft hovering over the lake. "It could get dangerous."

Tibboh spoke, "We need twice that many. A crash is irrelevant. Do it."

Mulendur was still looking at Majore.

"Do not look at zam," Fladnag ordered.

Zie turned and nodded. "It is done."

"Go there," Neiklot ordered.

The silver rings and the orbs vanished. Majore opened zas eyes. Zie felt the bed beneath zam. Zie rose. The room, like all such rooms, was sparse. Synthons relied on what was in their heads and little else. It was the same with Majore. Far from Arion, the strong Flow allowed every Inducer to report. No sign of the wratchet-gatherer. Zie looked out the window. Skyscrapers ran on both sides of the boulevard, each filled with similar rooms. Hundreds of thousands of wagers inhabited them, their entire purpose inculcated in Moving the Ball Forward.

The Fallen. A Benefactor. *The One Who Left.* When the anomalies began it was discovered that Uhlman replications contained a fault. Genetically altered chromosomes would not suffice. Early within the Evolutionary Leap, female to male cell equitability was disturbed.

This was the era in which Majore became a Benefactor. Was it the same with Mador? What was zas old name? So much to ask of one who was no longer there. One who gave up the Enhancement. Why?

And what of paper? Zie should have known of this substance, as well as the hieroglyphs that spread across it and the metal. Zie had never questioned vaulting. But it was beginning to puzzle zam.

The Benefactor stepped out of the building and

strode across the parkway to the waiting Silverstream. Zie had to find Bragen.

Chapter 12

Bragen opened zas eyes to a blinding sun. Turning, zie squinted down the mountain and found Rezcom Lake. Zas mind returned to the little girl with the hazel eyes. Bragen looked up the mountain. The image changed. Misla the woman. Two fingers touched her forehead. "Trust the Way," she said, dropping them to her chest.

Somehow, zie was back in the Interact. "I do not know it."

"You will," she said, grasping the same two fingers of zas left hand. She placed them on zas forehead, then moved them to zas heart. "Your friend will show you." The wizened appeared, staring into zas memcore. *How?*

"Go to the Goman Ruins," Mador said. Behind zam was the winding stairway that led up to Mythgarden Point. But the professor was looking in the opposite direction, into the small square room with the arched opening. Feelwin and Arena stood there with the other Humans, watching.

Mador said, "Look under the plaque."

The Humans disappeared. Now the wizened was in zas apartment, holding something in zas hand. A device of some kind. "This is not what you think," zie said, staring at the wall. "I do not know if it will work—" In obvious pain, zie raised the object, then turned and looked behind zam. Bragen heard a loud crash.

A thought command entered the Interact. "Stop it."

"I am—" Mador's image froze. Zie had turned toward the apartment door, yet zas eyes remained on Bragen. Someone else was there.

Bragen reached for the wizened and almost stumbled down the mountain. The lake shimmered in the sun. No stairway. No Humans. No Mador. Instead, a steep incline that led down to the lake. *Arion.*

"What plaque?" The thought was aimed at the blue sky above zas head. And the Goman Ruins? The shoreline loomed below. Zie stood up and started walking in the opposite direction. Bragen wanted to lose zamself in the forest. The pine trees closed in, growing thicker, their tall canopies completely covering the ground. Thick beds of needles and leaves crunched under zas boots. Zas mentor was more than a wizened. But what?

For the next hour Bragen fought the incline, walking sideways between the trees, the air thick and humid. Sweat ran down zas neck and back. Zas shirt became soaked. Not a good thing. Synthons seldom lost their fluids. Soon zie found a ravine that cut a vertical gouge up the slope. Taking advantage of the rocks lodged in the bottom, zie began to climb.

When the ravine tapered off zie stood on an overlook peering into a distant valley. Down below, much of the forest had been cleared, replaced with buildings of glass and metal. A facility town. A big one. This meant a lot of Synthons were there, working. Which meant a subroute back to Andrio was nearby.

Bragen searched the Flow, but could not find it. In its place, a sense of unease. This was different from a flip. Flips were short-term blocks purposefully instigated to avoid Locals and the Warp. Zie studied the outline of the buildings. *How had Mador entered the Interact without zam?* The wizened's thoughts hung there. *Go to the Goman Ruins and look under the plaque.*

Bragen started walking again. Those ruins were a popular attraction in West Andrio. The professor used to lecture there. Countless skyscrapers and interconnected tramways surrounded the site. It contained the remnants of an old Uhlman village. A series of collapsed walls and steps interlaced with bushes and flowers. Bragen searched zas memcore. Zie found the plaque mounted on a square base in the center of the park.

Tramping through the forest, it took zam a couple more hours to get to the valley floor. Once near the buildings, zie realized the largest was a magnetoid plant. While there was no discernible Warp, zie believed the Local would give zam enough information to make a decision on what to do next. Synthon teams housed in such facilities built the omitrons that powered magnetoids which every interplanetary vehicle relied on. Somehow, zie posited, this power source must be linked to what zie saw in the cave. The magatonom.

Like other wager facilities, each zone was made up of teams that competed for the Common Benefit. The same in the tunnels. Each worker wore the team colors. Zie saw some wearing red and green striped jumpsuits. Others were clad in pale blue. They were filing down the maze of wide walks that connected all the zones. A giant Dimensional was built into the side of the tallest one, posting each team's zone standings. Quota statistics flashed from one grade to the next. A large group of Synthons stood directly underneath. A rally. Above the posting ran the banner MOVING THE BALL

FORWARD. Blinking back the uneasiness, Bragen walked out of the line of trees and toward the crowd.

Zas Local kicked in, allowing zam full access to those nearby. They were focused on standings and evening projections. From wager to wager, conversations concerning speed ratios and endurance patterns bounced back and forth, a competitive spirit lacing it all together.

Bragen wedged zamself into the crowd, feeling the thrum reverberate from one team to the next as the statistic's changed. Amidst the thought-blurs zie picked up a nearby group had just ended their twenty-four-hour shift. They would head home soon.

Within minutes, they began to move away from the Dimensional. In their place others started crowding around Bragen, all eyeing the big screen. Zie turned sideways and wiggled through, catching up with the tail end of the Blues. While most of their thoughts remained on the standings, a few mentioned the void. It was clear no one wanted to address this peculiarity in detail, but that is what it was. Where was the Warp?

Zie followed them. Off to the left a column dressed in yellow and orange walked into one of the glass and stone buildings. Like everywhere, the landscape was perfect: flowers, bushes and zyglot branchings color-coordinated and symmetrical. It was the same with the Synthons, all moving in sync with their neighbors. No standing on the walks. Moving. It was like every hub Bragen had ever experienced. This plant was more than a facility, more than a community, or even a city. As every Synthon could recount, this was civilization within civilization. What was intended for colonization in the Glendom Valley and Mythgarden Point.

Odd, zie thought, *this is what drew me to the archodials*. Archies did not live in the present or the future. They lived in the past. Nature, not buildings, dominated that past. Rocks and mountains. Rivers and prairies. *What was wrong with zam*?

Up head a Directional indicated the drop. A blue clad Synthon tried to probe zam, "You're not from here," the wager said.

"No," Bragen said.

"I can't find you," zie continued.

Bragen searched, noticing it too. Apparently, the Synthon could not connect through the Local. Which was impossible. Zie felt it best to respond with a truth. "I'm looking for the sub route."

Detections depended on how interested the questioner was, but finding another's thoughts, not just their communication, also depended on what else was going on. Through the Local, this one should have been able to derive more information, whether Bragen wanted zam to or not. But it was not working. Then another turned and stared.

"Where are you going?" The second one asked. "I can't find you."

"Where are you from?" The first one interjected, an odd tone to zas thoughts.

"Back to Andrio," Bragen said, answering the first.

"We can't find you," the second repeated. They were still moving toward the drop. "Why?"

Bragen did not know. Deciding to play into their concern, zie shrugged, "Perhaps it has something to do with the absence."

The Synthons thought about this. No one wanted to mention the Warp by name. Was that it? Was their

191

inability to conduct a Local connected to the absence? If not, Bragen saw them thinking, *this oddly dressed stranger had another purpose*. One they did not wish to pursue.

"Actually, East Andrio," Bragen continued, trying to divert them. "I have an apartment there."

This was true enough. With only topical access, they could see no further, and looked away. Together they entered the loading station. Fumbling for the transpo coin, Bragen scanned the Directionals. Down on the left was the one that denoted the West Andrio River Station. Moments later zie was in the tube and holding on to the head-rail.

The coin buzzed. Bragen knew its activation would alert the Watchers. Perhaps whatever was wrong with the Warp would make it harder to detect. At some point zie expected to see lidscanners.

Lights flashed red and yellow as the tram flew through the tunnel, reminding zam of zas many projects in such places. Bragen's mind was filled with all the wagers zie had teamed with. Zie recalled watching the Dimensionals with zas fellow players, waiting for the standings update. The bond such competition forged among them. The common goal of working toward the future. A moment later the lights flashed on and off and they were there.

Bragen took the steps out of the loading zone two at a time, occasionally turning sideways to get around the masses that moved in the same direction. Instead of the normal oblivion, many Synthons stopped to watch zam bound up them. Why did they notice? Something, zie knew, about breaking the pattern. No one moved that way.

The evening sun's pink haze covered the sky as it sank behind the skyscrapers. The walks and rails were full of Synthons. Once away from the entrance the oblivion returned, but something was not quite right. Occasionally Bragen caught the eye of someone moving in the other direction, a connection that normally only happened while communicating. They were actually looking at zam. A few even tried to probe zam when zie passed. No luck.

The Goman Ruins were located in the center of the city next to the Goman River. Bragen approached the stone bridge that ran over it. Long ago, zie stood in that same spot with other students listening to Mador lecture about the early Synthons who founded the colony. Goman was their leader. After extracting large stones from the Western Mountains, they stacked them on barges and floated them downriver to this bend. Its blue-green waters ran under the stone arch before whirling north and then south around the eastern edge of Andrio proper.

The first moon rose over the horizon. Silhouettes of various crafts cut across the silver orb. Evenings were congested. Shifts were ending as new ones began. The buildings' skins began to glow, lighting up the walkways. It would take a while for traffic to subside.

Bragen walked away from the bridge, reviewing how some of the Synthons had taken notice. Unusual. Was it the absence? How did that affect the Local? Or was it something else? They had said they could not see zam. Zas thoughts. Yet they had seen zam, albeit differently. Something was coming undone.

The avenue paralleled the river. A mile from the bridge foot traffic began to thin out. Cockle trees lined the walkway, their red leaves flitting in the evening breeze. What would happen if the Warp was gone forever? Synthons were still tethered to the Flow, but the Warp was practically non-existent. Why? If there was no One Thought, what was there? Why was zie different from the others?

Shadow fell into shadow. The sun dropped behind the ragged metal and glass skyline, their outlines glowing golden in the dark. Bragen turned around. The lane was deserted. No meandering. Either home or work.

Bragen thought about the plaque. The ruins were divided by two walks that crossed in the center of the park. In that center sat the thick pedestal that held it. Bragen found it ironic that zas archived memories did not hold an imprint of what it said. Zie called up the Warp and blinked. Nothing. Of course. Zie could not find it. *And I brought nothing. No tools. Only Mador.*

The bridge was deserted. The river reflected back the moon. Still rising, it hung in the dark, watching zam. Bragen started over the bridge, so many lectures coming to mind. At the crest, one flashed up. Mador stood where zie stood, pointing into the park. The professor was lecturing about the Zofran oaks that once hugged the river. Long extinct, their exposed roots hung like tendrils from huge trunks before dipping over the bank and into the water. Both grazels and limpidmods cherished these roots. For centuries, long extinct species lounged along that very shore. The colonials had a hard time dislodging them from the area.

The Goman Ruins were a series of half walls and floors made up of blocks carved from boulders hauled there long ago. A significant archeological site. It was within walking distance of University. The archodial department oversaw the artifact museum on campus. Bragen had been there many times.

There was no one in the park. The pedestal was a bronzed likeness of the Zofran oak, its intertwined roots running around and down the trunk, spiraling down into the stone pavement. As was typical, the plaque was flat and smooth. Its center was dominated by a circle. If Bragen ran the palm of zas hand over it, the history of the Goman Ruins would come into zas thoughts. Instead, the archy bent and studied where the plaque joined the pedestal. There was little to no space between the two.

Bragen stood and looked around. No one. Across the river zie saw a few individuals walking along the avenue, oblivious to zas presence. Zie searched the Local. Nothing there. Zie searched the Warp. Nothing. Zie bent and placed zas hands and one shoulder under the plaque and pushed up. Nothing.

"Wake up!" Zie told zamself. "Wake up from this illegality! This… aberration." *Nothing.* Zie bent and pushed up again. The plaque moved about an inch. Bragen leaned down and grabbed one of the bronze roots and pulled up with both hands. Nothing. Zie put a boot on the pedestal and pulled up again. The root bent. Zie put both boots against the pedestal and pulled backward. The top part of a thick root broke away. Bragen got on zas knees and moved it back and forth until it snapped off at ground-level.

Zie looked up and scanned the park, then the bridge. Nothing. While the buildings on the other side of the river lit up the surrounding walks, only a few dim ground lights highlighted the ruins. Bragen inserted one end of the metal root into the space between the plaque and pedestal. *Why look under there? What had Mador done?*

Zie pulled up on the root until the plaque moved. Repositioning zas body, zie pried up on the root. The plaque came loose. Zie pushed it sideways until it revealed the top of the pedestal. A small, empty void appeared. *Nothing.* Bragen paused, ready to disappear across the bridge. Yet when zie looked that way zie saw Mador standing there, lecturing. Zie turned back, leaned against the plaque and gave it a shove. The plaque moved again. Zie bent and peeked underneath it. *There.* Something.

Bragen reached in and pulled it out. It was a clear sheathing, very small. Something was in it. At first zie thought it was the tharsonome membrane. But that could not be. That was in the bottom of Rezcom Lake. Zie slipped a finger into the package and pulled out what looked like a transpo coin. Similar to the one in zas pocket, it was about as big as zas thumb. Gold. Zie studied it. There was no imprint.

Every Synthon carried a golden transpo coin. It was used in all manner of transportation. Individual seri codes were embossed on each. This meant that everyone, including Bragen, was individually observed each time they operated any craft or took a tram.

Odd. This was the first time Bragen had thought of it that way. *Tracked.* But what did it matter? All Synthons carried one. Traveling required it. To report to a terminal without a transpo coin was unimaginable. And there was another consideration. To be caught without one led to lidscans and Watchers. No one wanted that.

Bragen pulled zas out of zas pocket. The numerals 1031 were embedded into it. *Archodialbragen1031.* There were no numbers on this one. Zas heart beat like a jackbolt ramming into liverock. Bragen ran zas hand under the plaque. *Nothing.* Zie scanned the bridge. No one. Mador was gone. Except zie was not.

The archy slipped the new coin back in its plastic sleeve. Zie noticed some digiscript on the sheathing. Bragen blinked. When held up to the moon, the script became a thought. K-E-Y. Mador had said: *We need fewer locks and more keys.* Zie wanted to sit down. Wanted to search. There was no time. Mindfully, zie put the packet in zas back pocket and the regular coin in zas front vest, swung the plaque into place, then studied zas work. It wasn't perfect, but it looked level. Bragen stood still, listening, for what, zie did not know. Zie heard the river gurgling as it wound its way south. When had Mador come? Bragen looked back toward the bridge and began to run.

Once across, zie forced zamself to slow down. No sense in drawing attention. *A coin with no seri.* Approaching the station Bragen realized such a device might not be tracked. That was it! No seri. No straight line. A lidscan buzzed over zas head, flying toward the ruins. Zie picked up zas pace and entered the terminal.

It was between shifts. The station was not crowded. A few Synthons in various types of attire strolled by, ignoring zam. That was the norm. Zie did the same, thinking of the coin. *It's to get me out of here,* zie thought, *to get me to Apollis.* Up ahead a series of directionals noted the incoming and outgoing trams. When the East Andrio liner stopped zie hopped on and grabbed the head rail. Several other Synthons crowded in. One dressed in the red and blue of a technician turned and looked directly at zam. Bragen stopped breathing. The lights dimmed, signaling their approach to the next terminal. The inquisitive Synthon turned away.

Still staring straight ahead, Bragen pulled zas transpo coin out of zas vest pocket. The tram slowed. Fingering it, zie studied the shoulders of the Synthon that had turned around. Zie wore a blue jacket. Zie placed the coin in the stranger's side pocket. The tram stopped. Oblivious, the Synthon stepped out and walked toward the East Andrio terminal.

Bragen stepped out too, but walked the other way. Once in front of a Directional zie studied zas options. One tram led back to West Andrio, as well as several outlying villages and facilities, and the ruins. Another led to the aerodrome. Removing the packet from the back, zie placed it in zas front pocket and stepped into the aerodrome. A minute later zie exited it and stepped into another tunnel. A distant alarm sounded. The archy looked back, as did several other Synthons. It was not their terminal. Zie visualized lidscans racing toward the East Andrio station.

Andrio's aerodrome looked like every interplanetary hub in the Prometheus. There was a terminal for each planet. Some were easier to access than others. Apollis was not easy. It was a colonial project, not a population center or even a habitat. Bragen was still the archy of record, or at least had been until recently. Cognizant of a weakened Warp and malfunctioning Local, zie pulled the packet out of zas pocket, removed the coin, and walked up to the boarding dock. Zie held it up to the screen's pupil. It blipped and turned green. Bragen walked through. At the next stage zie placed zas right palm on the boarding hand. It also turned green. If the Stellar Council had issued a trace it was not working. Perhaps a weakened Warp had something to do with it. Or that alarm. The starship told zam to board.

A few wagers were taking their seats. Zie pushed by them and found zas own. No Locals. No probes. Zie looked around. It was half full. Mostly wagers, clad in New World Design's red and yellow. A few purple outfits as well. The grinders. Bragen still wore archy green and orange. The Synthon next to zam looked straight ahead. *Good.* Bragen closed zas eyes. The craft informed everyone that the Galaxial Warp was at full flow on Apollis. Bragen found the absence quite odd. In a sense, disconcerting, but something else as well. The loss of the transpo coin played a role in this... feeling. The coin had been a part of zam since initialization. Why such emptiness? At the same time, something zie could only identify as ease also permeated zas system.

After lift-off, Bragen opened zas Recollect. The dreams were hidden as best zie could in the far corner of zas temporal lobe. After a moment the boat appeared. Then a lake, followed by charred ruins and a pock-marked road. There was a fire behind the ruins. A blue cloth flew through the air and wrapped around zas leg. A smock with a red M emblazoned across its skirt. Bragen jumped. The wager next to zam was shaking zas arm. Others were leaning over their chairs and staring.

"What is a soma farm?" Zas neighbor asked, eyes wide.

Bragen felt their thoughts. They could not see zam. Zie blinked. Could not see zas thoughts. *What was a soma farm?* Zie searched zas memcore. Feelwin's thoughts still echoed there. *The Benefactors, in league with their progeny, took our children to their somatic cell farms, as always, claiming it was for the Common Benefit, where animal burdens were eliminated and freedom replaced slavery.*

Bragen looked around, then answered the Synthon. "Not sure. I guess I am overly extended." It was the common term from zas wratchet-gatherer days, having to do with double and triple shifts. Neither the passenger next to zam nor the others seemed to believe zam. Bragen could not get the burning buildings out of zas memcore.

"I can't see you," the Synthon said.

"Nor can I," said the one in front of them.

Bragen looked out the window. They were in deep space. Somehow, zie had fallen asleep. What had happened? "It has to be the absence," zie said. "Why else would the Local fail?" Bragen studied them one by one. Could see their confusion. The loss of the Warp was bad enough. The inability to use their Local was more personal. Normally they would have understood zas reply to be little more than disinformation and made a report, but under the circumstances, that was impossible.

Both the cock of their heads and the penetrating stares informed zam zas reply was unacceptable, but no one thought it out loud. Slowly, they turned around. They did not have a way to assess zam, so they decided to leave zam alone. The next thought came from the craft, welcoming them to Apollis.

The sky was deep turquois. Soon it would turn green, then yellow-green. Enough time before the Sun ruled the sky. Ignoring the Synthon next to zam, Bragen settled deep in zas seat. The dream came back. The fire. The red letter. Zie studied the wagers as they prepared to deboard. All sat ramrod straight, focused on the future. Despite the distance, the Flow was getting stronger now. Everyone felt the thrum. Zie wanted out of there before they decided to try another probe.

Head down, Bragen followed everyone out of the craft and down a series of connecting corridors, wondering about Vatch, Bricksite1 and Cloyden. Zie stopped where the Mythgarden Point terminal was located. It was not there. Instead, the Dimensional declared this was the Aguila Terminal. Several New World Designs wagers walked past zam and filed out the opening and down to the tarmac.

Without thinking, Bragen searched the refreshed Galaxial Warp. Mythgarden Point was not there. Zie searched again, this time for Aguila. This initiated a stream. Aguila, it noted, was Apollis's first lifeway, so named because it overlooked the Aguila Coast. An image of Governor Radiwon was superimposed within the thought, noting that superconstructvatch2213 of New World Designs and zas team was building the site. The next image revealed wagers near the edge of the cliff, pouring a circular base into a large void. Here, the thought continued, was the foundation support for the viewing tower that would soon overlook the beach. There was no mention of ruins, or Bricksite1. A panoramic shot revealed about two-thirds of the enviro-dome was in place. This structure would deflect the damaging effects of the planet's harsh sun.

Bragen followed the yellow and red-clad wagers down the steps to the tarmac. They walked in the direction of the commuter craft zie knew well. It would take them to the base. Zie veered off to the left where the Silverstreams were kept. Three sat there. Bragen was sure zie had used each one at some point in the past. No one was around. The archy walked to the first craft. Its door opened. Zie slid in thinking of the blank coin. As zie strapped zamself in, the door closed. *Mythgarden*

Point. Nothing happened.

Bragen looked at the blank Dimensional and thought again; *Aguila.* The Silverstream launched. Climbing vertically, the screen lit up, revealing the mostly completed enviro-dome, lots of framed and partially completed walls, as well as several grinders and chain-gaugers working near the edge. Bragen magnified the image. No low course of earthen blocks. No ruins. Five minutes later the craft beeped. It was directly above zas destination. Bragen nodded, initiating the descent.

It was the first hour of the third moon. The worst heat had come and gone, yet thousands of feet up, the Hammerheads' wrath was still evident, spreading like a burn scar away from the Lifeway. Off to the east several dry river beds were evident, cutting across the rust-colored earth. For the next several hours, the sun would only become less oppressive. Zie did not have a visor. Bragen wondered about Cloyden, as well as Shyden and Loydback. Were they still there?

Before zie had left, the Council rewarded zam with a promotion to Menomis. It now seemed nothing more than another illegal dream from lifetime ago. Approaching the landing zone, Bragen took over the guidance system and veered east. Zie was still far enough away to avoid a Local and hopefully, Flarman. The Inducer might already know zie was there but it was possible the transpo-coin had shielded zas whereabouts. What was certain was the Hive was filtering through Warp metadata looking for zam. The Flow was working as well. It was only a matter of time before they got a ping.

Once away from the coast zie steered the craft lower, catching the last vestiges of the Highland Red

Grass that bordered the coast. Then zie was over the eroded plains. Bragen used the Dimensional to find Mavwa's Gulch.

Life changed when Cloyden found those bones tangled up in the blueweed. Was any of it left? Was it all dozed? Would it have been better if zie had not found the ruins? The readings? Majore had showed up twice in zas span, and twice, zas trajectory had changed. The non-definitive readings and the mitochondrial DNA results dovetailed nicely with Rawnswawn's assessments. Assessments the Galaxial Warp discounted and blank spotted.

In both cases, the Stellar Council informed zam that the tharsonomes were defective, or read wrong. On Apollis, they blamed the sun. Both discoveries, they told zam, involved Uhlman fossils. Instead of nonspecific DNA, Bragen had stumbled upon what survivors of the Pioneer Expedition had left on the planet. *Untrue*.

So, what about Mavwa's Gulch? According to Landerwin, that was where the Humans landed. If this were so, then Mavwa was a part of a larger mission. As to whether the anthrogenecist knew this, Bragen did not know. What zie did know was that when the search party arrived, the prey they were looking for was not there. They were hiding deep in the mountains. Sometime later, these same Humans returned to the Gulch and buried the Interacts.

One thousand years ago there had been scrub brush and thick grasslands in this region. And a faint trail that ran east to west. Range arths and steedfells roamed the prairies. Hundreds of years later, the Hammerheads struck, making most of the planet uninhabitable.

Bragen saw the large, black, and white boulder first.

It sat on the edge of the cliff that overlooked the gulch. Down below was a freshly dug, large gaping hole in the ravine. It was so deep it almost looked like a cave. A mound of orange soil rose next to it. An excavation. The icon noting Mavwa's original survey was gone. Bragen peered into the chasm. They had retrieved the Interacts. Zie looked beyond the ravine for the peak, the next landmark. Behind it loomed a hazy mountain range. *Aromla.*

Why must I go? Zie wondered. It was all so long ago. No one knew of them, so why would it matter? Bragen looked behind zam. The operational base zie had lived on for five years was just a few moments in that direction. Even closer was the construction zone they now called Aguila. Like the Humans, in this present, Sunbloom never existed. Zie thought of the low row of exposed dirt blocks. The children. Marabella. The Galaxial Warp did not acknowledge any of it.

Bragen initiated a long-range three-sixty scan. No incomings. At least not yet. If they found zam, as they surely would, what would they do? Majore's image came up. Basically, Bragen's replica with a different memcore. With just a few exceptions, all Synthons looked the same. Thoughts were more important than bodies. Flesh and what it contained was immaterial. It was the One Thought, the Flow that was important, not the conduit. What mattered was the Common Benefit. But if that were so, what about the baby?

Zie could not vault that image. No fable. In the cave, Tinda held a small blue bundle of movement. A noise maker. A thing the Warp did not acknowledge. An unthought. Yet this unthought had fingers, toes, arms, and legs. A nose and a mouth. A beating heart. But even more than that. Somewhere behind the gleam in Marabella's eyes remained an unknown the soma farms could not erase. Whatever it was, it reminded zam of Mador.

Bragen sent the Silverstream east over the gulch. Once near the lone peak, zie told it to land. Zie hopped out and searched the ground for signs of the trail. Zie knew that over time, wind and rain obliterated such paths. Zie walked one direction, then another. A soft cloud of dust followed zas boots. Everything was dead here. By the time zie returned to the Silverstream the third moon was falling and the sky was deep green. No trail. No indention in the earth. Too much time had passed. *They would find zas trace.* A warm wind blew a gust of sand across zas face.

Bragen stepped into the craft, turned on the scanner and flipped on the topography map. Keeping zas eyes on the base of the peak, zie pictured the trajectory zie had taken on Moon and lined it up with the screen, which took zas thought and translated it. A superimposed red line showed up on the map. It ran straight to a particular point in the mountains. Zie enlarged the termination target. The wall and the plateau below it flashed up. But another image, one in zas memcore, superimposed itself on top of the screen. In this one the red steedfell plodded up a rutted path, its mane bouncing as it moved along. They were close to Aromla, but not there yet. Landerwin's musical voice, full of excitement, echoed within the Synthon. Zie was in the midst of a story about zas first range arth hunt. Bragen replayed it for a moment, made zas decision, then walked back to the Silverstream.

Nodding, the door opened. Zie pulled the coin out of

zas pocket. Its golden sheen glimmered against the sky. No seri. A blank, yet certainly more than blank. *Where had it come from?* Zie flipped the coin into the craft and closed the door.

"Go to Manebeck," Bragen ordered.

When the craft lifted, a cloud of dust engulfed zam. Zie backed away and watched it shoot into the sky. Manebeck was ten miles down the coast from Mythgarden Point. At present, this second lifeway was little more than a landing pad and storage facility. Zie had been there a time or two, once to initiate a survey, once to talk preliminaries with Vatch and zas crew. The Silverstream would land on the deserted site and await its next command. A part of their search for zam had to include looking for missing Silverstreams. Perhaps it would buy zam some time.

Synthons utilized an internal system of regeneration that eliminated the need for exterior resources. Each body operated its own self-sustaining ecology. An ecology that placed them above the mammalians. Without need of bodily functions, the ultimate goal, Moving the Ball Forward, remained in focus. Even though the worst of the wave had already occurred, this system broke down when exposed too long to Apollis's heat. That was why all the planet's lifeways were along the coasts. Reviewing the Interact, Bragen calculated that Aromla was two miles to the east. The third moon trailed the sun as it began to sink beyond the horizon. Zie walked to other way, toward the mountain.

An hour later Bragen stood at the foot of the mountain. Zie had never sweated like this before. Zie was soaked. Zie looked for the half wall. Nothing looked familiar. No scrub brush. No grass. No wide path. Drifts of sand hugged the mountain's base. Looking behind zam, zie aligned the lone peak with Wasenah Rift and then followed that line to where it should terminate, looking for any anomaly that might reveal the road up.

Bragen saw the sled tracks before the cut. Several. The types built under a Silverstream's carriage. Zie followed them down the wall until zie saw a large pile of sand and freshly turned dirt. The opening was twenty-feet wide, exposing part of the half wall and the path, which ran up the side of the sheer cliff. Zie looked around. Other than the dunes and a few fallen boulders, it stood much as it had the day zie followed Landerwin up the trail. Bragen looked back at the coned-peak one more time before walking around the dirt pile and starting toward Aromla.

There were more sled and Synthon tracks at the top. Zie was not surprised. Across the way, large mounds of boulders covered the arched entrance. In between, a bed of sand covered the courtyard. Low dunes covered the parapets the Humans once patrolled.

They were here. Old and young. A thin film of sand blew across zas boots. Cognizant of Apollis's stronger Warp, zie flipped. Looking at the boulders, zie sent out a probe. *Nothing. I am standing where the Humans stood. Where they hid from the Uhlmans. What about the Now? Was Flarman looking for me? Did Apollis have lidscans?*

The archy turned off the flip and walked over to the boulders that blocked the entrance to the cave. Zie peered between them. Darkness. They were too large to move. Zie sat down. *What now? This could still be a dream. Wake up!* Bragen sat there, unsure what zie should do. If the universe was a lie what were Inducers really for?

Why move the ball forward? What was Majore really up to? Why did it matter? If zie just flew back to base what would happen? Perhaps if zie did they would take zam to Mador. That thought created a bubble in zas chest. Zie thought zie heard something. A gurgle. A shiver went down zas spine.

Startled, Bragen stood up. What was that? Zie looked at the boulders. Long ago, zie heard a similar sound. It came from within the cave. The sound Marabella made. Not a pleasant sound. Zie had jumped, but Tinda and Misla... laughed. *Laughed.* Bragen felt the heat on zas skin. Then another moment from the same Interact. "I am in you," Misla said.

Another warm wind blew sand across the courtyard. It skidded over the row of low dunes. Bragen walked over and dug zas hands into one of the mounds. The sand was hot. Zie pushed it to the side, finding something flat underneath. *The benches.* Zie looked toward the opening. The Council's doing. Or Majore's Continuing to push the sand away from the bench zie called up the last Interact, and retraced zas steps through the cave.

Zie saw the kaleidoscope of lights. Felt the platform lift and take them to the upper room. Followed Misla to the window that overlooked the rockets. A window that looked out the north side of the mountain. There was a ledge below it.

Blinking sweat out of zas eyes, Bragen rose up and dusted off zas hands. A self-circulating system could not afford much more loss. Looking over the parapet zie searched the side of the mountain for the same ledge. There it was, running east around a bend. About two feet wide. It must turn north on the other side, toward the window. Zie looked back at the isolated peak,

Landerwin's voice, or music, tickling zas thoughts.

Then zie walked along the parapet until it met the mountain. After pausing, zie stepped over it onto the ledge. A light bed of sand and a scattering of small rocks littered it. Bragen took one look down then decided not to do that again. Slowly, zie began to make zas way around the mountain.

Chapter 13

"We picked up a ping," Mulendur said. "The wratchet-gatherer's transpo coin activated outside a magnetoid plant on the other side of the lake. From there zie took the West Andrio route into the city, then boarded an East Andrio tram."

Majore brought up a grid map of East Andrio, then zeroed in on the streets around Bragen's room. "Misdirection."

"Yes. The Watchers picked up the Straight Line."

"To zas apartment."

"No. Three streets over. Perhaps another nest."

The Watchers called any place used to block the Flow a nest. Covering apartment walls with reinforced kulcat fibers went beyond normal black-market get-togethers. "That would not surprise me. Set up a containment. Not too close. Hold in place until I arrive."

The wratchet-gatherer's elusiveness was directly related to *The Fallen*. The mentor was captured, but the student escaped. Intentional?

The Straight Line led to a non-descript series of towers that housed tens of thousands of wagers. Each was thirty stories tall, all gray stone and green glass. Dark now, the buildings' walls, like the streets below them, emitted a dull yellow light. An ad-hoc command center was set up a block from the target. Mulendur and zas crew stood waiting, each lost in their part of the operation. Once the Silverstream touched down, the Inducer walked up.

A message concerning a technical glitch had already flowed through every inhabitant of the building. The Warp was off-line while an emergency update was carried out. Everyone knew to stay inside until further notice. Majore and Mulendur led the crew down the walk to the tower entrance. The trace led to the fourteenth floor. The lobby, hallways, and elevators were empty. Mulendur took the lead. At apartment 1411 the door opened.

Majore already knew.

"Yes?" the Synthon said. Bragen was not there. Puzzlement blocked the dweller's thought patterns, yet zie was keenly aware this was some type of official visit. Zie stepped to one side and let them in.

Majore switched to a different pattern. Nothing. Mulendur scrambled to assimilate and reorganize zas crew. While the Inducer put new orders in place, the Benefactor scanned the room. A table. A bed. A chair with a blue jacket draped over it. An orderly line of red jumps and blue jackets hung along the ceiling, dividing the room in half. A large plate glass window dominated the far wall, overlooking rows of similar towers, their rooftops glowing yellow.

Majore looked for the next best opportunity. There was information to be gleaned. High-level magnetoid technicians wore red jumpsuits with horizontal blue stripes that ran across their chests. They also wore blue jackets. Mulendur reached over and searched the pocket of the jacket that hung on the chair. Zie pulled out a gold coin.

"Where did you get that?" Majore asked.

Of course, the wager did not know. The Synthon removed a coin from zas front pocket and stared at it. Then zie looked at the coin in Mulendur's hand. The victim's thoughts ran rampant, searching the past several days for a clue. Nothing.

The Inducer handed it to Majore. Bragen's seri was embossed across one side. Zie looked at the Synthon, a prey to the wratchet-gatherer's deceit. "You do not know how this got in your pocket?"

"I do not. It is not in my memcore."

They already knew this. This was the archy's doing. Mulendur's crew arrived and began to inspect the walls and floors. The Benefactor was certain there was nothing there. Zie motioned for the victim to take a seat on the bed.

"We believe you," Majore assured. "But something happened. Either in the plant, outside of the plant, in the tram station, or in the tram. For the record, where do you perform?"

"Facility 106," zie said.

"How long?"

"Fifty years."

Mulendur stood next to the wager, tracing every thought. "Your incubate year?"

"3099."

"What is your expiration?"

"5010."

"So other than your boot up year, this has been your station."

"Yes."

Majore looked at Mulendur, who nodded.

"This has been your home for fifty years."

"Yes."

"When did your shift end?"

"Three hours ago."

"Afterwards, you left the facility?"

"Yes."

"Did anything strange happen after you left."

"No."

Majore leaned down and looked straight into the Synthon's yellow eyes. "Your seri label indicates you are Winnowager3099."

"Yes."

"And you know your teammates."

"Yes. A winning team must work together. Know each's strengths and weaknesses." This was straight out of the programming.

"And you would know the seri of any new player."

"Yes," the Synthon answered, again checking zas memcore.

"When was the last time a replacement came to your team?"

"Three zero four zero. Winnowager3090 lost a finger in the mold injector. Zie was replaced by Winnowager4089."

Majore thought about this. "Ten years ago. What about today? After your shift. Trace your steps."

Mulendur was capable of repeating winnowager3099's thoughts as they came out of zas memcore. "We walked over to the board and watched the stat screen. It was a good day. We are only a few points behind the leader. Then we broke and headed for the station."

"This is important," Majore began. "Did anything happen on the way to the station, anything unusual, or out of the ordinary."

Mulendur watched through the Synthon's memory. The wager walked away from the stat screen and between the buildings on the main path to the station. Nothing.

"What about in the tram?"

The Synthon shrugged.

"Did anything happen at the West Andrio Station?"

Winnowager3099 was about to respond in the negative but stopped. Majore saw it in zas eyes. Mulendur saw it in zas head. The Inducer repeated the memory. One moment zie was in the tram holding on to the head rail, looking straight ahead. The next zie was looking behind zam. At archodialbragen1031.

"What did zie say?" Mulendur asked.

The Synthon paused, then shook zas head. "Nothing. It was just a feeling."

Synthon vocabularies did not account for such descriptions. The Inducer looked at Majore for an explanation.

"No thoughts?" Majore asked.

"No," zie said. "An absence. Zie looked right at me, but I could not see zam."

"You mean the Warp? That's explainable," Mulendur said.

"No," winnowager3099 answered. "The Local. I could not see zas thoughts." Zie looked straight at Majore. "That was... odd. I got off at my station and came home."

Majore stood and looked out the window.

"And something else," the Synthon added. "Others noticed zam."

Majore stared at the towers that covered cityscape. "Noticed?" Zie watched the Synthon's thought process stop, as if surprised. Synthon's seldom noticed *anything* that was not in front of them, or not a part of the Flow.

"I guess that is what I thought. Perhaps I was mistaken."

The Benefactor looked back at Mulendur. "We have our answer. Order a remboot then proceed to the West Andrio Station with your lidscanners. There has to be a trace of some kind. Without a transpo coin zas options are limited. Get me a shadow. I am going back to the apartment."

"Archodialbragen's?"

"The wizened's."

The shadow met Majore on the first floor and followed zam out the door. The streets were clear. This included all manner of vehicular traffic. A clean, antiseptic order permeated the block. The Benefactor approved. Such order was critical. The soles of their shoes clattered across the pavement as they made their way to Mador's building. *I noticed others were staring at zam.*

Majore let the shadow enter first. They walked through the lobby and into the elevator, taking it to the second floor. Synthons did not look left or right. They conversed with coworkers, not strangers. They did not look in windows. They followed the Galaxial Warp. Whatever had caused this was not related to the weakened Flow. *I could not see zam.*

The door had been changed. There was no handle. The Benefactor told it to open and it did. The walls were stripped bare. The kulcat fibers were gone, as were the digibits and digaforms. Two upside down chairs sat in the middle of the room, their coverings removed. Majore inspected them. Not the chairs of a wager. The bed was standard, as was the table. Zie walked to the patio door and opened it. Down below, the trees gave off a soft green glow. The park was empty.

Data confirmed the wizened had lived there forty-five years. Other than zas time at University, which was little more than academic hooha, there were no other records. Nothing on previous assignments or domiciles. Outside of the academy, Mador was a ghost.

Everyone in the apartment building had been scanned. The wizened with the silver braids was an obscure figure who seldom shared thoughts with zas neighbors. Majore stared at the park bench. Two neighbors noted zie often sat there with a bag of brittle feeding the birds. They found this odd. Synthons walked through parks. Benches were aesthetically pleasing but seldom utilized. Both seemed especially distraught that the wizened fed the birds. They solved this by closing the blinds and ignoring zam. That was it.

Across the room, zas shadow inspected the long rectangular hole in the wall. Majore walked over. That is where zie hid it. A small piece of Ariztex sheathing. Rocket ship sheathing. *Apogonos.* It had been taken to Dalimath. Linatin was there. Majore reviewed Mulendur's report. Spare and to the point. Nothing about the sheathing. Why? Zie thought of the vaults. A tingle ran up the back of zas neck. *I need to see it.* No time.

"Linatin?" zie thought.

Linatin flashed up.

"Can you meet me at Wahlgahlen?"

"Soon," the other Benefactor answered.

Majore motioned toward the door. The shadow left the apartment, all data already transferred to its Inducer. This meant the information was also in the minds of the

Watchers, the Hive's eyes and ears. Yet there was an additional path to the Seers.

A Benefactor's enhanced telepathy was embedded within the pineal gland, also known as the Third Eye. Through this signaler, Majore, Linatin, and their cohorts maintained constant contact with the Hive. Early on, this enhancement proved so powerful that it interfered with Local activity. Progressional scientists solved this with a genetic alteration called the neural clip. This alteration removed interference, filtering high-level Locals to Inducers and Watchers while at the same time establishing a stronger connection between Benefactors and the Hive. At some point, *The Fallen* disabled or shielded the Third Eye. The Seers immediately adjusted the alteration so such alterations became impossible.

The shadow stood in the doorway watching Majore. Benefactors were control agents. Flow managers. They stored information no Synthon could conceive of. And more. Arms outstretched, zie squatted. With palms facing the ceiling, Majore began a crab walk around the room, searching for echoes.

Echoes were thought wakes. Flow remnants, electrical charges connected to the Warp. Over time they fell apart, leaving silver particles that only Benefactors and Seers could see. Eventually they dispersed or evaporated. Majore scanned the entire apartment, picking up isolated snatches of conversations that did not make sense. The kulcat fibers were responsible for this inefficiency. Zie stood. The shadow leaned on the door frame, watching. In the last fragment of the Interact discovered within the wizened's shield, Mador was looking at something else when Mulendur rammed the door. Majore shook the image out of zas thoughts and stood up. "Let's go."

The command post was breaking up. The unsuspecting Synthon was already on zas way to the remboot. Linatin flashed up. "Ok. Ready."

Mulendur stood by Majore's Silverstream, flipping the transpo-coin up in the air and catching it. Zie tossed it toward the Benefactor.

Majore caught it. Studying the coin, zie said, "Follow up on the interviews."

The Inducer turned and gave the commands to zas crew. Majore was already getting in the Silverstream. A moment later zie was several thousand feet above the buildings. After a few minutes of darkness, the craft began to descend. Wahlgahlen loomed below.

The boulevard in front of the facility was empty. Linatin stood at the entrance. Zie nodded. Majore searched zas thoughts, looking for the results. Ariztex was a common material used in a variety of applications, from transportation to manufacturing. The piece found in Mador's apartment was mined on Lark. Nothing unusual about that. But thirteen-hundred years ago only one forge operated on that planet. Its skins were used to clad that era's starships. Linatin had the inscription in the front part of zas memcore. Majore studied it. Searched the Record and zas old self. Zie could find nothing on it. No meaning.

The hallways were deserted. Once on the fifth floor they made their way back to the Wake Room. The Dimensional flashed up three images of Mador's memcore. The first revealed the partial Interact. But more had been extracted.

The professor was in zas apartment. Zie was speaking, but not to the Humans. "Go to the Goman

Ruins. Look under the plaque." The scene changed. The Human called Feelwin stared back. *This is not what you think. I do not know if it will work.*

Fladnag's order pierced the image. "Stop it!"

Mador's last words followed. "I am—" the cylinder in zas hand began to leak smoke. The image froze, then turned black. Another instant and they would have known much more. The Goman Ruins were in West Andrio. The pedestal?

The next digibit showed an intertwined wall of veins and vessels obscuring the purple shield. It resembled an impenetrable web of vines and leaves. Transfixed, Majore stared at the barrier several seconds before moving on to the final image, a small gray lump. The memcore. Zie leaned in for a closer look. It was different. Shriveled. Zie looked at Linatin.

"As soon as we opened it the inner core collapsed."

"Air?" Majore asked.

Linatin nodded. "A self-destruct."

Majore looked around the room. "I remember a similar technique."

"From the war years." Linatin said.

"Hostages developed it."

Linatin nodded. "Which verifies the era."

"It may help pinpoint how zie cloaked zamself."

"Those years are blank-walled."

Majore totaled up the vaults that were hindering the operation. "True."

"Should we?"

Majore shook zas head. Extracting information from the Hive would set off a long series of inquiries and time-consuming answers. Both could feel them watching, analyzing their methods and assessing true intent. As to the other, Majore could now see that Mulendur was already at the ruins, studying the pedestal. The plaque was not completely in place. Zie found there was a void underneath it.

Majore stared into Linatin's eyes. Another vault. Why? "Do we have any idea?"

"No," Linatin answered, zas own shield up.

Decisions had been made. It was best to move forward. Bragen was formulating a counter-thought. "What about the term? Apogonos. Anything?"

"If it is there," Linatin answered, "it is well hidden."

Flarman flashed up. "We've got a ping."

Majore felt Bragen's transpo-coin in zas pocket. "Apollis?"

"Yes," Flarman answered. "The aerodrome."

"The hand ident?" Linatin asked.

"Yes. And a Silverstream is missing."

Majore nodded to Linatin. *Just like the boat.* It would not be long now. "And?"

"A transpo-coin of some kind started it. It does not have a signature, but it has to be zam."

"We will be there shortly," Majore said. Arion was not the place to puzzle over such a coin.

Flarman's image evaporated. Majore and Linatin were already out of the Wake Room before they agreed, *we've got zam.* They quickly moved to the transit.

Majore had never seen the value of placing lifeways on Apollis. The coasts were quite nice but a majority of the planet was not habitable. The Hive saw it differently. Expansion furthered the future, which was certainly true, but mineral rights also played a role. Particular types of ores needed for magnetoids and other power drivers lay beneath the planet's eroded plains. Wagers were second stage emigrants, to be scattered among the arroyos and plateaus within domed encampments along with their borers and grinders. All for the Common Benefit.

Their craft slipped through the Black Hole and zeroed in on Apollis's aerodrome. The sun was slipping over the sea's horizon, yet there was still plenty of light left. Wagers were everywhere, going about their business. No one noticed the Benefactors' arrival. They walked through several corridors to the conference room that overlooked the skyway.

The first time Majore came to Apollis, it was nothing but rocks, sand, and lonely strips of prairie grass. That landing zone was adjacent to Mavwa's Gulch. The anthrogenecist toured zam through the crash site. Zie was shown the burn scars and excavation trenches. Zie never expected to return. That was thirteen-hundred years ago.

Flarman was waiting in the conference room. Zie and Mulendur were perfect clones of each other. From a distance, this was true of all Synthons, from their blue skin to their silver hair. Yet the various castes recognized their own. Inducers always appeared to be leaning forward. Their crews emulated them. That was the case when the Benefactors entered the room. Several held a particular bent, looking for thought trails. Others searched the Warp for the Silverstream.

The first ping, Flarman reported, a hand ident, alerted them to Bragen's presence in the aerodrome. From there, they back-tracked to the magnetoid station. "I linked up with Mulendur. The coin-trace provides the following timeline. Zie entered the tram station near Rezcom Lake at four p.m. Zie exited the West Andrio River Station at four-ten. Zie re-entered the same station and boarded another tram at four-fifty. Zas transpo-coin got off the tram and left the East Andrio station five minutes later. Digi eye coverage confirms that, by then, the now rembooted Synthon was carrying the coin, not archodialbragen1031. At four-thirty the perp's hand signature pinged Arion's entrance port to the Apollis starship. Zie landed here at five o'clock."

Majore and Linatin stared at each other, sharing everything they knew of Andrio proper, West Andrio, and the West Andrio River Station. Somewhere between four-fifty and four-fifty-five the archy ditched the coin. Occasionally coins were misplaced or lost. Synthons reported such losses immediately. Most factories and processing centers were too far from apartment cloisters to walk. Neither knew of an instance where the coin was purposefully placed on someone else. Majore looked away. *So, the wratchet-gatherer had another coin. A very dangerous one.*

Watchers were scanning data from the one-hundred and ten West Andrio digi eyes located around the station. Coin idents were the usual source for such tracking. Linking it to a particular craft on Apollis would make it easier to find the archy, but would not help the retrace process on Arion. Digi eyes required a seri. There was no seri. Thus, each digi eye scan for the period in question was being reviewed. They were looking for movements out of the norm. Black-marketers and purveyors or unthoughts did not move in the manner of Synthons focused on Moving the Ball Forward.

Outside the aerodrome's skyway, wagers were unloading the last of several hundred boxes from the belly of a transport ship. Dressed in New World Designs red and yellow, they stacked them on a flatbed cruiser.

One signaled the pilot to close the hatch. Instead of Mythgarden Point, they were on their way to the newly named Aguila.

Majore switched thoughts, bringing in Mulendur. "University is nearby."

The Arion Inducer nodded. "We went back." Earlier, another crew had searched the professor's office. This was during Mulendur's original ransacking of the apartment. "It's as it was. Nothing to report."

Majore could feel the Seers' probes. Bragen spent forty minutes near the Goman Ruins. Was this coin found under the pedestal? How did that happen? Recovery of digi eye data would take hours. "And the lidscanners?"

"The same," Mulendur answered. "And I have boots on every street, including the river boulevard. Once we've culled through the data, we'll start the interview process." A list of every Synthon who ventured into the vicinity would receive a thought query. A hit initiated a personal follow-up.

"Take us to the bay where the Silverstream was found," Majore said. Benefactors never stood still. They followed Flarman down the gangway to the tarmac. Two similar crafts sat by the vacant slot.

Linatin walked over and looked into one of the crafts. Zie studied the instrument panel, then looked at Flarman. "We know the Silverstream zie took. We know the coin that activated it. What's the trace? The Straight Line ends at the Point or the gulch. Which is it?"

They all knew, including the Seers, at the same time. A line from the aerodrome to the gulch ran across their thoughts. From there it moved to Manebeck. A surprise. As to why, there was no consensus.

"Linatin has something to tell you," Fladnag said, interrupting their thoughts. Seldom did a Seer use the Warp to communicate to groups.

Majore looked at the other Benefactor. Something in zas appearance was different. Linatin was still shielded. "I recently oversaw an excavation at the gulch and other work while you focused on the wratchet gatherer."

"What other work?"

"Derived from the Interacts."

"Return to the skyway," Tibboh ordered Majore. "A room is prepared. Flarman, set up a perimeter around Manebeck."

Derived from the Interacts was no answer. But there was nothing to do but follow directions. Zie nodded at Linatin and returned to the skyway. Off the main room a small apartment with a bed, a table, and a chair was waiting. It overlooked the tarmac. Majore walked in, closed the door, and lay down on the bed. On Apollis, it took a moment longer for the concentric rings of light to come into focus.

A river of incandescent thoughts materialized, rushing through the rings. Larger orbs of light clung to the outer bands. All the Seers probed zam.

"Only five feet deeper," Neiklot said. "The scans missed it. We do not blame Mavwa. We sent you there to ensure all was in order."

"The Interacts."

"Yes," Fladnag responded.

They blamed zam. Majore ran the review of zas inspection. Meeting the anthrogenecist. Walking the gulley. By then, the extracted cultural materials were enroute to Dalimath. Zie recalled the deep trench the crews cut down the middle of the ravine. How deep? Three feet. The Seers watched zas thoughts. Majore was not a true archodial but over the eras had inspected fifty-one excavation sites. None were deeper than three feet. It did not matter.

"I don't think we missed it," zie said.

"Look," they thought.

A more recent Recall, this one carrying Linatin's imprint, flashed up. Deep in the gulley, Vatch stood over a large hole. Tall piles of dirt surrounded it. Two of the superintendent's crew were lifting a long, rectangular box out of the ground. Several other wagers came into view, as well as Governor Radiwon. Acendoth and Linweil were also there. A gust of wind whipped dust through the ravine and kicked up a whirlwind. The reason for the dust was a slowly descending heavy-lift hovercraft. Its arm dropped down and picked up the box. A new image flashed up: the same skyway adjacent to Majore.

The top end of the rectangular container was gone, having been removed. Vatch, Radiwon, and the Council members stood on one side of the room, watching wagers carefully pull a clear tube of some kind out of the box. About three feet tall and several inches in diameter, it took a moment for them to lift it over the rim and set it within a small apparatus that kept it upright.

Upon closer inspection, the tube had a green tint, yet its contents were what captured the Benefactor's attention. Several multi-colored layers of a gelatinous substance filled it. In rhythmic cadence, the red, blue, green, yellow, white, and black sections glowed back and forth at each other.

"The box is made of ceramalic," said Tibboh. "A

product of the Sal Sagev Mountain Range. We are not sure what the tube is made of. It resembles glass, but seems impermeable."

"Regardless of the container, we know what it holds," Neiklot added. "Humans developed this means of preservation during the Uhlman Wars. These are the first Interacts. They are composed of plasmain. Each of the colors represents a different communique. This is what Bragen downloaded."

"So, you are aware of the content." Majore was fascinated. "All of it."

"No," Neiklot said. "Only Synthons can open. An old genetic anomaly. Long ago we replicated the design, but never their contents."

"Yet *The Fallen* entered them."

"Zie gained access through the wratchet-gatherer."

Access to an infection, thought Majore. Vaulted concepts concerning Humans, the Carriers, the Stain. *Words*. The Benefactor's throat clenched. *Words*?

"What do you mean?" Tibboh asked.

Zie did not know. Whatever it meant, Majore sensed they already knew. Zie was certain it was from the Long Ago, but could not provide an origination point. Zie had never thought such a term. Linatin was thinking what the Hive was thinking: *Contagion*.

Majore returned to the Interacts. "Archodialbragen1031 was not in the fragmented communique. The one in which the wizened's black-market device incinerated itself. Where did zie get it?"

"That is an Unknown," Fladnag admitted.

Another silence. Their minds were one. Majore moved on. The image of the ditch running down the middle of Mavwa's Gulch flashed up. "I think they waited until we were gone."

"Why?" They asked in unison.

"The Humans knew we were coming. They prepared a ruse. The scars on the gulley's walls, the charred artifacts. Even the bones. Enough material to confirm their presence, as well as their end. I think they planned it that way. Why hide them there if they knew someone was coming?"

The Hive was silent. Majore watched thoughts from across the Prometheus fly through the rings. The Seers' probes became more intense. In the Now, they decided it did not matter when the Interacts were planted. Only consensus mattered. They deemed this was Majore's mistake. There could be no counter.

Majore looked at Linatin. "What is next?"

As one, Tibboh, Fladnag, and Neiklot nodded, "Run it."

Linatin opened the Recall. The first image flashed up the base of a mountain wall. Through Linatin's eyes Majore watched a dozer dig large boulders and dirt out of a vertical cleft. Red and yellow clad wagers worked nearby, removing debris. All wore visors. Time advanced. In another image Vatch stood where the dozer had been digging. A wide path ran up the inside of a half wall. Time advanced.

In this flash up, Flarman, Acendoth and several of the wagers hopped out of hovercrafts and began walking up an elevated plain toward another dozer. It was clear they were higher up. The dozer's claw dug into the mountain. Boulders, rocks, and bits of a metal grate were pulled out and piled next to an emerging cavity. Time advanced. The dozer was off to the side. Linatin walked under an arched opening and into the bowels of a large cave. Everyone flipped up their visors. Lightglobe's hung in the air, illuminating a huge chasm.

Linatin, head up, made a 360-degree turn, inspecting walls, windows, walkways, and ceiling. There was a discussion with the others about the ceiling. Extraordinary chisel work was evident. Every surface was as smooth as glass. An unknown source was instrumental in creating this finish. In the center of what appeared to be the ceiling, a large square seam was cut, indicating there was an upper level. Time advanced.

A sophisticated scaffolding system that included a stairway and flat-lift dominated the center of the cave. It ran up through the large square hole in the ceiling. Linatin led a delegation that included Radiwon and several of the Stellar Council up the stairway to the next floor. Then the Benefactor turned and looked back down.

The cavern floor had been scraped clean, revealing several holes, one larger and deeper than the rest. It was clear that much of what ever was rooted there had been taken or reduced to rubble. Rubble and dust that could not be identified. Only the carved doorways and windows remained. A discussion revolved around the spherical apparatus archodialbragen1031 saw in the first Interact. No such device was found in the mountain.

Linatin led them through another arched entry. A larger room. The only object, the crumbling remains of a stone desk, most of it covered with sand. More impressive was the large window that took up the north wall, revealing distant mountains and a yellow sky. They all walked over. Council members commented on the warm air. Far below the opening, wind whipped the tops of several large sand dunes into vertical cones. Individual vortexes swirled halfway up the mountain before falling apart and repeating the process.

The discussion continued. They did not know what had happened to the Humans. They might never know. Acendoth wondered about remains. Bones. None had been found. Radiwon asked about other artifacts.

"Only this," the Benefactor answered, nodding at the desk. Linatin's eyes swept around the room. Unlike the cavern below, this space did not have a finished appearance. Large and small boulders poked out of the walls. The same with the ceiling. It appeared to be an observation post of some kind, yet why face north? Away from the sea?

The tour ended. Everyone started back to the stairway. Majore did not want it to end.

Neiklot read Majore. "Why?"

"There is an answer for every question," Majore replied. No Seer could deny this statement. It was ingrained within the Galaxial Warp. "Why face north?"

"A ruse," Linatin answered. "Like the gulch."

"A one-thousand three-hundred-year-old ruse," Tibboh added. All the Seers agreed. Whether true or not, they were ready to move on.

Majore was not. "There may be clues within the artifact manifest." Material culture inspected, analyzed, and removed from Mavwa's Gulch was taken to Dalimath's Processing Laboratory on Dwarth. Mavwa's report was also there. The report Rawnswawn had sourced. "I would like to go there. Perhaps the answer is there."

"Linatin already checked," Tibboh said. "The report is gone. Perhaps Rawnswawn took it. Or Sarkasian. Looking backwards is seldom productive. The ball moves forward."

"Something has been missed," Majore insisted.

"Much has been missed," the Seers replied as one voice. "The future has no use of this past."

Linatin broke in, "Flarman has the perimeter set up."

There was a pause, one Majore deemed a threat to zas span. Everyone was gauging zas reaction. "I will defer to Linatin."

Fladnag addressed Linatin. "Ensure the Inducer has blocked the Warp and set up a series of mind traps. Take zam with you."

Majore opened zas eyes and rose from the bed. The decision had been made without zam. A shift. There was nothing zie could do but report. Linatin was waiting for zam. Without exchanging thoughts, they left the skyway. A Silverstream was waiting on the tarmac.

The trip down the coast was short. Only the tip of the sun was visible, the rest having sunk into the sea, casting a red glare across the water. The white shoreline that rimmed Manebeck's inlet was deep in shadow when the craft began its descent. Flarman and zas crew were already there, stationed beyond the dunes, about a mile from the beach.

Majore brought the craft down next to the Inducer's. After the dust settled both hopped out and gave the greeting. Flarman already knew, focusing on Linatin.

"The signal is strong," zie said, referring to the transpo-coin. "But nothing else."

Linatin looked toward the beach, its dark brown dunes casting off darker shadows. "No trace?"

"No," Flarman answered.

"Let's deprogram," Linatin said. Circumstances seldom called for a coin to be wiped. It eliminated records that might be needed later. Flarman walked back and reached into zas own craft. Zie pushed a couple of buttons on the instrument panel and turned around. "Even though no thought is tied to it, the coin is still alive."

Linatin looked at Majore. They had no answer.

Neiklot broke in, "The wizened's doing," not acknowledging Mador's true nature. "Go ahead."

Followed by Flarman and zas crew, they tramped across the dunes to the shoreline. The Silverstream sat next to a small metal building. The group cautiously approached the craft. A gold coin sat in the passenger's seat. When Linatin walked over, a door appeared, then slid open. Zie picked up the coin and inspected it.

There was no seri. The Benefactors exchanged looks. The Seers, as one, explained, "it is from the production centers."

"Before origination," Majore realized. "*The Fallen* had something to do with a production center?"

"It appears so," the Seers admitted. "A search team has been notified."

Majore thought of the unsuspecting Synthon's pocket. Flarman unlatched the door to the building. Two of the crew members went inside. Empty. Bragen did not come to Manebeck. Had never intended to. They came back out, trying to keep their thoughts neutral. Everyone would be slated for a clean scan. Including the Inducer. Flarman looked at Linatin. "Which way?"

The shift continued. Majore studied the waves that pounded the beach. A hazy mist of foam hung over the breakers. *Odd,* zie thought, studying the mist. *I never noticed that.*

"Irrelevant," the Seers said as one.

Majore looked northeast. Those rusty plains led to

the gulch. The trace told them the Silverstream landed there before coming to Manebeck. Further east were the mountains. Was zie there? Or had zie doubled back to Aguila? Zie scanned every file in zas memcore, then reviewed everything regarding Mythgarden Point. Did the wizened bury something there as well?

"Linatin," Fladnag broke in, addressing both. "You should return to base with Flarman and crew. Enlarge the thought perimeter. Majore, take Zawn with you to the redoubt."

Majore did not know the term.

"It was their last known location," Tibboh answered.

"The cavern Linatin just surveyed?"

"Yes," they all answered.

Fladnag called it Zawn. Majore watched zam approach. A copy of the others, certainly a Synthon. But what else? Zie recognized its thought pattern. A Watcher.

Watchers were intermediaries. Galaxial Warp gate keepers. They funneled information between Seers and Inducers. At the behest of the Seers, Watchers inserted thought messages into the Flow. They coordinated searches for black-marketers, and controlled lidscanner records. Perhaps that was it. Perhaps more than that.

"It is unlikely," Neiklot said, answering Majore's thought regarding *The Fallen*'s intention. "Yet possible. It does seem clear this trick leads back to the ruins. Zie is looking for something. Capture is imminent. Linatin, take the balance of the party there. A large crew awaits your instructions."

That is when Majore realized *they were all Watchers*. Zie studied their stiff legged gaits as they trampled back to their hovercrafts, their thoughts locked and seamless. All but Linatin, who already knew. Black-marketers called them sniffers. The Seers believed Bragen had returned to Mythgarden Point, now Aguila. They wanted Linatin in charge of that operation.

What then? The two Benefactors shared a thought that took them back to their first encounters. They first met during the last years of the Uhlman Wars. They worked in tandem to stamp out the Stain and push toward the Common Benefit, eradicating misinformation and along the way, the misinformed. After victory, history began. The answer to every question soon resided within the Galaxial Warp. Majore and Linatin acknowledged this commonality, then walked toward their respective hovercrafts, certain this was their last encounter. Zawn slid in beside Majore. The last remnant of light was leaving the eastern plains when the craft rose and flew toward the mountains, now shrouded in darkness.

Chapter 14

Arms outstretched, Bragen hugged the mountain's steep face, zas nostrils moving in and out, drawing air into zas lungs. Every few feet zie stopped, blinking the sweat and dirt out of zas eyes. After a brief respite, zie started again, sliding zas boots along the ledge, pebbles and stones dropping into the abyss. Zie never heard them hit. One incautious step and zie would no longer worry about what a cleanscan felt like. Rounding the bend, a hot wind blew sand into zas eyes. Squeezing them shut, zie hugged the mountain, resting. *What am I doing?* Afraid to look back, zie blinked away the dirt and began again, moving one slow slide-step to the right.

The scorptor changed everything. Zas five-year assignment was over when it found bones in the blueweed. *It was better before. Working underground, boring tunnels, watching the stat screen with fellow wagers .Everything was better. Moving the Ball Forward beat any freedom the archodial life provided. It was not worth it. Mador's fault.*

Each time Bragen slid zas right boot along the ledge, zie grabbed for a root or rock to hold on to. Like the wind, the mountain was warm. Several steps later, zas bleeding fingers found the framed opening. Zie slithered over the window ledge and fell on the floor. Exhausted, zie rolled onto zas back and closed zas eyes.

A low, distant moan cut through the silence. *The*

wind. Several seconds later, Bragen opened zas eyes, rolled over and stood up. *Misla's room.* Everything was gone but the stone desk. Legless, it sat like some ancient, wounded animal near the window. *Get out of the dream!* The wind reminded zam it was not a dream. *And I am not in an Interact.* Zie saw the arched entry that led to the other room. Zie saw the opening, the square hole in the floor. Nothing else anywhere.

Bragen turned. One wall jutted out near the crumbled desk. *That's the one.* Zie walked over and studied it. A rock face, just like the others. *More than a wall.* Zie touched the stones. *I am an archy. I know rocks.* Zie ran a hand over their rounded edges. Pushed on a select few. Some were no bigger than zas thumb. Others were larger than zas hand. Gray, black, and rusty orange stones covered all the walls. *How many hundreds of years had passed?* Zie placed the flat of both hands on one of the larger rocks and pushed. Nothing. Over the next several minutes zie twisted and pushed several of the grays and blacks, all the while looking for a seam. Nothing. Zie kicked the wall. Silence. Disgusted, zie limped over to the window.

Looking over the edge, zie remembered rockets. Steam rising from their engines. Recollected their nosecones. The etchings. And the mountain backdrop. Zie looked north. The sky was dark green. Soon it would be black. Watching the sky change colors, zie recalled her thoughts. Heard the musicality.

A moment later a star blinked. Zie did a double take. It was gone. Zie squinted and looked some more. *Nothing.* Yet zas memory saw it. *An arc.* On the benches, the Ollepas mural, and the nosecones. *The hidden room.* Bragen turned. Zie studied the wall that jutted away from the rest of the study. Zie walked over and looked at its face. Looked up. There it was. Small black stones curving into a larger, rust colored one. Bragen reached up and grabbed the larger one. Nothing.

Standing on zas toes, zie tried again. Nothing. Tiny dots of blood remained on the rocks. Bragen snorted. It sounded so simple. *Twist it. All will be revealed.* Zie rubbed zas hands on zas jumper. *Mador had left a gift?* Behind the wall? An image of Manebeck flashed up. *They will come. And soon.* Zie looked back. Several constellations were winking at zam. To the right of the Rising Steedfell was a glittering arc. *The Horn.* There. It was not a part of the Galaxial Warp; therefore, it did not exist. Yet there it was. How could that be? It appeared as if the Steedfell's front hoof was going to crash into the largest star, the one on the end.

Bragen looked at the desk. Zie found one of the broken legs half buried in the sand and picked it up. *Sturdy and thick.* Brushing it off, the archy looked up at the thin line of curved stones. Zie raised up and smashed the leg against the large, rust colored one. Shards of stone sprayed across the room, followed by a large grinding noise.

Dirt began to fall from the cave's ceiling. For a moment, it seemed like the entire room was going to collapse. Instead, the portion of the wall that jutted out began to move. The grinding noise grew louder. As it moved to zas right, stones began to pop off, cutting lines of sand across the floor as they rolled away. The grinding turned into a high-pitched screech. Bragen backed toward the arched entrance. The façade exploded, sending splintered stones through the window. The noise stopped.

Dust filled the air. Bragen snorted out a wad of dirt. Bits of multicolored rocks and stones were everywhere. Taking a wide angle, zie walked around the opening. Tattered strips of black cloth hung in the void. It reminded zam of kulcat fibers. Bragen pulled a large strip down, revealing what looked like another wall. A wooden wall. Zie ripped the remaining cloth down and threw it out of the way.

Two heavily scratched wood panel doors filled the void. Each with a silver handle. Bragen wiped zas hands on a piece of cloth then grabbed one of the handles and pulled. The door opened. A soft orange light painted zas face. All the shelves were empty save the middle one. Two objects sat there, one emitting the orange glow. A tube of some sort. The other looked like one of the red cylinders Misla had shown zam.

Not so easy. Bragen bent over. Although it was getting dark, the tube lit up the void. Zie touched it. *Warm.* Zie pulled it out. About the diameter of zas arm, one end was pointed, the other triangulated and flat. Zie kicked away loose shards of broken stone and sat it on the floor. The tube dimmed.

Bragen bent down, studying the odd markings that ran down its length. They were different from the symbols found on the Interacts. But they reminded zam of something. Zie looked at the only cylinder. *They took the rest.* Zie pulled it out and sat it on its side next to the tube. One half of the pipe was made of metal, casting a silver sheen. The other half was red, yet made of some translucent material. Zie could see that something was inside it.

Bragen took another piece of discarded cloth and wiped off the desk. A seam separated the metal part of the cylinder from the translucent part. Placing it between zas legs zie twisted it one way and then the other. Nothing. Grabbing the red end, Bragen walked over to the alcove and whacked it against the stone shelving. When it broke into two sections, a small pointed instrument shot across the floor. Zie knew what it was.

Bragen was able to remove a lid from the other cannister, tapped the bottom into zas palm, and removed tightly rolled material it contained. Then zie strolled over and picked up the tool. It turned orange. Placing the scroll on the desk zie scooped up some of the stone shards. Getting on zas knees, zie rolled the material out and placed the shards on its corners to hold it down.

Two columns of hieroglyphs made of dark curves, circles, whorls, half-lines and dots flowed down its thin surface. Hand trembling, Bragen ran the instrument over the scroll, its orange light lit up the markings, turning them into understandable streams of thought. Just like the voices, a musicality pervaded their meaning. Without the instrument, no Synthon could translate. Bragen knew what zie was seeing were words. Somehow, zie also knew that words were thoughts memorialized on something other than a digibit or within the Flow. Zas eyes ran across the script. This, zie somehow understood, was reading.

In those last days preparations became more intense. Discovery was only a matter of time, Uhlman search craft were already in the Sal Sagevs. The deep valleys served us well, but the Apogonos is beyond hiding. Thus, during the first quarter of the blue moon's crescent in the year 3150, fifty-five adults and fifty-one children left Lark. Thirty men, twenty-five women, four of whom were pregnant, thirty-one boys and twenty girls.

We were always going Home, and planned to do so in the Spring. Yet their flyovers were getting closer. Winter was fast approaching. We could not wait. Provisions and equipment were loaded. As was your source into The Way.

We left for the wildlands of Apollis. The journey was fraught with difficulty. Flying blind, the target was missed. Instead of the valleys that lay north of the Black mountains, Wasenah sat us down in a deep rift near the great sea. Upon inspection it was determined that the ship could not be retrofitted. This meant our original destination, beyond the mountains, remained out of reach. Instead, we moved to the coast and started our settlement along an escarpment that overlooked the ocean.

Despite the lack of protection, the plains and coastline had much to offer. The soil was fertile. Above the grass line herds of range arths and steedfells grazed. Below it, erzatz and desert rinks prowled their underground tunnels and burrows, in constant watch for hawks and sea fowl. This coast and its inlets also provided a variety of finscale and marmaks, both the blue and black skinned. Thus, from the beginning, we did not want for provisions.

While those first years were challenging, they were nothing like the wars. In this new world our children remained our own, not the products of conception. Instead of malleable pieces of biology defined by others they grew into their true selves.

We flourished in Sunbloom. This was due in part because of The Source, spinning light into thoughts and elements into objects. Like gravity, the unseen presence held us together as a people. Those who call our offspring the Stain also use it, but in detaching the mind from the body they have lost the connection, the essence. Fabrication of the animate into the inanimate may create the efficiency they seek, but in the process, they lost their True Selves, as well as the Forever we have maintained to present to you within The Way. Your experience within The Way means we have preserved the Truth. A Truth painted across Aromla's walls, etched on the foundation blocks of Sunbloom, traced across the nosecones of our ships, and memorialized within your essence.

We saw them coming. Detected the starship long before it arrived and set about destroying, burying, and removing all traces from the Wasenah Rift and Sunbloom. We hid in this mountain. They came. They searched. They left. In 3151 we buried The Way, below the rift. In what you call Interacts we left our Truth. Which you found.

We never intended to remain on Apollis. Your arrival was the signal. Subsequent returns confirmed this. As did your friend's appearance. We accelerated our efforts and prepared Aromla for your last visit to our Now.

Landerwin awaits. That moment will be memorialized with the rest. As my father reminds me, the Truth is not burdened by the constraint of time. Like the purple fliguan, it may lay dormant for long periods, but its beauty remains, waiting for the sun.

You have seen that beauty, have heard Marabella's cry, and watched her take her mother's milk. Such is the fruit of life, bearing the bitter and the sweet, the sadness and the joy. All of it is in you, as it is in me, within The Way. Do not listen to the silence. Just like The Horn, we were always here. Listen.

While Bragen was searching zas memcore for reference to the purple fliguan, a wailing, sand-filled gust of wind caught the scroll and blew it off the desk. With bits of stone and sand, it rolled across the floor. Bragen jumped for the script but missed it. It skidded under the arched entrance, whirled up for a moment, then fell into the hole. It floated down and landed face up on the floor below. Looking down, Bragen realized the tool was still in zas hand, glowing. Far below the scroll lay in the darkness. *Thirteen-hundred years.*

Bragen turned. A billion stars lit the sky, yet it was The Horn that stood out. An orange hue filled the room. Zie dropped the tool. *Words. Paper. Voices.* All blank-spotted. Stunned, zie sat down and crossed zas legs. The cylinder stood in front of zam.

Sucking air deep into zas lungs the archy placed both hands on its tapered neck and closed zas eyes. *What else?* A warmth flowed through zas fingers and into zas arms, neck, and skull.

The ocean's roar filled zas ears just before a wave rushed past zas ankles and crashed into a line of boulders behind zam. Zas eyes followed a series of steps that ended at the bottom of a rift, a void. A hooded figure stood in this opening, watching zam. A Human. It waved, then descended the steps and walked across the beach toward zam. Bragen stood there, waves rushing past zas feet. Zie looked down. *Where are my boots?* The figure removed the hood. It was Feelwin. An orange glow surrounded his neck.

"We thought it best to start here," he said. Bragen looked up the face of the cliff. *Mythgarden Point.* "Your friend was in a hurry," Feelwin continued. "With good reason. Walk with me."

They walked along the shore. "You mean Mador?"

Feelwin's blue eyes found zam. "That is your name."

"What is yours?"

"You are about to find out."

A gull dipped into the swale between two waves and ripped a finscale out of the roiling sea. Bragen pondered Feelwin's words. The wizened had somehow broken into an old Interact, what the Humans called The Way, and left two messages. One involved the Goman Ruins. *The other must be here, on this beach. No. In Aromla. I am in Aromla.*

"Misla knew zam," Bragen said. An image of the alcove flashed up. "She knew zas name."

Feelwin made the trilling sound. *Laughter.* "True. But she is not here. She is—"

"In the mountains," Bragen said, finishing the thought. "Looking for a new place. A cave. Is that right?"

"It is true she is not here. But as to where, that is not for me to say. Unlike these Interactions, life is more random. The Way is simply a guide. Your friend charted zas own way, as you will in your Now."

Bragen looked back to where Feelwin had emerged from the gap in the cliff. The place where the scorptor spotted the blueweed. "It seems my Now is different from yours. Is it?"

Feelwin looked straight into a deep blue sky, his neck ring glowing bright orange. "Not so different. The Now comes from the Long Ago. Which connects us all through The Way. And leads us home."

More gulls patrolled the coast, occasionally striking the water before soaring into the sky with their catch. Feelwin turned. Bragen followed. Following their footprints, they walked back. Zie looked up. "You mean The Horn?"

"Yes," Feelwin said.

"How is Mador connected to all this?"

They were back in front of the steps that led to the void. Feelwin placed a finger on zas forehead and nodded at Bragen. "You will have to ask zam."

Bragen did the same. When the Human dropped the same finger to his chest the archy repeated the motion. An instant later zie was not on the beach. Instead, zie was bumping along a tree-lined road in the cab of a large transport, fast approaching a massive iron gate that was guarded by several large, helmeted individuals.

"What is this?" Zie asked Feelwin.

"Don't think anything. They can't see you."

Bragen almost jumped out of the seat. It was Mador. Sort-of.

The wizened pulled to a stop in front of the guards. One walked over and peered in.

"Transport or delivery?" When it spoke, a muffled noise came out of its jaw-line.

"Transport," the sort-of Mador answered. "One-Zero-Five to Oceanview."

Frozen, Bragen stared at the guard's face. This was no Synthon. Nor was it a Human. Neither was Mador. The guard and the driver studied each other. Both had very small ears and a slight protrusion above their chins. *What is that?* A sound, not a thought.

"Ok," the guard said, waving at the gate. The others pushed it open.

The sort-of Mador pulled the lever and drove through the opening. Low-level stone and glass buildings sprang up on each side of the road.

"I know," the not so-Mador said, looking over at zam. "My name is Rodam. And yes," zie said, turning left into an alley that ran between two of the buildings. "In this Now, I am an Uhlman." Bragen barely heard zam, still trying to process the strange sound coming out of the lower portion of its mouth. *Zie understood it! Uhlman?* Zie watched zam whip the vehicle into a parking lot, turn around, and back up to a building dock. Rodam hopped out. Bragen heard other sounds in the back. Musical sounds. Zie opened zas door and got out.

Rodam was standing on the dock, opening the transport's back door. "Just watch. No one can see you. I will explain once we get out of here."

The archy bounded up the steps in time to see several black-garbed Humans pile out the back of the van. Rodam was already at the door, manipulating some type of screen, then pulling it open.

"What is this?" Bragen asked.

"A Somafarm," Rodam said. The Humans that had bolted out of the back of the vehicle were already inside. "This way."

Hundreds of cubicles filled the brightly lit room. An explosion shook the floor of the building. The screams of fifty babies subsequently erupted across the room. Bragen shook zas head. There were no orange rings. *Sound?*

"This is my memory, not yours," Rodam answered. Zie turned zas attention to one of the Humans, a woman. "The pre-natals are over there." A series of clear-glassed cabinets hung on the wall. "Ten boys and thirty girls." There was another explosion. Just as zie lost zas footing Bragen realized the woman was Misla. More screams. Other than dust falling from the ceiling, everything seemed intact.

Rodam helped zam up. "A diversion," zie said. "Just stand next to me and watch."

Misla was gone. Several of her companions were unfastening the clear tops of the cubicles. Others were opening the cabinet doors on the walls and removing rectangular containers that glowed red and blue. Others wheeled elongated carts into the center of the room. One by one, the babies were removed from the cubicles and placed into individualized compartments with the carts. A wailing cacophony of distress filled Bragen's senses.

Rodam addressed zam. "This is the bay that leads to the tissue transmission centers. Do you know where you are?"

Zie did not. But zie knew what was happening. "You are taking them."

"We are," Radom answered.

Bragen's memcore could not provide zam with the term zie was looking for. "Where are the... who watches... oversees?"

"They're called production managers. This room operates on its own. Unfortunately, corridor guards had to be neutralized. They will wake up later. The explosions have drawn the attention of the majority who work at this plant. That includes the managers."

Bragen saw her enter the far side of the room carrying a small child. Older children followed, some barely able to walk, some as tall Misla. Their various hair colors were just as fascinating now as they were on Opellas. The last one sent a tingle up the back of zas neck. A little boy with a shock of white hair and equally white skin. They all lined up against the wall and listened to her. Except this one, who seemed to be staring straight

Bragen with eyes so light gray they appeared as translucent as his skin.

"You said they could not see me."

"They can't," Radom said. "Where?" Zie followed Bragen's eyes. The boy was no longer looking at zam. Instead zie was looking at the woman. Misla was bent over, speaking intently to him. She turned and pointed at the wizened, then Bragen.

"I do not know everything," Radom said.

"Time?" Misla yelled.

"Two minutes," Rodam answered, nodding toward the door. Then to the archy, "I don't think she can see you. That child seems different. Look at the others. They cannot." Zie looked at the exit sign. "Go stand outside."

Bragen followed the older children, the white-haired boy was up near the front of the line. They stopped at the end of the dock and watched several of the dark-garbed adults slide rectangular receptacles into form-fitting slots that were built into the sidewalls of the transport's cargo bay. Once secured, each was lit by an orange glow.

"Those are the pre-natals," Rodam said, suddenly beside zam. "These are the newbies."

Several carts of squealing babies whirled by, their tiny hands waving in the air. The transport's interior was surprisingly large. Carts four rows wide and five deep were soon packed with newborns.

Bragen felt Rodam's fingers squeezing zas arm. "Come on. We're leaving."

Zie felt like zas boots were stuck on the loading dock. *Fables?* The older children, including the only one with white hair, rushed past with the remaining adults and crammed themselves into the last few feet of cargo space. What about Misla?

A guttural command came out of Radom's throat, "Now! Don't interfere with my focus!"

Bragen hopped off the landing. The cargo's doors slammed shut behind zam. Rodam was already behind the steering device, energizing the vehicle. Beyond the parking lot a cloud of smoke rose over the buildings. Most of the sky was already black. They lurched forward, speeding out of the parking lot. Bragen stared at zas hands, but only saw tiny pink ones reaching up and out of the compartments.

The large van roared down the alley. Jerking what looked like some sort of steering device, Radom avoided bits of metal and broken glass that were strewn across the road. A few seconds later they veered onto the main road. The transport accelerated. Several white clad guards were standing in front of the gate. One pointed an object in their direction.

"Get ready to duck," Rodam said. Something hit the front of the transport just before the guards jumped out of the way. When it crashed into the gate, iron pickets and posts shot into the air and flew over the cab. Rodam made a chortling sound deep in zas throat. Bragen still stared at zas hands. "I know," Rodam said. "But this was the best way. The best Now I could pick. Once we're clear I will explain."

Bragen studied Radom's face. There was a bump of skin above zas chin. At its center a small hole moved in and out when zie breathed. Nothing like the Human mouth. No slit. No teeth. No tongue. When zie talked the lower portion of zas face moved. Rodam swerved around another smoking piece of mangled metal. Quite an explosion.

A spiderweb of cracks ran across the windshield.

There were no more buildings. Elderwoods lined the road, little more than blurs. Bragen checked the sky for lidscans but of course there were none. *This*, zie realized, *was happening more than a thousand years before zas origination. What would they have used?* The trees thickened; they were larger. Zie kept looking up. Nothing. Zie had heard the term Somafarm before. It seemed clear this one was not close to a city.

"Another few minutes," Radom said, zas eyes searching up ahead. Not long after, the vehicle slowed and turned onto a dirt trail that led into a wall of Wedge Pines and Giant Oaks. Their canopies covered the sky and blocked out the sun. The transport bounced in and out of several holes, precipitating several bangs against the metal that separated the cab from the cargo hold.

"You're welcome!" Radom roared, whipping around a large rut. A few moments later they rolled to a stop under a large shed-like overhang built of logs and branches. Several dark clad Humans emerged from the shadows. A few held pole-like devices. Zie noticed a larger building, also made of logs behind the overhang.

"Ok," Radom said. "A few more minutes and we'll talk."

Bragen hopped out and ran to the back of the vehicle. A ramp was already in place and they were pulling the first cart out when Radom came around the other side, ducking underneath the ramp and placing a hand on zas shoulder. "You can't," zie said. "That is not why you are here."

The archy was looking into the cargo hold. The children were climbing down with help from the adults on the ground. Wailing now pierced the forest. Radom pulled zam by the arm away from the ramp. "Stand over here and observe. I will be right back."

The boy with the white hair and skin walked out of the bay with the older children and followed some of the adults beyond heavy-planked doors that led into the log building. Rodam stood there, talking to two dark clad Humans. The boy stopped inside the doorway and looked back in Bragen's direction, then disappeared. Bragen shuddered, turned, and watched the rest of the children come out of the cargo bay. Almost empty. *Where was she*? Zie walked over and looked inside. A dark-headed man stood in the hull by zamself, fastening several ties and straps to the exterior walls. Zie paused a moment, looked in Bragen's direction, then continued about his business.

Walking up, Rodam said, "It doesn't matter." Zie placed an arm around the archy's shoulder and guided zam away from the transport. "Let's take a walk."

Bragen looked back one last time. The man with the dark hair was out of the transport, and walking toward the double doors, a large coil of rope wound over zas shoulder. "I know him."

Radom stopped and looked back. The man was gone. "Who?"

The archy thought a moment. Landerwin. It looked like Landerwin. No. It was not Landerwin, zie realized. *Reenquo.*

The vehicle's engine clicked on. Someone was in it. A moment later it rolled by them. The driver waved. Not too far down the trail it turned left and disappeared into the forest.

Rodam shrugged, as if to say, that is not why you are here. Zie motioned with zas head toward the road. "Come. I wanted you to see that."

They were in a very thick forest. One that contained the biggest trees zie had ever seen. It was midday, yet due to the canopy, they remained in complete shadow. Beams of light cut through the overhang, painting silver circles on the ground. Several yellow birds flitted about. They looked familiar.

"Those are sea merchants," Radom said. "Each night they hit the beaches for sand crabs, which seem to be their main dish."

"There is a coast. Which one? Where are we?"

"The West."

Bragen caught a whiff of salt, "Arion?"

"Lark."

Zie thought about that. Zie had never seen Lark's coasts.

"The closest city is Seaport. A few miles to the north. Here." Radom nodded toward the large split log that rested near the trail. "Have a seat."

Bragen did so. Radom sat next to zam. Bragen stared at the small hole below zas nose. "You're an Uhlman."

"Yes," came the muffled answer. "I wanted you to know this place." Zie looked back, toward the log building. "That's a holding facility. They'll be out of here as soon as the sun falls."

"You work with them? The Humans?"

Radom looked straight ahead. "I do."

"You're Mador?"

"Yes."

Chapter 15

"Why didn't you tell me?" Bragen asked.

Deep in zas throat, Radom made a clucking sound. "It would not do. Telling is not seeing. It is your own experience that bears the weight of Truth. I have been struggling with how to do this. The lidscan forced my hand."

Bragen thought a moment. Two yellow sea merchants landed on the trail in front of them and began pecking in the soft dirt. "Brinslow Park. Your apartment?"

"Yes," Radom answered. "I am afraid events overtook us. They found your trace. I had to improvise."

"The Goman Ruins."

"Yes, after sending you to Maice, I visited the ruins."

"That coin. It was different. Where did it come from?"

Radom sat up straight and sucked air through hole, then blew it out. "We should start at the beginning. Otherwise, you will remain lost. Are you ready?"

The two yellow birds twirled up into the air, fighting over a worm. One broke free and shot into the canopy. Squawking, the other followed. Bragen nodded.

"I was processed in as a Black Hole manipulator. It was an era of great biological and technological leaps. From the beginning my focus was solving the time gap puzzle that prevented straight line transits. Just as the war broke out, I found the way through. The Ruul knew the value of instantaneous delivery of high value assets from one end of the Prometheus to the other. This led to being enhanced, which meant a greater lifespan and higher-level extrasensory communicators. In other words, I became a Benefactor. Benefactors oversee societal functions such as travel, industrial capacity, and biological processing. All in the name of control and oversight. Warp oversight. In those first years, I was in charge of all Black Hole Transits, which helped to facilitate victory.

"Afterward, still in charge of these transits, I became instrumental in product redistribution to the somatic cell farms. Timing was crucial regarding the prenatals. In this Now, exo-wombs are scarce, particularly on the outlying planets. The transits provided the answer. Until, that is, a worm hole entry point collapsed. Weeks passed. Thousands expired. Up until then, I remained oblivious of the process. My focus, like all Uhlmans, was the end result. The Common Benefit.

"Once the new transit was up and running the spoilage came to Dalimath. Several of the parts were salvageable. Here was the key: the progressional leap. Dissection. Distribution. Utilization. I oversaw this process. Afterwards, I began having dreams. In each one, I saw them running down the transport ramp and into the woods. Woods like these. Even the prenatals. The Ruul noticed, assuring me the loss was insured and it was time to move on. Yet I could not get beyond the reality. This was no trope. My oblivion abandoned me. A few moons later I was informed a remboot was in order. That is when I broke the neural clip and fled the city."

Cones of light moved across the dirt road. Bragen stood. Zie stared back at the cabin. Wondered what was going on back in the building. What were they telling them? What did the little ones think? Zie looked back at Radom's face. Studied the many similarities between Mador and Radom, but could not get over the hole above zas chin. "What is this... clip?"

"The Ruul anticipated that their overseers might occasionally... have questions. Questions are not good. To solve this, a genetic enhancement specific to Benefactors was inserted within the pineal gland. This enhancement created an inseparable link, similar to the Galaxial Warp. Yet our thoughts were indelibly tied to the Ruul, what became the Hive. Yet evolution is not a straight line. On its own, our brains sought a way around this connection, creating a blind spot. I became aware of this possibility during one of the dreams. The children were fleeing a transport. I ran after them. At some point I realized I was not chasing them. Instead, I too, was being chased.

"In this dream a wire ran from the back of my head and into the sky. Running through woods like these, I reached up and jerked it loose. When I woke the link was still there, but so was something else. Something new. An original thought. And the images. What they called spoilage. A part of the new equity.

"Despite my brain telling me this was Right Thinking, I knew otherwise. Images of the spoilage remained. I knew it was not Right Thinking. And they *knew* I knew. So, I told the link to stop. Something within my manipulated pineal gland responded, for a blind spot interrupted the connection, leading me to conclude that science and the evolutionary leap it created do not always operate in tandem. One does not control the other. The neural clip came apart. They could not see my thoughts. Immediate adjustments were made before other Benefactors became aware. By then, I was gone."

Bragen began to understand, but the chronology was wrong. A black crow flew down the road, followed by several yellow sea merchants. "You became a wizened."

"As you can see, not immediately. The wars were not over. My remaining enhancements kept me shielded, and gave me the talent needed to create a new identity. I became a member of the wager class. And spent those first years underground." They exchanged a look. "Yes. That day in the park was quite interesting. I knew more about what was going on in those tunnels than I let on.

"A Benefactor has many advantages, one being an almost unlimited span. Unlimited unless caught. The tunnels became my refuge, where, as they say, I began Moving the Ball Forward. The wars continued. The images remained inside me. While they could not see my thoughts, I retained access to the Galaxial Warp and certain priority channels few were privy to. Over time I gained a sense of where the resistance was strongest, the West Coast, and used my talents to find positions that might lead me to them. One of these talents was the ability to manipulate my own seri. Benefactors often utilized this tool to maintain proper oversight over the general population.

"Once situated, I pinpointed where the cell farm was located. These types of facilities attract the briganders. After transitioning in as a transport wager, I used my oversight talents to locate them. It took a year. And that is how we got to this bench."

Bragen needed more. "So, you met Misla. How did

that happen?"

"Not important at this point," Radom answered. "I will not go into it. Suffice to say I did. After the war, and beyond this memory, I slid back into the shadows for a few more centuries, every so often, changing my origination.

"A Benefactor's ability to shield past histories and most thoughts provided me the cover needed to remain undetected, yet I sometimes wondered if it was worth it. Longevity for what? For a while I worked at a facilities plant on Arion making transpo coins. I scooped up a lot of blanks during that period, which have proved most useful.

"Long after the wars, I pretended to work toward the singular purpose of bringing about the future. An Uhlman's span is only a few hundred years, which makes such an existence more palatable. The unlimited nature of mine made it worse. With the advent of the Synthonic Age, I saw an opportunity to make life more interesting.

"The Galaxial Warp was in full roar. The entire Prometheus became connected. The Seers replaced the Ruul, using the Hive mentality as its operating structure. Here, the One Thought flowed unimpeded into each new memcore, which accelerated the next evolutionary leap. This included the end of vocalization. First generation Synthons maintained this facial orifice for some time; thus, I was able to pass as one of the new species. When your kind evolved, I managed to replicate the facial changes, yet I will not get into that.

"Devoid of the link but in possession of other talents, I changed identities, using past experience with Black Hole transits and distribution systems to relocate to the Dalimath processing center, my old center of operations. Uhlmans with any knowledge of my person were long out of service and not a worry. As a result, the unlimited nature of my span did not seem as onerous. I made myself indispensable.

"Ages passed. I moved up, controlling all incoming material to this facility. That was my function when special cargo arrived from Apollis. The shipment included Mavwa's discoveries and zas report. My function included curating, labeling, and distributing materials and data to their intended bins and councils. The report was interesting, but it was a particular artifact that drew my attention.

"A piece of metal wrapped in clear sheathing. Its edges serrated, as if torn or blasted away from a larger section. There were unique markings beneath the wrap. I removed this artifact from the collection and took it to my office. Why? Perhaps my unlimited span once again provoked me into doing something irrational. Or perhaps doing so gave me a purpose other than Moving the Ball Forward."

"What was it?" Bragen asked.

"I think it was a part of a ship. When I oversaw the transits in those early years of the war, I came across similar markings of Human origination."

"What did it say?"

"Benefactors are programmed to understand many archaic languages. I knew what it said, but not what it meant. Translated, the markings refer to something they called Apogonos."

Bragen recalled Mador within the Interact, studying one of the women's swollen mid-sections. More to zamself than Bragen, the wizened had thought, *it is somehow related.*

"I was thinking about the worm-hole collapse," Radom said. "And that some Humans had escaped."

"You never mentioned it."

"The damage related to gaining knowledge without context can prove more harmful than no knowledge at all. Events overtook us."

Bragen thought about Mavwa's Gulch. "It was meant to be found. They left it on purpose."

"I began to sense that," Radom agreed, staring at the forest. "I don't know why. A message. I did not curate the metal, or Mavwa's references to it. In a manner, I blank-walled it."

"You joined them again?"

Radom snorted. "Not physically. I could not return to this Now. All evidence of their existence was eradicated. Over the centuries, I continued to puzzle over the metal and the inscription. *Apogonos*. It drew something out of me. Something tangible and of great meaning. Why were they erased? Was it linked to the spoilage? Or what the spoilage represented? Of course it was. But what good was this knowing?

"I began to use Dalimath to launch illegal thoughts into the Flow. Whispers of other species. Species similar to Uhlmans and Synthons, yet different. When Rawnswawn inserted zas treatise, I began to float my own shielded thoughts into the Galaxial Warp. Bits about Humans and Mawoans. They were blank-spotted, but not before circulating a few days. Then I became more creative."

Bragen recalled the lidscan patrolling through Brinslow Park. Inducers and Watchers were woven into the fabric of each Synthon's span. Flips could not have hidden such egregious unthoughts for long. Only a

Benefactor could avoid capture. "How long did this go on?"

"Several spans. My talents kept them at bay. Working in distribution I was able to acquire a ream of blank digibits, which are similar to the transpo-coin blanks. I placed these untraceable images into the Warp and watched them drift toward the distant parts of the Prometheus, floating information on mysterious beings who produced their own progeny. Despite the Hive's best efforts, the seed was planted.

"As a result of these subtle successes, I grew bolder, sending the vague term Humotzero into the Flow, along with rumors that Uhlmans were once capable of ingestion, excretion, and propagation. Watchers always found these thoughts, and continued to take them down, so I decided that each should be preserved in some manner. Using a blank digibit, I began to store them all in one place. For no particular reason, I began references to the storage as The Symporous. Thoughts inserted into the Warp were eventually removed, but like the piece of metal, I refused to give them up. They have always been with me. I plan to share them at some point. Perhaps in this Now."

"I remember that term, Symporous," Bragen said, recalling one of zas evenings in Mador's apartment.

"I wanted the Hive to know," Radom said, "that I was still out there. That they were not completely successful. So, I inserted that name into the Warp."

"It was a ruse, this Symporous."

"Remember," Radom said, "this is *my* memory. One I will eventually share." Zie looked back at the log building. "Notice I said memory, not memcore. Like the Ruul, completely organic repositories of information were already on the way out when the Uhlman Wars began. In this Now, new science allowed the manipulation of receptors and the creation of synthetic repositories, which they called memcores. Programed assumptions and instincts inserted into you at origination and maintained throughout your span created a new yesterday. Synthons only know what the Galaxial Warp wants Synthons to know. Unless a black-market Thought tells them otherwise. Intentional or not, it is more than a ruse."

Bragen thought about the children coming out of the cargo hold. The children at Opellas. "It is hard to process."

Rodam continued staring at the building. "In this Now, children are looked upon as nothing more than a resource meant to promote a future that does not include them. Uncomfortable realities lead to uncomfortable questions. Eliminating the reality eliminates the question. Those who fight back against this Unreality are labeled the Contagion. Their offspring the Stain. Labels help with control. Which reminds me of a passage within the *ruse*, 'they will take the I out of you and replace it with the We that only They control. Every discordant note will be replaced with a thrum. Everyone will bleat the same answer to the old question and the people will lose their voice.'"

"Mador, I mean... you, said that once."

"Yes," Radom said. "Vocalization is more than a way to communicate. If that is all it was, you would still have a mouth. They took the I out of your species and replaced it with the We only They control. Everyone bleats the same answer, 'Move the Ball Forward.' Archodialbragen1031, you have lost your voice."

Radom paused. When zie did, Bragen saw the wizened's golden eyes, not Radom's yellow ones. Incandescent particles swirled around Mador's pupils, reminding the archy of the shafts of light that penetrated the canopy. "I have been working toward this last span for centuries. At University I used all I learned from past ages to bring forth a new respect for what came before, albeit in a subtle way. How odd that a wratchet-gatherer led me to the sound that comes from their mouths. When the lidscanner appeared, I knew this was my last span."

Yet it was Radom, not Mador, that walked across the road and stared up into the branches of a Giant Oak. Each branch, two feet thick, stretched across the road and co-mingled with similar branches from the other side. Winding cords of vines covered with thick green leaves wrapped around the branches and with each other, blocking out the sky.

Bragen followed the wizened's gaze. *So familiar. From where? The dream. And Opellas.* "What does it mean?"

"Perhaps," Radom began, looking at the canopy, but studying zas thoughts, "we all come from the same vine." Radom was no longer there. Instead it was the wizened who looked into Bragen's eyes. "You left my apartment. Minutes later, I did too, by another route. One that led me to Goman Ruins. I could have vanished again after leaving you the coin, but the collapse of the worm hole and what it wrought, images I cannot forget, demanded I do otherwise." Zie looked over at the log structure. "I was complicit. Images of mothers never known and tomorrows never seen. By then my purpose had evolved, so I used my Talent to get back to Mythgarden Point. When the Inducer broke down the door, I feared I was too late. But you found the memgit that led to the coin, and you are here, which tells me the Humans kept this memory for your return. How, is irrelevant."

Radom was back, nodding toward the cabin. Zie began to walk in that direction. Bragen followed. "When they hauled me off," zie said, recalling zas capture, "it was like the last day before forever. In many ways, a relief."

Bragen stopped, once again looking for Radom but finding Mador. The Uhlman with the hole above zas chin was gone. The wizened stood there. Blue face, golden eyes, no mouth. Pigtails winding around the back of zas head and down zas neck. Synthon. Wizened. Mentor. "Eliminating vocalization was key to gaining control of thought. This leap broke the bond between body and mind."

Bragen looked at the cabin. It seemed time had also bent. How else would Mador know this? "How?"

Mador shook zas head. "I do not know. It has something to do with the connection between flesh and the sound it emits. Words. The body is the conduit from which Thoughts once flowed, producing the musicality called language. Once that bond was lost, the creativity inherent in the species broke down. Except in a minority of instances, such as the one you have experienced within the Interacts and this Now, Human progeny became product. No longer creators, they bowed to the science that led to their demise. Archodialbragen1031, what is the purpose of One-Zero-Five?"

Bragen thought of Aromla. "Misla said the Uhlmans needed them. Human children were needed."

Mador nodded. "True. For the progression. To

rectify a chromosome imbalance. Yet the original tissue transmissions did not solve an imbalance, it created one. One the Humans, in this Now, are determined to stop. You saw her at the One-Zero-Five."

"Yes."

"They call her the Lifegiver," Mador said. "She did not believe in the Common Benefit. This belief, in an absurd turn, made her a traitor. As you have witnessed, she is one of many. The Ruul branded her with their own title. They love branding those they hate. Stainspreader. What do you think she is spreading?"

Bragen thought of the little girl who reached up and grabbed zas fingers. "Something not in me."

"But it is. Preborns and Postborns are more than biological goo to be formed into whatever the Common Benefit requires. She put that in you."

"You helped them."

Mador was now Radom. Zie nodded. "I did. In the Now, and certainly before I bent the clip, talent gained as a Benefactor provided me a clearer Flow. Those who Know refuse to express any concern about what is going on. I find it quite ironic that in the Tomorrow, this vocalization, a mode of expression, becomes extinct. So yes, I was very much a part of the… progression."

Radom began walking toward the cabin. "And, as is apparent, still am. But only in You. So, there you have it. It is your time now. As it is those who remain, which is why I returned to Sunbloom without you."

Bragen felt like the soft dirt under zas boots was falling away. "You interacted with the Humans. Why not do the same in the Warp?"

"My clip does not work as it was designed, but it still works. The evolutionaries made sure Benefactors could not *corrupt* the Flow." Mador, not Radom, touched a finger to zas forehead. "It is up to you."

It was too much. Bragen searched through zas mentor's thoughts for something that would sway zam. "What happened after they broke into the apartment?"

"I moved on. It is left to you."

"That is not an answer."

"It is all you are going to get."

"The object you used to get me to this Now. Is it a part of the Warp?"

"No. Remember. Benefactors cannot spread such... knowledge within the general population. You must do it."

"I can't," Bragen said.

"Yes, you can," Mador said. "This type of knowledge is not given. It is experienced. You must live it. You just did." Zas finger left zas forehead. "You are the vessel, not me. But I prefer the term ark."

Bragen reached out, but zas hand swiped thin air. Mador was gone. So were the Edge Pines, the Giant Oaks, the log building, and the beach. Zie was back on zas knees in the stone room. The upright tube sat amid the spray of rocks and rubble, glowing bright orange.

Chapter 16

The Silverstream shot across the dark plains, its screen picking up the lone peak that stood over Mavwa's Gulch as it moved north toward the mountains. Thirteen hundred years ago Majore walked in that ravine, half listening to the anthrogenecist point out where the artifacts and fossils were found. Zie should have listened more closely. Where was Mavwa's report? It did not appear to be in the Record. Until just a few hours ago, no one knew and no one cared. Prior to today Benefactors had always paid more attention to Rawnswawn. Sarkasian's official rebuttal was never questioned but whisperings continued. Black-market thoughts occasionally tainted the Galaxial Warp. That was what Inducers and Watchers were for. Deep in zas hidden brain, Majore realized the source of those whisperings. The wizened. A few minutes later they reached the mountain.

Aromla was cloaked in darkness. The Silverstream lit up, revealing the remains of the courtyard. Zawn watched zam. While both read the other's mind, neither chose to interact. Majore ran the light down the path that led to the bottom, then back up and across the plaza to the cave opening. Vatch's work was evident. Large mounds of dirt and rock filled the entrance. Zie looked at Zawn, then directed the craft to land. Once on the surface, they got out. Majore walked over to the large mound. A thick quiet hung over the mountain.

Zawn walked to the dunes that covered most of the parapet. The Synthon flipped on zas hand-held illuminator and ran it down the wall. The Benefactor glanced back, unable to read this Watcher. The air retained a hint of the heat that dominated this planet during the worst part of the day. Silence. No thoughts. No engines. Nothing. Majore gazed toward Manebeck, then Aguila. Linatin was at the Lifeway, leading the real search. Zie looked up. There was the Flying Erzatz. To its left, the ten-starred Ram with Arion positioned between that constellation and the Long Brow.

Stars remained a consistent reference point within a galaxy filled with evolutionary leaps. While genetic manipulations Moved the Ball Forward, the Brow never changed, nor did the Raring Steedfell, which hid somewhere north of the mountain.

Majore blinked, then again, zie studied the Watcher. It did not appear Zawn was paying zam any attention, but zie could feel the probe. Of course, Benefactors could block such traces, but the Seers would immediately know, so what was the point? Zawn was a high-level thought breaker, but that only pertained to Synthons. Majore looked up at the stars. Zie clicked back to Linatin's inspection of the cave. The other Benefactor stood in the carved-out room on an upper level. Acendoth and Radiwon were there. Some type of ancient furniture lay on the floor. Rubble. A large window faced north, which should give a clear view of the Raring Steedfell, as well as the Labyrinth, and the Five-Fingered Hand.

"The Labyrinth?" the Watcher asked.

A tingle ran down Majore's back. No Synthon knew

of it and would never see it. It was not a part of their memcore, no matter their level of enhancement. The Benefactor ignored the query and walked back to the Silverstream.

"What?" Zawn asked, coming away from the parapet.

"We need to be on the north end," Majore said. "Something was missed."

"What is the Labyrinth?" the Watcher asked.

Zie continued to ignore zam, sliding into the craft. A moment later Zawn did the same. Try as zie might, no Synthon could reach all parts of a Benefactor's mind. The neural clip prevented Watcher's like Zawn from scouring a Benefactor's hidden files and conversely, Benefactors could not insert Right Thinking or unthoughts into the Galaxial Warp. The clip was a twofold Hive control meant to check the power of both.

Gaining lift, Majore turned on the light beam and floated the craft into the darkness, washing the mountain with brilliant white light. Zie saw what looked like a small ledge protruding out of the rock face and followed it north, studying each crevice and shadow as they moved away from the courtyard. After rounding a large bend, a soft orange glow came into view. It was midway up the mountain. Majore reversed the Silverstream and moved back around the bend. Both studied the Dimensional's analysis. The light was superimposed over a dark rectangular opening. *The window?*

"No one is there," Zawn said.

"That is what the readings say," Majore agreed. Both sent out additional traces. *Nothing.* "But the stone is thick. We may not be picking everything up."

Zie flipped the screen and studied their

surroundings. The craft was approximately two-hundred feet above the ground. Zie edged the craft away from the mountain.

"What are you doing?" Zawn asked.

To the north, the dark outline of a distant mountain range was still visible. Seldom did clouds form on Apollis, yet the stars created a milky aura of light that gave off a cloud-like appearance. Majore studied the constellations. *There it was.* A curved string of stars, the last much larger than the rest . It hung between the Hand and the Raring Steedfell. Zie remained silent, trying to puzzle out the connection between this arc and Aromla.

"What are you looking at?" Zawn asked.

Majore ignored zam. Their prey was close, but solving this puzzle seemed just as important. Six smaller stars made up the arc. The larger one on the end, was also much brighter. *The Labyrinth. They do not call it that.* Zie made sure Zawn could not read zas thoughts. *The Horn. They called it The Horn.* Zie looked at the Dimensional again. *What else?* Redirecting the light beam, zie ordered the Silverstream to descend.

"You're going to let zam escape?"

"I do not think that is possible," Majore said. The wratchet-gatherer sent zas hovercraft to Manebeck. Zie must have walked here. Clever. The Watcher's flow streamed back to the Hive. Did it matter? The craft dropped down the wall, dust rolling up around it.

After touching down, Majore waited for the area to clear. The light beam illuminated the base of the mountain. Zie studied the Dimensional. It scanned the craft's perimeter and several feet up the face of the cliff. It detected a void at the bottom. The craft's visual zoomed in. Beyond a pile of dirt and boulders was the outline of a door. Zawn saw it too. They got out.

Hands on hips, Majore looked up. Craning zas neck, zie could still see the orange glow. The window faced north. Zie walked in a large circle, looking from the window down to the door, then back at the stars.

Zawn stood on the mound of dirt, bent over, and looked at a stone slab. "It leads to something. An entryway of some sort. It's been here awhile."

Majore looked at The Horn. "A long while."

The Watcher leaned in with zas shoulder and pushed on the door "It's not going anywhere. Vatch's crews will have to open it."

"No time for that," Majore said, now rubbing the sole of zas boot back and forth across the earth. It was a very flat space. Even in these wastelands, this ground seemed unusually hard. Compacted. Zie bent and flicked away some rocks, then ran zas fingers below a thick layer of sand. Zie moved over a few feet and did it again.

Fladnag broke into zas thoughts. "What are you doing?"

Majore looked over at Zawn. "Come on. Get back in."

"Answer." The command came from all the Seers.

Zawn stood on the mound, waiting.

"There is information here," Majore replied, looking up at the orange glow. "Important data."

"That you missed," all the Seers replied.

The Benefactor studied the stars. "Yes." Zie stared at The Labyrinth. "It is all connected."

The Seers watched zas thoughts. Zawn could not.

"What?" The Watcher asked, still standing on the mound. Zie searched the same sky the Benefactor studied. "The archy is an infection. What does zie have to do with those stars?"

Majore paused, waiting for the Seers response.

Intrigued, they did not make one. The Benefactor watched as they reassembled priorities. They agreed. Mavwa's Gulch, Mythgarden Point, the briganders on Lark: all were connected to the Labyrinth. Their Horn. The depictions on the benches. The etchings were not digibits. What they created were not within the Dimensionals, nor the Warp.

Such creations were... what? Illegal? Of course. What else? Majore looked up the mountain's face. The orange glow was still there. Such creations, those replications, were reason enough to snuff out this contagion. Yet zas moment had passed. They did not want a discard to apprehend the wratchet-gatherer. But Linatin was not there.

Majore calculated the odds based on the Seers' pause. Zie looked at the Watcher. "Come on."

The Hive's inaction meant approval. Zawn came off the mound and followed zam to the Silverstream. Both hopped in. Majore guided the craft into the air, then tilted its nose toward the same stars. The thruster, pointed down, ignited, and began to blast the area. Dust clouds roiled up and made the mountain and everything else disappear. A minute later Majore cut off the thruster and bent the nose toward the earth. The magnetic stream had obliterated sand, rocks, and small boulders, bringing visibility to zero. Zie placed the craft in landing mode, sat it down, then waited for the dust to settle. They got out.

"You were right," Zawn said. "Look."

Atomized rock particles still floated in the air, but the surface they stood on was as clean as a table top and just as flat. Several colored etchings were visible, each with considerable detail. *Planets*. A string of them. The first six were about three feet in circumference, ten feet apart. Red and green ones. A brown one with two golden rings. An orange one with blue and white rings. The seventh was larger. A blue and green ball with smatterings of white. As always, blue signified water. Green, vegetation. White, clouds.

"I have never seen that string," Zawn said, wiping dirt from zas eyes. "Or that planet. What is it?"

Majore looked closer. *The Horn of course*. The Watcher could not read zam. Instead of answers, confusion clouded the Synthon's thought pattern. Nothing in zas memcore prepared zam for this. The Benefactor knew a cleanwave was in this one's immediate future. The Seers' probes left zam and found Zawn. They watched thoughts. Majore looked at the depiction. Did the wratchet-gatherer play a role in this surprise? Majore did not see how.

"What are they?" Zawn asked, turning from the ground to the northern sky. No matter how long zie looked, zie could not see it. Long ago the Hive assured such knowledge was vaulted from all Synthon memcores.

Majore ignored zas question, still focused on the etchings. The spacing between them indicated that whatever the area had been used for, it was quite large. Just as interesting was the large swirling pattern of lines that ran around the planets. The Benefactor squatted down and rubbed the heal of zas boot over them. The lines crumbled. There was more there than etchings. Hundreds of years ago, something cut those lines deep into the surface. Zie moved a few feet over and did it again. The indentions crumbled. Zie looked up. Some type of propulsion system did it. Zie looked back down, then over to the slab. Zie bent and gently ran a hand across more of the lines. *Rockets made this.*

"Perhaps," Tibboh said, making sure the Watcher was still blank-walled, "you should return to Aguila. Linatin has been informed."

They want me out of here. Majore looked up. The orange glow was gone. *My span ends today.* "Bragen is in there," zie said. "Zawn and I could hold zam until they arrive."

"Go to Aguila, Majore1074," Tibboh ordered.

Fladnag broke in. "Wait. What would you do?"

Majore looked at the half-buried door. Zawn was allowed back into the Flow. "There is no place to land up there. I doubt the back side of the mountain will do us any good. Not unless you left the scaffolding."

Silence.

The foot of the mountain was less than a rock's throw from where they stood. "Try to open that door," zie answered. "It has to go up. We need in there."

"How?"

Zie looked at the Silverstream. "The thrusters."

"The quicker loose thoughts are... blanked," Neiklot thought, "the better."

Majore waited. Silence. Again, such a pause was as good as approval. Zie looked at Zawn. "Get in."

Once both were seated, Majore floated the craft up and again pointed the nose toward The Horn. The thrusters blew magnetoid rays at the half-buried door. In return, a spray of dirt, rocks, and other materials shot in all directions. After several minutes, Majore tamped down the thruster, then sat the craft back down. The

Dimensional revealed the mound was gone but the door was still there. A crack ran down its center.

Majore ordered the craft up, titled it so the thruster aligned with the slab, then ignited it. An explosion of rocks and rubble slammed into the Silverstream. An avalanche of dust and rocks from above clattered onto the roof. The Benefactor shut it off, turned around, and focused the light beam on where the pile of stones had been. As the dust cloud settled, a dark void emerged. The door was gone.

"There," Zawn said.

"Hurry," Tibboh ordered.

Majore sat the craft down. Keeping their eyes on the opening, they grabbed nose wraps and visors before climbing out and scrambling over the new pile of sand and rocks. Both stopped at the void and probed it as the Seers probed them. Once they entered the dark space, the Flow weakened. Ahead, the shadowy outline of a stairway appeared. Majore looked at Zawn. "We have to go up there."

Unsure if the Watcher would follow, zie pushed by zam and started up, zas visor adjusting to the darkness. The steps were narrow and steep, winding up and away from the opening. The Flow vanished, cutting zam off from the Hive.

"What will they think?" Zawn asked, yet to follow.

"They approved. We have no choice." A few steps later, Majore heard zam coming.

It was a circular stairway, clearly cut out of the mountain with the same type of tool used to make the rooms zie had seen Linatin and the others exploring. A Human device. Their visors cast a dim light on the smooth honed walls. An unknown talent, achieved prior to the leaps, was responsible. Much was recovered after the wars, but neither the Ruul nor the Hive knew this technology. Unlike tissue transmissions, a Carriers' cortex could not be extracted in the same manner as a Synthons. Thus, even in victory, much was lost. Many of their contraptions were never replicated.

Majore bounded up the steps two at a time, all the while winding up and around. Zawn labored up behind zam. A concentric line of steps led deep into the mountain. After a while, zie slowed, each step becoming more challenging. Disconnected from the Warp and those who controlled it, their senses began to play tricks on them. Sometimes it appeared they were going down steps. Not up them. Majore began to lose zas equilibrium. Zie stopped.

Zawn bumped into zam. "How much further?"

"Not sure.

"I have lost something," the Watcher said, sucking deep drafts of air through the nose wrap.

"It is momentary. Once we are out of here the Flow will return."

"What if the room is barred?"

"It may be," Majore admitted, also sucking in air. The Local seemed fine. "Archodialbragen1031 saw or heard us. But zie must be close. We have to try. If the way is blocked, we will come up with an alternative."

"Linatin will get here soon," the Watcher informed zam.

Majore's visor lit up Zawn's face. Zas large yellow eyes glowed in the dark. Of course, this was what the Seers would want. They let zam go up the stairs, but that did not mean they had given up on Linatin. Perhaps the Watcher knew more. "When?"

Zawn replied to zas thoughts, "Soon. With one of Vatch's crews."

Majore turned and looked up the dark passageway. Zie started up again. After several more revolutions the dizziness returned. Zie was about to sit down when a cool breeze washed over zas face. *Fresh air.* Zie rounded another bend and saw an oblong swath of gray light. Stumbling forward zie hit zas head, ducked and fell into a larger space. Distant stars were visible. The window. *The room.* Zie felt the Flow. "We're in."

"Not the Watcher," Fladnag said.

The Benefactor rolled over and sat up. Pain shot through zas right knee. Large rocks and rubble were strewn across the floor. Zas hand hurt. Rising, zie pulled a shard of glass from zas palm. Green glass. Zas visor illuminated a dark hole in the wall. *Where was Zawn?*

"Call zam," Tibboh said. "We cannot."

The place zie had just crawled out of was surrounded with broken pieces of planking. They were covered in orange goo and bits of glass. The planking. What as it? *Shelves?* Majore ran the visor light up the void zie had just crawled out of. A space within a space. *Once hidden.*

Zie called out, "Zawn." No answer. "The Local is not working. The walls are too thick."

"Go back and get zam," Tibboh ordered.

Majore turned around. The room was empty except for a legless stone desk. Zie looked out the window. "Where will Linatin land?"

"Out front," said Fladnag. "Vatch is bringing the scaffolding."

No Bragen. Zie scanned the broken shelves, then studied the floor. The rocks lay in a spray pattern. *What went on here?* Zie looked at zas hand. Wiped away the blood. Zie walked over to the alcove, boots crunching on green glass, and bent over and peered into the crawlspace. "Zawn?" *Nothing.*

"Go back and get zam," Fladnag repeated. "If you can't see zas thoughts, something is wrong."

"It's the walls," Majore replied, looking back at the remnants of what was once a desk. Linatin would be there soon. That meant discard and emulsion. To zas right was an arched opening that led into another room. A faint orange glow emanated from that void. *The wratchet-gatherer.* Ignoring Fladnag's order, zie ran under the arch and lost zas footing. At first, zie thought zie had tripped. Zas last thought came from Tibboh telling zam otherwise.

"You fell in a hole."

Chapter 17

The light from the tapered glass tube painted Bragen's hands orange. Mador's last thoughts hung in zas memory. *I moved on. It is left to you.* Globules floated within the tube's viscous liquid, blinking to the rhythm of zas heart. *Human technology.* Zie remained on zas knees. *Now what?* The wall of rocks had exploded, revealing the alcove. *I cannot give it to you. You must live it.* Bragen touched zas forehead. *Nothing.* Zie touched zas chest. *Nothing.* The globules turned red, solidifying as they changed colors. The archy's heart began to jump around like a wild animal caught in a sack. The tube cracked. *What?* Zie again grabbed the neck with both hands. The glass crystalized. Warmth flooded through zas fingers and up zas arms.

The adult Misla flashed up. She wore a shiny black, one-piece suit, loosely grasping a face shield of some kind. Behind her loomed the window zie had crawled through. "Despite our realities, we stand in the same room," she said. No orange ring, yet zie understood every word. "What does that say about time?"

Bragen followed her eyes to the alcove. "I am not sure. Of anything."

"You understand what comes out of my mouth."

Bragen stared at her neck. "Yes. How?"

Zas memcore returned to the last Interact. The stack of scrolls. All were gone, save one. The one that had blown out of zas hand. "It has to do with Truth."

"Speaking it?"

"Knowing it."

Misla disappeared, replaced by Radom, sitting on the bench admiring the canopy that spread over their heads. The intricate web of branches, vines, and leaves blotted out the sky. This image was replaced with another. Leaves and branches etched into the bridge rails that ran over the Ollepas River.

Misla returned. The brigander. Bragen studied the face. Intense and resolute. Zie asked, "How do you know what is true?"

"Truth is a living expression. It cannot be killed. Effort to silence it only makes it stronger. Makes you stronger. Thus, we live. That is how you know what is true."

Bragen thought about zas life as a wager. Every communication. Every thought. The silence. No musicality. "I cannot speak it. You have to do it. They must hear it. They must see you. Not me."

"Science requires such demands, archodialbragen1031, but Truth does not. They will see the me in you. The vine that connects us. That is all that is required."

Bragen shook zas head. Zie did not have a mouth. Did not have a tongue. "They will not."

Misla nodded toward the alcove. "The wall behind the shelving looks as solid as the rest of the room. Correct?"

Bragen looked. Nodded.

"Remember, everything is not as it seems. Beyond the veneer is a stairway that leads down to the platform. To the launch site. It serves as another passage out of the mountain. Once through this veneer, before descending the steps, you will find a corridor that angles off to the right. It leads to an upper room. The Truth resides in that room. Go and find it."

"Show me," Bragen said, lifting zas hand.

"It is in you. You are the Ark. Do not be afraid."

Misla was no longer there. Bragen's knees bit into the floor. Zie looked at zas hands. The tube was gone. The wind made a moaning sound. Zas palms were full of red crystals. As they lost their glow, they turned green, then black.

The archy closed zas eyes, trying to bring her back. *Nothing.* Zie stared at the dark bits of crystal that clung to zas palms. The wind brushed against zas face. *She does not know the scroll blew away.* Zie stood up, wiping zas hands. *There was more to translate, something important. Get the scroll.* But zie did not move.

An orange glow caught zas attention. It was the translator. The oblong tool. Zie walked over, picked it up and studied it. There was some type of etching on it. Something Bragen did not understand. Zie looked at the wall the shelves were fastened to. *Everything is not as it seems.* Hesitating, zie turned and walked to the window, boots crunching on bits of glass and stone. Still holding the tool, zie leaned out, half expected to see three nosecones. *Nothing.* Zie looked across the sky. The Five Fingered Hand and the Raring Steedfell hung in the dark like an accusation. Between them The Horn glittered like a beacon in the night, calling zam home.

Bragen blinked. A moment later, after forgetting to breath, zie snorted. No mural. No scratches on a dirt block or the nose cones of rockets. There they were, blinking back. Six distinct glitterings arcing across the night, the last larger than the others. Something wet ran down zas cheek. Zie touched it. *What?*

A cone of white light shot passed zam and lit up the room. Bragen ducked, crawled under the window to the corner, and looked around. Zie knew that imperceptible hum. Zie looked at zas glowing orange hand. It was a hovercraft. Bragen stuck the translator into zas pocket. Zas hip glowed orange. The beam of light painted most of the room a moment longer, then disappeared. The archy scooted over and peaked out. Down below, the Silverstream glided toward the base of the mountain, its beam moving up and down.

No getting the scroll. Mador flashed up. The wizened's eyes bored into zam. Zas hands clasped Bragen's shoulders. *You have to go.* Zie did. But the professor never left zam. From the Goman Ruins to Somafarm One-Zero-Five, zas presence remained, guiding zam forward. *Where are you?* There were no more blank transpo coins, no trams to catch or hovercrafts to steal. Zie felt a terrible weight and sat down on the floor. The orange light lit up zas midsection. Bragen placed zas head between zas knees and waited for the end. The weight pressed down on zas chest. *Of what?* Zie knew. *Knowing.*

Remboots and cleanwaves were considered a normal part of Synthonic spans. Moving toward the future required such sacrifices. Without them, the Common Benefit would fly apart, bringing progress to a halt. Bragen shuttered. *Let it happen. Let the forever sleep take me.*

Zie opened zas eyes. The glow seemed to come from zas body, lighting up the room. *Everything is not as it seems.* Certainly true. Zie shook zas head, trying to eject the weight that pressed against zas heart. Zie listened for the hovercraft. *Nothing.*

Sucking in a deep draft of air, zie started crawling across the floor. Twice zie stopped to pick crystals and wood splinters out of zas palms. Zie moved under the archway and stopped once zie arrived at the opening in the floor. Zie pulled the tool out of zas pocket and dropped it. It made a loud clang when it landed. Still glowing, it revealed several sheets of the scroll moving across the floor.

Bragen backed up, stood, and returned to the other room. Much darker now, zie carefully found zas way over to the alcove. Once inside zie felt along the shelving for the back. Smooth. Zie found a brace and pulled, jerking it loose, throwing it on the pile of rubble that was once a desk.

A loud roar followed by a blast of light sent zam back to zas knees. Bragen crawled over and looked down. The hovercraft was encased in a rising cloud of dust. Covering zas nose, Bragen returned to the void. Slipping into the area where the shelf had hung, zie gave it backward kick. It cracked. Outside, the roar grew louder. Rocks fell from the ceiling. Bracing zamself against the alcove's interior walls, zie kicked backwards again, shattering the wood façade.

Snorting out dirt, the archy turned and began pulling large sections of the broken panel away from its framing. Zie stuck zas head in the newly created hole, searching for air. A cool gust caught zam in the face. Bragen turned sideways and crawled into the darkness.

As zie scooted inside, one of Mador's lectures came to mind. The wizened stood in Artifact Hall, pontificating on the various types of caves found throughout the Prometheus. Caves were different than canyon or prairie surveys. More preparation was required because archodials did not know what might await them around the next dark bend. Proper preparation was a critical component to any survey, but particularly so when it came to caves. Working without light in tight spaces, Mador reminded them, was not only challenging, but dangerous. Yet the benefits derived from such work, zie continued, almost always proved the most fruitful.

Running zas hand along the floor, Bragen found a step. *It must lead down.* To the right, the floor widened. Crawling forward, zie found another step, this one leading up. *The upper room.*

The roar stopped. Bragen remained still for several minutes. *Had they left?* Zie scooted forward and crawled up three steps, then listened. Nothing. Looking back, zie saw light filtering in from the hole zie had just crawled out of. No more noise. No more dust. A light breeze touched zas face. Zas eyes adjusted to the darkness. Along with pieces of wood, bits of crystal lay glittering on the floor. Turning, zie squinted down the unknown corridor. It was not as dark at the end. Bragen stood and walked toward the light.

To zas right, an eye-level portal opened into another void. Bragen poked zas head in and peered down. The orange glow permeated the space. Below was the entrance hall zie had followed Landerwin into. Other Humans had followed them in. Bragen's eyes adjusted. Above the floor, zie began to see shadowy forms built into the walls. A balcony. A bridge. And down below, spots of white flittering across the floor. Remnants of the scroll. Bragen looked for a way down. *Nothing.* Zie turned.

Another light, different, came from across the corridor. A doorway. The archy walked over and peered into a room. Multicolored lights greeted zam. Reds and blues. Yellows and greens. They came from seven translucent stones embedded in a far wall. Zie walked in, reached down, and touched one. All were round, their luminescence enough to illuminate the small interior. When zie bent down, they washed across zas face. *Where have I seen that?* Zie searched zas memory. *The octagonal spheres.*

Their gleam revealed the walls were covered with a series of colorful objects. Synthons did not use color in this way, so it took the archy a moment to assess what zie was looking at. Nor was such a talent found within any Synthon's memcore. Bragen wished zie could get an explanation from Feelwin or Misla. Where did it come from, this talent? Zie needed an answer. An answer left out of the Galaxial Warp. Instead of constellations, zie realized these were crude depictions of the creatures who once roamed Apollis.

Thin and thick lines, as well as large and small circles, using a variety of pigments, created the images. An orange and brown range arth. Yellow swirls interspersed with blue dots represented two desert rinks. Four red and yellow steedfells were in the background, and above this scene broad black strokes created an image of some type of rooker or hawk. Bragen touched the range arth. *I know.* Children did this. On the wall by the opening, another image. The archy stepped back.

It was clear the circles were heads. Splashes of color for hair and skin. Stick arms and feet. The blue swatches represented clothing. All stood in a field of tall grass.

Red painted the tips of the grass they stood in. Each figure gave zam pause, yet it was the one in the middle that stunned zam. Here, a blue-skinned Synthon held an equally blue-bundle. A small hand peaked out of the blanket. There was an attempt to place an M on the cloth, but the last leg of the letter ran down the wall. It did not matter. It was the blue-faced character's face that captured zas attention. More specifically, what was below its nose. *A mouth.* Like the others, its lips were upturned. *Smiling.*

The Watcher filled the doorway. "Who are you?"

Bragen jerked back, hitting zas head on the wall. A Local pierced zas cerebral cortex. Zie tried to flip, but it was too late. The other Synthon's eyes moved to the wall. Studied the figures. The archy lowered zas head and bowled into Zawn's midsection.

****

The Watcher felt more than saw the blow and grabbed onto zas prey. Both fell into the corridor. Bragen managed to wiggle away, but not before Zawn grabbed zas leg. A moment later, zie held Bragen's empty boot. The archy was gone, disappearing into the darkness. The Local came undone.

Only minutes earlier the Watcher was following the Benefactor, Majore, up the winding steps. When Zawn stopped a moment to suck in air, zie lost zam. Majore had kept going, putting a distance between them that interrupted the Local. And the Flow had left them as soon as they entered the mountain. The walls were too thick. By then, Linatin was in charge, and on zas way. Zawn started up the stairways again, trying to tamp out the inferno in zas chest.

The Watcher's instructions were observational in

nature. The purpose of their trip to Aromla was little more than a way to keep the ex-Benefactor away from Bragen. The Seers believed the wratchet-gatherer had returned to Aguila and wanted Linatin to oversee the capture. Zawn was unaware as to why that Benefactor was put in charge and did not care. It was not zas place to question the Common Benefit.

Pounding up the steps, zie finally reached a platform of some kind. Zas left hand felt some steps and turned in that direction. A hallway. A light. Zawn followed it to its source and stumbled into the room.

Bragen was there. Trapped in a haze of multicolored lights. Zawn looked at the strange images on the wall. Not digibits. Archodialbragen1031 knocked zam down. The Watcher grabbed at zam. Came up with zas boot. Threw it away and got up. Out of the darkness came a muffled crash, followed by several thuds. Zawn moved cautiously down the corridor, pointing the handheld toward the steps. Once zie found the platform zie veered right and began to retrace the way they had come. Down below, something made a scuffling noise.

The handheld's light found Bragen in a crumpled heap. Zawn looked up, searching for the Flow. Nothing. *I have to get out of here so I can link up.* Zie illuminated the perp's face. Zas yellow eyes stared back.

They connected. "Can you walk?"

Bragen shood zas head. "I might have broken my leg."

"Try," Zawn said, slipping a hand under zas arm. Bragen did not resist, but the stairway was narrow, dark, and treacherous. After some effort, zie managed to get the target into an upright position.

"You need help," Bragen said. "I will not make it

down without falling."

Zawn knew the archy was right, but wasn't sure what to do about it. Watchers functioned as observers, not problem solvers.

"Go ahead," Bragen said. "I'm not going anywhere."

Zawn noticed the small gash on zas head, then looked at zas bootless left foot. The ankle was clearly puffed out at an odd angle.

"Sit back down," zie said. "I'll be right back."

Zawn left zam in the stairway and followed it down to ground level. Once outside, zie walked over to the Silverstream.

"What has been going on?" Fladnag demanded.

"I can't find Majore."

The Seers were not concerned with the Benefactor. "Where is the Contagion?"

"I've got zam."

"We do not see zam," they said.

"Zie is up in the stairwell with a broken leg or foot. I couldn't move zam by myself. I need Majore to help."

"Majore is no more," Fladnag said. "Zie fell in a hole."

"What?"

Altogether, the Seers said, "It is not your concern."

"We are landing," Linatin interjected.

Zawn felt their Local, their Flow, and their location. "Not that way. Come around the north face of the mountain."

"And Majore?" Linatin asked. "What happened?"

"Your object is the Contagion," the Seers replied. "The Watcher is correct. Go to the north side of the mountain. Time is critical."

****

Bragen woke up, zas eyes fixed on a blinding light. For several seconds zie searched zas memcore for answers. *Nothing.*

"You are not in the cave." A Local.

Zie could not blink. Propped up in a chair of some type, zie tried to turn zas head, but could not. A blurred image rose up in front of zam. "Is this Aromla?"

"Finally," said the blur. An outline began to crystalize. It was a Synthon. Blue skin, yellow eyes, large nose. Another, similar, but distorted image flashed up, but this one was in zas mind, not in front of zam. It had a mouth. *The drawing.*

"What is a drawing?" The blurred Synthon asked.

The archy searched for an answer. "I do not know. Where am I?"

"Not Aromla."

Bragen repeated the name. It had come out of zas memcore, but zie did not know it. *Where had that thought come from?*

Another Synthon stepped into view. "I am Linatin. This is Barnam. What is your ident?"

Bragen shook zas head. *Blank.*

"And your seri?"

"Seri?" zie asked, even more confused.

Barnam's memcore extraction gave the Hive the details needed to clean up the riddles. The subsequent cleanwave was the first step in the elimination process that would end with an emulsion. A few disconnected thoughts remained. Barnam would take care of that as soon as the Seers gave the signal. *The Fallen*'s discovery had altered the usual protocol. No emulsion until this Synthon's every thought was thoroughly analyzed.

"What is the Apogonos?"

"What?"

"Where is The Horn?"

"I do not know."

"Who is Misla?"

"I do not know."

"What is a baby?"

"A what?"

"A baby."

"I do not know."

The wratchet gatherer was clean. Linatin observed the Seers' thoughts. They agreed.

"Continue to probe," Tibboh ordered. Together, they studied each thought that ran across the Dimensional. Clearly, control had been restored, as had the reestablishment of order and Good Thought.

It was all there. From the meeting inside *The Fallen*'s apartment, to each Interact encounter. Human technology contained an archaic quality, but there was no denying the innovative aspect, from orange ring communicators to the multicolored tubes that immortalized them. All agreed that species used parts of the brain Uhlmans and Synthons could not. The Seers were at a loss as to how either the orange rings or the tubes operated. The animal mind was beyond comprehension.

Information gleaned from the wratchet gatherer provided troves of data. Additional information regarding non-specific DNA, Cloyden and Maice's culpability, revelations concerning the Human colony on Apollis and so much more was already being analyzed. Toponyms such as Sunbloom, Aromla, and Opellas, when coupled with the Human names Feelwin, Arena,

Misla, and Landerwin filled in gaps of time the Hive was only vaguely aware of. Knowns were easier to blank-wall than Unknowns. *The Fallen*'s surprising association with Somafarm Zero-One-Five, as well as zas rather insidious alias, Radom, provided fresh insight into how black-market thoughts were bled into the Flow long after the Carriers were gone.

Linatin observed the last sections of Bragen's memcore pass through the Dimensional. The screen turned gray. It was clear that many strange thoughts had bounced back and forth between the archy and *The Fallen*. All to no avail. The threat to the Common Benefit had been eliminated.

"Go ahead," the Seers said.

Linatin nodded to Barnam, then stood and watched the physical extraction. The Guide placed the memcore in the center of the table and opened it. Through Linatin, the Seers searched for more hidden files and shields. None were found.

Linatin got the message and looked at the Guide. "Proceed with the emulsion." The Benefactor remained in the Thought Room while the process played out. Afterward zie checked with the Seers, then made zas way down the hall to the prepared room. Laying down on the bed, zie closed zas eyes. A second later zie floated up through the concentric rings of light. The Seers hung on the rings, probing every inch of the Benefactor's thoughts.

"You have done well," Fladnag said.

"Control has resumed," Tibboh added.

"The Stain remains a stain," Linatin said.

"Yes," Neiklot agreed. "And truth remains the Truth."

"The ball moves forward," Fladnag added.

"And the Future is preserved," Tibboh confirmed.

Mulendur's face flashed up. This was the second time this Synthon had gained entrance to the Hive. Very unusual. Zas eyes expressed puzzlement. Zas thoughts explained why. Within them was a crude representation of a Synthon surrounded by unknown beings and animals. It was clear this image came from the Galaxial Warp. The Seers studied it. So did Linatin. It was fastened, or embedded into something. Perhaps a wall. The Synthon was holding something.

Linatin opened zas eyes. Zie was still on the bed. The Hive was gone. Even so, the image remained. It sent a shock down the Benefactor's spine. Jumping up, zie ran to the Wake Room. The body was gone, as was the memcore. Barnam was looking at the Dimensional, but zas mind was elsewhere. *Inside the Warp*. Linatin saw it too. A blue-skinned Synthon, surrounded by smaller characters. It held something in its arms. The beings that surrounded it, as well as the Synthon, had a mouth. Even what it held had a mouth! For the first time in zas span, Linatin grew dizzy.

The Seers were back in zas brain. "Tell us what you know."

"I have seen this," Linatin said.

"Where?"

"In Bragen's thoughts. During the inspection."

"Yes," Fladnag agreed. "But it was contained there. So how is this possible?"

"What is it?" The Guide asked, still staring at the image.

"A virus," Linatin answered.

Barnam ignored the Benefactor's response. "Those

appendages are arms and legs. What is the opening above the chin?"

The Hive remained focused on Linatin. "And the origination point?"

The Benefactor hesitated. Majore was discarded. Was zie next? Zie searched the galaxy for Watchers. "It is too soon."

"It has legs," Fladnag said. The Seer was not talking about appendages, instead zie referenced high-level black-market links. Which meant it was spreading.

Mulendur joined them. "I see it. The origination point is Lark."

"Where?" Fladnag demanded.

"Kilgahlen. But it is loosed."

"I see it on Arion," Tibboh added. "And Thon. Only Watchers are capable. Where is Zawn?" Watchers maintained constant contact with the Flow, Synthons, and the Hive.

"I flew here with the Contagion," Linatin explained. "Zawn returned to Kilgahlen." Kilgahlen was that Watcher's station.

"Who ordered that?" Tibboh asked.

Again, Linatin hesitated. Zie knew the answer, but knew better.

Reading zas thoughts, Fladnag said, "That is not so."

"I sent zam there," Linatin lied, following proper protocol. The mantra went, *A lie to preserve the greater Truth is not a lie.*

"When?"

"No more than two hours ago. We left the Apollis aerodrome at the same time. A debrief was to take place here after the emulsion. Zie is waiting for my thought."

"Do it!" Neiklot demanded.

Additional reports began to flow into the Hive. They came from Dwarth, Thon, Arion, and Lark. Even the Lifeway on Apollis was seeing the image. Linatin tried to fight back the implications. "The Watcher..."

"Zawn," the Seers said, more an accusation than a reply.

"Is on zas way," Linatin said.

Like everyone else, the image still hung in the Benefactor's mind. It carried significance beyond zas comprehension. *The Carriers*. Zie felt a sickness in zas midsection. What was the image? The colored whorls, lines, and circles began to make sense. *That was Bragen*. Holding some small thing. *The Stain*. Heresy. Bragen had transferred some strange thoughts on the way back from Apollis. Before the extraction. When had Zawn been infected?

"It's changing," the Guide said, stepping back from the screen.

The image split and morphed into another. No crude scrawl this time. A woman walked out of a crowd of Humans carrying a blue bundle. Linatin snorted and stumbled backwards. Little hands and feet poked out of the bundle. The Benefactor knew zie should turn away. There was much to do. From Zawn's interrogation to zas own discard. But zie kept looking. *Woman* was a term from the Long Ago. She pulled back the blanket. The baby nuzzled her breast. Linatin felt a constriction in zas throat. *Zie* knew what it was doing, but the hundreds of thousands of Synthons throughout the Galaxial Warp absorbing the Flow did not. Curious, Linatin turned to Barnam, a high-level wager, but a Synthon all the same. The Guide was searching zas own memcore for the reference that was not there.

Linatin searched back through the last few hours. To the capture. And that conversation with Bragen.

****

Once Linatin's craft touched down at Aromla, the Seers ordered zam to the north side of the mountain. The Benefactor met Zawn in front of an opening of some kind.

"It's a stairway," Fladnag informed zam. "Get up there!"

With Zawn in the lead, they scampered up the dark steps, two of Vatch's crew members behind them. Halfway up, Linatin found Bragen sitting crossways on the steps with zas back against the wall.

"What took you so long?" The wratchet gatherer asked.

Hands on knees, snorting air into their lungs, the Benefactor and the Watcher pondered this question. The thought contained a tone they did not know. One they could not interpret. Vatch's crew came stumbling up behind them.

"Go back down," Linatin ordered. Zie worried about the spread.

"So, you are more than a Council Coordinator," Bragen said. "That means you are not an archy, correct?" After the bones were found in the blueweed, Linatin came to Apollis as the new Council Coordinator. Zie oversaw completion of the excavation.

"You know I am not," Linatin replied.

"Are you all frauds?"

The Benefactor looked at Zawn. "Help me."

One on each arm, they struggled to get the Synthon down the narrow steps, stopping every few minutes to catch their breath.

Near the opening, Bragen asked, "Why?"

Still in the spiral enclosure, Linatin looked at Zawn and contemplated a response. The Seers were still shut out. "It is not in you to know."

"They are in me."

"Who?"

"And in you," Bragen said. "Whether you know it or not."

Linatin could barely see the wratchet gatherer's face, yet zas yellow eyes glowed in the darkness. Getting a better grip, zie nodded to Zawn and they started again. Each tried to find the Warp. *Nothing.* The Benefactor knew the faster zie got to Arion, the better. The archy wreaked of contagion.

Once outside, Linatin told Vatch's wagers to stay back. With some effort the Benefactor and the Watcher carried zam to the hovercraft and slipped zam into the passenger seat.

Looking at Zawn, Linatin said, "I'm taking zam to Wahlgahlen."

Oblib spoke to the Watcher. "Return to Kilgahlen."

Linatin slid into the craft and looked at the wratchet gatherer's ankle. It was turning purple. "They will repair that."

"Really?" Bragen said. "I'll be cleanwaved first."

Linatin directed the Silverstream back to the aerodrome. The trip was short and thoughtless. A starship waited on the tarmac. This time Linatin allowed wagers to pick zam up and take zam over to the larger craft.

They soon sat next to each other in the back of the starship. Neither chose to share their thoughts in the Black Hole transit, yet when they began to descend, the archy looked at zam.

"Do you know what a drawing is?"

Linatin ignored the question. It seemed a ruse, one meant to open zas mind.

"I'll take that as a no. I didn't either until today. Remember that image on Mythgarden Point? We both saw it. On the blocks. Check your memcore, or whatever it is you have. Those scrawls in the dirt. We hypothesized about it. Remember? That was a drawing. I have seen several others since then."

Linatin could not resist. "More stars. Where?"

"In several places. All different, yet the same. But there was something else. Different. A representation of a face. Mine, I think. Humans put it on a wall. I was surrounded by children. Do you know children? And babies? I was holding one in that drawing. One more point about that image. Everyone in it had a mouth. Including me."

"Ignore zam," Tibboh ordered. They were out of the Black Hole transit.

"Different colors were used in this rendering," Bragen continued. "Red, brown, blue, and yellow, I think."

"Blasphemy!" Fladnag said. "Get zam down."

Linatin felt the starship's wheels hit the ground and began to unbuckle zas bracing. *The wratchet gatherer knew something.* Something zie did not know. "We are getting some help."

Bragen's thoughts continued to flow. "They were using their brains, or something inside them, to make those drawings. What an odd thing, to make something outside of the Galaxial Warp."

A red and white clad wager rolled up to the ship's

ramp and Bragen's chair. Zie bent over and helped the archy get up and settle into the device.

Bragen looked up at Linatin. "An independent creation."

The wager rolled zam down the ramp and out of the starship.

"It seems a repetition, this creative act," the archy said, looking back at the Benefactor. "What do you think it means?"

"A repetition of what?" Linatin followed zam down the ramp, aware of the Seers presence.

"Everything," Bragen replied.

"A waste," Fladnag interjected. "Block zam."

Several probes moved into the wratchet-gatherer's neck and zie went to sleep.

****

Two hours later Linatin stood in the room with Barnam, transfixed by the archy's last thought. *Everything.*

"Jibber jabber," Neiklot said.

The Benefactor thought about Zawn. "They were in the mountain together. Before I got there."

"Correct," Tibboh said.

"Zawn is a Watcher." Watchers were the conduit between them all, with access to everything.

"And?" Fladnag asked.

"Well," Linatin began apprehensively. "Zie was infected."

"The Benefactor is right," Tibboh interjected.

"In the cave," Linatin began, "he saw something. What did zie see?"

Silence. Then, all together, the Seers replied. "Everything."

Epilogue

It came to Siwel when the warning bell rang. She stood on the dirt trail that rounded the pond, watching tadpoles skittering around its bank. She thought, *metamorphosis.* As if on cue they shot into the deeper part of the pond and disappeared. *Soon you will crawl out of there and chase grasshoppers.* Smoothing down her new blue smock, she looked across the school yard. Welba, Pia, and several students she did not know scurried up the building's steps. All wore the same blue smocks. Pia looked her way, gave a quick wave, then darted through the double doors.

Hesitating, Siwel looked back at the benches that rimmed the pond. Forty years of memories filled her. Early on, she began to take her lunch to the bench on the far side of the water so she could keep an eye on the children. Later, she led her class to the same bench, where she talked to them about pollination, how clouds were made, and of course, metamorphosis.

Out of the corner of her eye she saw movement and turned. Principal Aden was holding the double doors open and waving toward her. This was her last day. She waved back and started walking across the grass.

Smiling, the principal said, "Morning Siwel. It's a beautiful day."

She looked up at the cloudless sky. "It is."

She stepped into the wide hallway. Teachers stood at the entrances to their classrooms, all wearing similar smocks. All smiling. She smiled back as she passed each one, again wondering if this was a mistake.

"There is a special luncheon in the breakroom," Aden whispered. "And this afternoon the assembly."

Siwel stopped and looked into the principal's blue

face. "I was thinking I might leave after the students settled into the gymnasium."

Aden's mouth popped open. "Oh no. I am afraid you have to be there."

"You have already done so much. All of you have. I was just thinking…"

The principal put a gentle hand on her shoulder. "Absolutely not. The children would throw a fit."

Siwel couldn't see her way out of it. She didn't want to disappoint them. It was as much their day as hers. Several papers were stuck to the back side of her open door. Drawings. In some fashion each represented someone with blue skin and a large smile. Many also included children wearing blue smocks. She sighed, then nodded at Aden.

"Have a great day," the principal said before striding down the hall.

At sixty-nine, she could have retired five years earlier. Boren's sudden death was the original reason she decided to continue working. Each subsequent year Siwel promised her three daughters that she was only going to work one more semester. Which always turned into another. Then another. In between, she plotted out month-long trips to her grands and worked on designs for a new backyard garden. Smiling, she walked into the room.

"Good morning class."

Thirty-five students replied, "Good morning."

Once again, she wavered. All wore their special blue smocks and large smiles. Sitting in their seats, waiting for the question.

"What is today?"

Some said, "Your last day." But most said, "Waking

Day."

Siwel walked around her desk and sat down. Ignoring the part about her retirement, she answered, "That is correct. Waking Day. What do the drawings have to do with Waking Day?" She pointed to the tall, dark-haired girl on the left. "Yes, Kawtren."

Kawtren pointed at the drawings. "They help us remember."

Siwel looked up at the class. "And why is that important?"

From the last row, Zeleden blurted out, "It's the last day of school."

The children burst into laughter.

Siwel playfully rolled her eyes, which sparked more laughter. "Yes, but that was not the question." Half the class raised their hands, but the same boy, half out of his seat, frantically waved both hands above his head.

"Go ahead, Zeleden" Siwel said.

Several of the children moaned and gave the boy ugly looks.

"Quiet," the teacher said, straightening in her chair. "Tell us Zeleden."

Zeleden stood up. Smoothing down his smock, he said, "They woke us up."

"Better," Siwel said. "But how. What did they do?"

"They sailed into the galaxy on the Ark."

"Yes. Why is that significant?" The teacher looked up at the portrait that hung over the learning vials. "Who is this? Aaren?"

The girl with the dark pigtails and the green eyes sat up straight and studied the image. The man's skin was even whiter than his hair, which was thick and long. His eyes so light gray they were practically clear. This part of the ritual was playing out in every class across the Prometheus. "Long ago, most people did not know they were human. Once they forgot, they lost their humanity." She stood, still looking at the face. "Rendaway and a few others escaped on the Apogonos, thus were saved from the Blank Spot. We know this because he wrote it all down in this." She tapped the small blue pamphlet on her desk. "He also wrote about the two times he encountered the Ark. But no one knew about his book, about the *Symporous* for hundreds of years."

"What happened when the Ark came?" Siwel asked. Moedan waved his hand. "Go ahead Moedan."

"It broke through," the boy said, pointing toward the door, "and delivered the Truth." Pleased with zamself, Moedan smoothed down his smock.

The teacher nodded. "Yes. Now someone else. We wear these garments on this day only. Why? Go ahead Milben."

"Rendaway wrote about it. It is what they were wearing when the Ark sailed into the Opellas Valley. And they left a drawing on the wall."

"When did the Ark see this drawing?"

The entire class answered, "On the Last Day Before Forever!"

"Yes, class. On the Last Day Before Forever the children, wearing these smocks, sailed into the Prometheus and woke everyone up." The children began to clap. This part of the ritual was coming to an end. "And what did we gain as a result?"

Everyone replied, "Our voices."

Afterwards, the class pulled out special treats prepared by their mothers and placed them on the assigned table directly under Rendaway's portrait. Siwel supervised the division of goodies and even took a few morsels back to her desk. Savoring a sweet bread, she sat back and soaked it all in. Various hues of blue faced children sat at their desks munching away, at times giggling at their neighbors or whispering something in their best friend's ear. There was no lunch on Waking Day, just a short get together before the assembly closed out the year.

Later, she sat up front with the principal in the gymnasium listening to several of her cohorts and a few students expound on what a great teacher she was, both pleasurable and awkward at the same time. Next came the pageant. All the grades played their usual parts, from the Ark's arrival on Sunbloom to their leaving the Sal Sagevs for Apollis. Lastly, Lifegiver, wearing a blue smock with a red M emblazoned across her chest pocket, gave the address to the audience, closing with, "Before Waking Day, everyone bleated the same answer to the old question and people thought they had lost their voices. You have proven that this was not, and is not, true."

Siwel's favorite part involved the departure from the Sal Sagev Mountains. The students worked all spring creating the rocket that dominated the stage. Lewina, a tall lanky boy played the robed adult who stood by the vessel's door greeting everyone as they stepped on board. Only the stage crew could see them filing out the back and collecting behind the curtain. The teachers, students, and some of the parents watched as little Amena, the last in line, stopped at the bottom of the steps and pointed up at the vertical letters that ran down the rocket's side.

"What does it say?" Amena asked the robed figure.

In his gruffest voice, Lewina, playing Feelwin, replied, "Apogonos."

"Apogonos?" Amena asked. "What is that?"

"An old word from the Long Ago."

As rehearsed, the little girl stepped back and craned her neck up. "What does it mean?"

"Offspring," the robed figure answered.

"Like me," Amena said.

In dramatic fashion Lewina nodded, "Yes," as the applause began. "Like you."

In the final scene the blue-faced Synthons pulled the patches off their faces, revealing their mouths. The student playing the Lifegiver then returned to the stage and they all sang, *I Am the Me in You*, ending the day's festivities.

Afterward, Siwel stood on the track by the pond watching the children filter out of the building for the last time. She clutched the stack of drawings to her chest. She was not going to change her mind this time. Siwel would spend more time with her grands and her own children. It felt good. She looked into the sky, still very blue. That evening, as she did on every other Waking Day, she stepped out on her back porch and looked for the arc of stars that guided the Lifegiver home. Once she found it, like Humans everywhere, she gave thanks to the Ark for carrying the Truth into the Prometheus. Then she went inside and read the Symporous.

A word about the author...

James Bailey Blackshear is an award-winning author, historian, professor, husband, father, and grandpa who loves reading, writing, autumns in Texas and summers in New Mexico. His history books and journal articles focus on nineteenth-century Northeastern New Mexico, yet as *The Last Day Before Forever* attests, his writing interests are varied. He believes reality is often found somewhere between fiction and non-fiction, between a past we cannot return to and a constantly changing future.

jamesbaileyblackshear.com